DARKNESS
BURNING

By Delilah Devlin

DARKNESS BURNING
SEDUCED BY DARKNESS
INTO THE DARKNESS

Don't miss the next book by your favorite author.
Sign up now for AuthorTracker by visiting
www.AuthorTracker.com.

DARKNESS BURNING

Delilah Devlin

AVON

An Imprint of HarperCollinsPublishers

This book is a work of fiction. The characters, incidents, and dialogue are drawn from the author's imagination and are not to be construed as real. Any resemblance to actual events or persons, living or dead, is entirely coincidental.

DARKNESS BURNING. Copyright © 2009 by Delilah Devlin. All rights reserved. Printed in the United States of America. No part of this book may be used or reproduced in any manner whatsoever without written permission except in the case of brief quotations embodied in critical articles and reviews. For information address HarperCollins Publishers, 10 East 53rd Street, New York, NY 10022.

HarperCollins books may be purchased for educational, business, or sales promotional use. For information please write: Special Markets Department, Harper-Collins Publishers, 10 East 53rd Street, New York, NY 10022.

FIRST AVON PAPERBACK EDITION PUBLISHED 2009.

Interior text designed by Diahann Sturge

Library of Congress Cataloging-in-Publication Data
Devlin, Delilah
    Darkness burning / Delilah Devlin—1st ed.
        p. cm
    ISBN 978-0-06-149820-6
    1. Vampires—Fiction. 2. New Orleans (La.)—Fiction. I. Title.
PS3604.E88645D37   2009
813'.6—dc22
                                            2009002484

09 10 11 12 13   OV/RRD   10 9 8 7 6 5   3 2 1

*For my "Roses" at www.RosesColoredGlasses.com
for being there to listen
while I whined my way through this book,
and who offered me support, advice,
inspiration, and true and loving friendship.*

PROLOGUE

Destiny sucks.

Being an uncrowned prince of the Undead might get you laid, but it didn't win you friends. Instead, you stayed on the down low, hiding in plain sight from enemies who'd kill you just because you existed. Not an easy task when you still had a duty to protect the innocent and demolish the misbehaving.

Which was why, when Alexander Broussard crept deeper into a dark, dank alleyway just outside the French Quarter, only half his mind stayed with the prey he'd tracked for nearly a mile. The other half wondered whether this was just another demon hunt or the opening salvo of "the great battle to come."

Although he was aware that lack of focus could land him in deep shit, an odd restlessness gripped him. His destiny awaited him —or so he'd been told for as long as he could remember—but that promise was as unproven as the *protective amulet he wore on a slender cord around his neck. Unproven, untested; would the moment ever come?*

Perhaps he'd messed the whole thing up. Made a misstep that would cause all their carefully laid plans to fall like dominoes. After all, he wasn't the one who'd seen what lay in store for the future. Simon, his mentor, teacher, and his friend, had that angle all wrapped up and wasn't sharing what he knew, afraid he'd somehow change the course set before them all.

Time, even repeated, never moved forward quite the same. Or so Simon often said.

Missteps, mistakes . . . Alex prayed he hadn't already made things worse.

Concern for his unborn child ate away at his gut. That neither the baby's mother nor her lover wanted him around sat heavy on his conscience. He'd used them both for his own ends. Their seduction had been necessary, part of the bigger plan, but that didn't matter. Leaving them trapped, dependent on the mercurial Inanna's mercy, undermined his resolve.

Nothing he could do about it now. But soon, all the players would gather at Ardeal, the place "beyond the forest," named for their last kingdom on Earth. A little more patience and he'd have it all—the girl, the power, and the bloody damn crown.

That was the future he wanted, the one he'd waited for these seven centuries.

In the meantime, he'd keep his head down and follow the scent of any trouble that might complicate his quest. Like the sharp, musty odor he'd trailed beyond the Quarter into the meanest streets of New Orleans—dangerous before the flood, infinitely more deadly now.

A heavy footpad rasped on grit, dragging his thoughts back to the danger lurking in the shadows. Alex's body tightened. He crouched, shifting his weight to the balls of his feet, getting ready to make his move—but where was the bastard?

He forced himself to concentrate, directing his senses to search for a darker shadow in the pitch blackness, sniffing the humid breeze to catch the scent of the beast.

A steamy breath gusted against the back of his neck.

Fuck.

Alex leapt to the side, took a single running step, and planted his foot on the wall of the alley. Then he climbed up and somersaulted to land behind the creature.

Only it had disappeared again. Now the cagey beast hunted him.

Alex's lips stretched into a feral grin. His teeth slid deeper from his gums, curving over his lower lip. Adrenaline seared his veins. His heart rate surged. At last, he'd found a challenge to refocus him—if only for the moment.

A low, grating snarl gave him a second's warning. He whirled to meet the massive creature as it launched from the ground ten feet away.

Alex thrust up his arms, slamming the beast in the jaw to deflect a vicious bite, but he was carried to the ground by the force of its ballistic velocity.

The cord around his neck broke when the wolf's serrated canine tooth scraped the base of his throat. Alex ignored the scratch and the blood soaking into his shirt collar, but noted where the amulet landed on the ground. He wrapped his hands around the creature's thickly muscled neck and squeezed.

The beast screamed as loud as a hellhound, forcing air past constricted vocal cords to gust in steaming clouds above Alex's face. It was scented with its doggy breath and echoes of its last meal. Sausage perhaps. Shrimp or crawfish, for sure. No hint of human.

Alex ground his heels in the gritty muck beneath him, straining with his thighs to roll over, but he never got the leverage he needed to put the creature on its back and knock it out quickly.

Instead, he held tight, shoving the wolf's head and snapping jaws as far from his face as he could, until at last the choke hold did its job. The beast deflated like a balloon, landing limply against Alex's body.

He pushed it away and climbed to his feet, immediately searching the ground for the amulet. With only minutes to spare before the wolf revived, he needed to retrieve the precious stone and flee. Without either a proper weapon to finish the were-creature *or a silver linked collar to capture it, he could spend hours battling the beast. Although the fact griped his ass, he'd have to kill it another day. No one could come prepared for every unearthly contingency.*

At least he'd confirmed his suspicions after reading the reports that Ruby had left on his desk back at the station house, telling of packs of wild dogs roaming the streets. Werewolves had infiltrated New Orleans.

Just another breed of scavenger descending on the city when it was at its most vulnerable.

Alex caught a glimpse of the shiny, round stone wedged between a box and a trash bin, and he knelt to retrieve it.

At the first sounds of a scuffle from the other end of the alleyway, Alex ducked low, peering into the darkness, waiting to determine whether the combatants were human before deciding to enter the fray. They were too far away to tell at first, so Alex tamped down his impatience, glancing back to assure himself the wolf still slept. Then he stared ahead, waiting.

A heavy hand fell on his shoulder, and Alex inhaled a familiar scent. Father.

"How many times have I told you not to come to a fight without the

proper weapon," Rene Broussard *whispered in his Cajun-laced accent, an ironic note in his voice.*

"Who said I meant to kill him?" Alex *replied dryly, looking over his shoulder.*

Rene grunted and knelt beside him behind the him.

"Why are you here, Rene?" Alex *asked, careful as always not to signal their relationship should anyone be listening.*

"Makin' sure you aren't so pumped up with your own self-importance you get yourself killed."

"How long have I been patrolling?"

"Thirty or so years less than me, mon fils."

Alex's *lips stretched into a rueful grin. While Simon had honed* Alex's *otherworldly skills, Rene had been there to remind* Alex *he'd been born of a vampire and a human man. Rene's teachings and the example he'd set inside their small, tightly knit family unit had been just as important to keep* Alex *grounded, reminding him constantly of his duty to humanity, as well as feeding a yearning for something he could never truly have.*

"We should go," Rene *said, lifting his chin toward the ruckus beginning at the other end of the alley. "Not our fight. Not your time."*

Alex *speared one more glance into the darkness. "Let's wait a minute or two, just to make sure."*

Rene gave him a short nod and hunkered down beside him, his hand still pressing down on his son's shoulder.

Alex *didn't fight the cautionary hold. A male Born vampire couldn't be too sure whether a fight erupting so near was an inconvenient coincidence or all about him.*

CHAPTER

I

The profound silence struck Mikaela Jones first. Her own booted heels clapped on the pavement, but the sounds she associated with The Crescent City had vanished, along with most of its inhabitants.

Instead of the blare of blues and tinny Cajun music from the bars along the street, and the voices of people laughing and shouting as they ambled by, barhopping in the late-night hours, a muffled hush blanketed the city. There was a watchful, pregnant quiet, like the breathless, relieved lull after the powerful storm—the day before water had consumed life as she'd known it.

The inky, thick shadows at the edges of the streets also creeped her out. Without power, alleys and deep doorways were impenetrable to her gaze and could hide many creatures of the night—street thugs, looters, gang-bangers. She carried a hardened leather blackjack deep in her jacket pocket—her weapon of choice should anything jump out from the pockets of darkness.

She'd worn her weathered leather jacket despite the muggy heat just for that purpose; she needed storage for her weapon and the tools of her trade. But she also needed comfort, and the jacket was the first piece of clothing she'd bought with her first paycheck. Not the nicest item in her closet now, but familiar. A little worn, but resilient, just like her.

As the silence and darkness closed around her, she reminded herself why she'd decided that this excursion would be such a peachy idea. Reports of the crime-ridden streets—the wanton attacks and rampant looting—were known. Every major news organization had descended like locusts on a killing field to cover the tragedy and the painful recovery.

But other whispers had reached her ears. Less newsworthy, but definitely more intriguing, made more believable by the fantastic events of the past days.

Whispers said magic was in the air. Monsters were on the loose. Perhaps the dreams that plagued her had a basis in reality.

Miki turned up her coat collar to ward against the prickling disquiet lifting the fine hairs on the back of her neck. She tried concentrating instead on the details she needed to remember for the next piece she'd write describing life in the aftermath of the great storm.

Like the twinkling stars she'd never seen above New Orleans's light-polluted streets. They speckled the damp, cobbled pavement, resembling muted fireflies. Or the unchanged aroma of sewage emanating from the grates beneath her feet, ripened by the added odor of the contaminants swirling in the black waters covering large portions of the city.

Twin beams flashed as a vehicle turned onto her street.

Miki trotted to an alleyway to avoid the National Guard patrol rolling by in a camouflaged Hummer. Being caught breaking curfew might make an interesting story, but she didn't want to waste hours cooling her heels, or worse, being evicted from the city.

She turned the corner and pressed her back against the wall of a brick arcade, waiting for the vehicle to pass, when muffled sounds came from behind her. For a second, she froze.

Low, heated murmurs. The scrape of a zipper and the rustle of clothing. Soft laughter cut off by a deep moan.

Someone enjoyed the anonymous shadows.

Curious, she crept closer, edging along the wall, her eyes adjusting slowly to the near-pitch darkness until she spotted a couple further along the opposite side of the alley. The man stood with his back against the wall, a woman nuzzling the side of his neck as he groaned. Metal glinted from his opened zipper, and Miki guessed where the woman's hand roamed.

She nearly groaned. The urgent sounds tightened her already restless body.

Deciding she'd leave them to their tryst, she edged backward, hoping the patrol had passed, when something rushed by her so quickly that she saw only a blurred, grayish streak. The man's next moan was cut short by a shout. The woman cursed.

Miki froze until sounds of a fight erupted, nearly making her leap back into the street. At first, she didn't see anything.

Then a dull explosion where the woman had stood illuminated another blur of movement too fast for her gaze to follow. A second gray figure streaking to the right had her narrowing her eyes to peer into the gloom. Fists connected with flesh, and were followed by another burst of light. Fiery ash settled to the ground.

A battle ensued, but one unlike anything she could have imagined.

Excitement started a slow, heavy thrum pounding in her chest. Had she found what she sought? Then a footstep scraped behind her.

It was too late to run. She gasped when a strong arm wrapped around her waist, pulling her back against a wall of solid muscle. With her arm clamped to her side, she couldn't reach for her blackjack. Acting on instinct, she lifted her foot and slammed her heel onto her assailant's foot.

A soft chuckle in her ear turned her fear into panic, and she struggled against his hold, wriggling hard, jabbing elbows at steel-plated ribs. The man behind her didn't budge. He simply tightened his arm until she slumped against him, panting breathlessly within his embrace.

So she couldn't beat him in a fight. Thinking fast, she relaxed in his hold. "Not gonna ask me what a nice girl—"

"Nice girls don't walk alone after dark," he told her, his voice deep and silky.

The thought occurred to her that only a truly attractive man could muster a voice like that—a ridiculous thing to note, given her circumstance. Her rising panic made thinking hard. "That's rather sexist," she blurted out and nearly groaned at her inane comment.

His hand slid inside her jacket and slowly up her belly to clasp her left breast. "Your heart's beating so strong, I'm thinking you're scared."

"Duh," she gritted out, trying to stretch away from his grasp. She gave up when soft laughter stirred the hair beside her ear. "Look, just let me go. I have some money—"

"I don't want money." His nose trailed along her neck, pushing past her collar.

"Guess not," she said weakly, a shiver working its way up her spine. "You know, I haven't washed in a couple days. No water."

"*Liar.*" His soft, warm tongue lapped the side of her throat. "I taste soap."

Miki nearly wilted in his arms, which set alarm bells ringing. How could she be turned on by a man who appeared bent on molesting her? "Um . . . my name's Sarah."

"Don't think so, but Sarah's pretty. I like the tat."

She bit her lip as he mouthed the tiny sickle-shaped moon and stars behind her ear. "You can see that? It's pretty dark . . ."

"Shush. It'll be over quick. I just need a taste."

"Taste?" Her voice tightened to a shrill squeak as his lips slid down and his cheek nuzzled the edge of her jaw. When teeth pierced her neck, her knees buckled. The sharp sting of the bite faded in seconds. "What the hell?" she said, her voice oddly breathless.

A murmur that sounded like a sexy reassurance rumbled against her skin, calming her. His mouth began sucking, drawing on the wound.

Miki felt dizzy, faint . . . and incredibly, instantly aroused. His hips pressed against her ass, making her aware of the thick, hard ridge of his cock. His hand cupped her breast and squeezed, shaping its fullness with his broad palm.

Her fear faded, overwhelmed by his sensual assault and the tingling awareness sweeping downward from where he sipped at her neck, winding tightly inside her belly and releasing a trickle of desire that dampened her cotton panties.

The attack continuing just feet away didn't seem nearly as important as her arousal bloomed, spiking higher along with the nipple he rubbed.

"Alex, isn't it?" came a masculine voice tinged with amusement.

Alex growled against her neck, eliciting another shiver of a different sort. Miki would have told the other man to beat it, but she was nearly boneless, nearly *there*.

Alex's teeth slid gently from her neck, and his tongue licked the wounds he'd made. One hand squeezed her breast, and the other patted her butt. "Sorry, sweetheart. Another time." To the man hovering at his elbow, he said, "Malcolm, you're a dead man."

"Too late." Malcolm chuckled. "Fancy seeing you again so soon. I'd be flattered if I thought this had anything to do with me."

"We'd better move along."

Before Miki opened her eyes, both men were gone. She reached behind her, pressing a hand flat against the wall to steady herself while her trembling legs remembered what they were for. She took deep, reviving breaths.

What the fuck had just happened?

A moan from further down the alleyway pulled her toward the man slumped on the ground.

"Hey, are you all right?" she asked, keeping her distance.

"Name's Leo," he said, his voice sounding weak. He held a hand against his neck, and dark, trickling liquid spilled from between his fingers. "Can you help me?"

Miki's "spider sense," the instinct she'd trusted before tonight, told her "Leo" wasn't anything more than what he seemed: a man caught with his pants down and a neck wound bleeding into his shirt. A wound like hers. Only when she touched her neck, she felt nothing, just cooling moisture from Alex's final lick.

Once again, curiosity and a shivering excitement built inside her.

Decision made, she held out her hand and helped him to his feet. Once she had him cleaned up, Leo was gonna do a whole lot of talking.

From the entrance of the alleyway, Alex strode in the opposite direction from Malcolm and his men. He wasn't sure how, but the scent of the wolf hadn't attracted any attention. Perhaps the men had been too distracted by the adrenaline zinging through their veins or the delicious aroma of "Sarah's" arousal to notice.

Whatever the explanation, he was glad the beast hadn't been discovered. Not yet, anyway. Not until he discovered why *weres* had broken treaty and entered vampire territory.

Rene slipped from a shadowed stoop and fell into step beside him.

"Recognize the man who led that patrol?" Alex murmured.

"Malcolm," his father growled.

Alex nodded. Malcolm was one of Nicolas's rogue vampires,

one of the group that had attacked *Ardeal* a few nights ago for a show of strength against the Born vampires. They'd wanted to win the right for one of their own to sit among the ruling *sabat*, the vampires' council—a right reserved for millennia by those born to the night.

Their plan had been doomed from the start, because Inanna, the matriarch and Queen Bitch of the council, had learned of their attack and prepared. No one, not the rogues or Inanna's minions, could have know that the *Grizashiat* demon who'd been steadily stalking closer to *Ardeal* would unleash a host of zombies at that exact moment.

Nicolas's rogues had been forced to protect the estate, battling alongside The Born, when the zombies had crashed their party. All had ended well, it seemed. The rogues hadn't been destroyed and instead were now patrolling as part of Inanna's security force, all under the leadership of Nicolas—who'd won his spot, at last, on the council.

"Couldn't resist playing hero, could you?" Rene muttered. "Looked like Malcolm had it handled."

Only Alex had wanted to do all the "handling"—Sarah had been too delicious to resist. "Just making sure the girl stayed out of the cross fire."

"Uh-huh."

"She was a tasty bit," he said, shrugging off the attraction that had sparked hot and irresistible when he'd held her in his arms. She was human, therefore not for him.

"So long as you keep your eye on the prize. Can't afford too many distractions now."

Alex nodded, tamping down his irritation at yet another reminder of his damnable destiny. His father hadn't had a choice once his mother had sunk her fangs. He might have resisted, at first, but his future had been decided in that one sensual act. No way could Rene understand the multitude of choices and temptations that lay in front of Alex.

A final glance over his shoulder assured him that the two humans were safe for now; they were moving away. He caught one last glimpse of the woman's sleek curves and sighed. Nice, but not for him.

Alex melted away beside his father, shedding regret and leaving it with the werewolf slumbering alone in the darkness.

CHAPTER
2

Alex winced as he pried away the shirt collar stuck to dried blood at the base of his throat.

"Quit being such a pussy," came an amused drawl from behind him.

"I seem to remember locking the door," Alex muttered, turning to scowl at his mentor.

Today, Simon Jameson bore the face of his video-store-owner persona. Short brown hair stood in stiff, gold-tipped bristles on top of his head. He wore a T-shirt with a Hurricane Party Here slogan and an arrow pointing toward his groin.

Alex didn't bother wondering why the mage had shifted. He thought that sometimes the long-lived Simon was just plain bored.

"I have a key. I'm your landlord, remember?" Simon leaned his shoulder against the doorframe. His forehead furrowed as he peered at Alex's wound. "That nick should have healed quickly. How'd you get it?"

"A werewolf bite," Alex said, turning back to the bathroom mirror.

"A werewolf inside New Orleans? Interesting." Only he didn't sound so surprised. And why should he have sounded surprised? Despite their treaty with the Wolfen Nation, they'd had other rare appearances in "N'awlins" lately—zombies, demons . . . a Born vampire of the male persuasion.

Alex skimmed off the shirt, wadded it in his fist, and tossed it on top of the growing pile of dirty laundry. "What else aren't you telling me?"

"You know I can't—"

"Yeah, yeah. Too much knowledge of what will pass might affect my course," Alex said, his tone sour. "You do know I'm getting just a little sick of that line."

"Did you meet the girl?" Simon's sharp gaze conflicted with the casual tone of his remark.

"The one who got dusted or the one I felt up?"

Simon's eyelids shuttered his gaze, then rose slowly again. "What did you think of her?"

Alex wished like hell the mage would simply tell him what he needed to know. "Why? You planning on setting me up on a blind date?"

"Just curious."

"Right." Alex snorted. "Let's see. Slim. Black hair, gray skin. It was a fucking alleyway. I couldn't make out much detail, colors anyway, in the dark. Probably wouldn't recognize her if I did see her again." *Liar.* He sighed, picked up a washcloth, and soaked it with the bottled water he kept on the floor beside the sink.

"Pity." Simon sniffed. "You'll be meeting her again."

"At last. A hint." Alex paused to stare back at him in the mirror. "That's all you're going to say?"

"It's all you need to know."

Screw him and the girl. He scraped the cloth across his wound. "Anything else I don't need to know?"

"They've beefed up patrols at Inanna's compound. Inside the perimeter and at the gate."

"How'd you get that intel? Thought you weren't welcome there any more after you aided my parents' escape." At the tightening of Simon's jaw, Alex grunted. "You sent your familiar to spy."

That Simon would put Madeleine at risk meant the stakes were indeed high.

"Seemed too risky to slip inside myself," Simon said, his tone even. "I let the kestrel be my eyes."

Alex forced his gaze back to his own reflection before he asked the question burning a hole in his gut. "Did she catch a glimpse of Chessa?"

Compassion softened Simon's usually passive expression. "No, sorry, Alex. Inanna will have her on lockdown to assure Nic's good behavior—and to keep her present condition under wraps. A mature, pregnant vampire will be hard to explain to the *sabat*."

Alex's irritation drained away. "I don't like it, Simon," he said softly.

"She's safe for now."

"You can't know that for sure." Alex lifted one eyebrow. "Something may already have changed."

Simon shrugged. "Inanna will keep Chessa safe for now. She's curious about her child. How it was conceived. Born females aren't supposed to get pregnant more than once."

"Why will she care about the how?"

"Inanna wants her secret. She might suspect a Born male exists, but there are other ways for a female to conceive more than once—dark ways."

"Does she want to use the child?"

"She never misses an opportunity to increase her power, but that's not what she wants right now. She wants to conceive herself."

"Should I be paying careful attention to how you just worded that?"

Simon's enigmatic smile irked.

Alex tossed down the washcloth. "I have to get to work."

"Alex," Simon said, his nonchalant expression changing subtly. "There will be a meet 'n' greet at the estate tonight."

At last the wily mage had gotten around to the reason for his visit. Alex narrowed his eyes. "The council is arriving?"

"All the members are in the area. They'll converge at the compound after dark."

"A welcoming party, then. They'll need snacks. I want to be there."

Simon's smile flashed. "Thought you might. Erika's trolling the Quarter for young, handsome men to serve as blood hosts. She doesn't know you."

"What about the rogues who were captured at the zombie fest? They'll recognize me."

Simon's smile broadened. "I'm a mage, remember? Let me take care of that little detail."

More magic. An uneasy premonition crept along Alex's spine. He unbuckled his belt and gave Simon a glare. "I'm gonna bathe. You staying to watch?"

"Stop by when you're ready to head out." Simon slid away, no doubt to prepare the spell Alex would need to cloak his identity among the vampires. Alex knew it would be up to his own wiles how he kept his neck out of reach. One bite would spell disaster.

Distracted and filled with an edgy, unsettled energy, Alex's mind wandered as he bathed street grime and sweat off his skin.

Lately, he'd been consumed with seeking new challenges while sifting through memories of the past—not all of them his.

With his destiny at hand, he couldn't shake the feeling they'd missed something. That *he'd* failed to widen his scope beyond prophecy and his mentor's insight into the future. That perhaps they hadn't predicted the true path he should seek.

Adding to his unease, he wondered what was so damn special about "Sarah." He didn't like surprises, even when they were sexy and wrapped in a whiskey-soaked voice.

Miki helped Leo, a slim man with shoulder-length dreadlocks, into the slouching recliner in his small loft apartment. "All right, Leo. Gonna tell me what the hell happened back there?" she growled.

He leveled his coffee-colored gaze on her. "You been walkin' dese streets after dark," he said, his voice flavored with Caribbean syrup. "You don't know?"

She had more than an inkling, but she wanted him to say it. Make it real. So she waited while he settled into his chair.

"Hon, I'm an addict. Needed my fix. My *vampire* fix." Leo rested his head on the chair and closed his eyes. "Need to stop the bleeding. Get a dishtowel from the kitchen."

Miki fingered the nonexistent wound on her neck. "How come you're still bleeding?"

"Lady didn't get a chance to lick me up after she fed."

She remembered the incendiary flares. "Where'd she go?" she asked, not sure she was ready for the answer.

His eyes opened, a stark expression on his face. "I'm wearin' her dust."

Miki swallowed, her glance raking his thin T-shirt. Ash streaked the black cloth. She turned on her heel and hurried to the kitchen, a thousand questions screaming in her mind for answers. Vampires. She'd really been bitten by a damn vampire.

She found a towel in a drawer beside the sink and rushed back to Leo, who wearily turned aside his cheek to expose his neck. Blood trickled in a sluggish but thinning stream from two small punctures.

"Think she took a little too much B-pos. Tired."

Miki's hand shook as she wiped at the wound, then pressed hard to slow the bleeding. "You've done this before."

"Told you. I'm hooked. I spend my nights in blood bars waitin' for an invitation. Most of dem are polite. Take only a few ounces so I can keep in the scene." His lips curved in a mirthless smile. "This one was . . . *da-yum hot*. Took so much I came before we . . ."

"Before you had sex?"

"Yeah."

Recalling how her own arousal had been manipulated, Miki thought she understood his peculiar addiction. "Where do you find them? The vampires?"

"Not so many places left. One just off Bourbon Street in the Quarter, called Aftermath. They play nice."

"So why were you in an alley with her?"

"Like I said, she was hot. Thought we might have a party. At my place. Never got this far. She had someone waitin' in that alley. Think they meant to make a meal of me. I was too far gone to care."

"What happened? I couldn't see very much. Blurred movement." She hesitated before adding, "Flashes of light."

"Move quick, don't they?" he said with a weak smile. "Never saw it before. Heard things. Never saw 'em killed. Those were the flashes you saw." His hand slid beneath hers, taking the cloth, and he turned his head toward her. "Get your first bite tonight?"

Miki swallowed hard and nodded. "Yeah."

"So, now you know," he said quietly.

"Guess so." She nodded toward his neck. "Are you going to be okay? Do we need to find a clinic?"

His full lips opened, large white teeth gleaming. "And tell them what? We all keep under the radar. I'll be okay in a week or so. Can hold out here for a while."

Miki straightened, already impatient to get back out on the street now she that had a lead. "I'll check back in on you to make sure you're okay."

"Be careful. Pretty lady like you . . . dey'll eat you all up."

Somehow, the thought didn't frighten her. She let herself out of his apartment, climbed down the narrow steps onto the street, and headed back toward the Quarter. She thought about hitting her apartment first, checking in with her neighbors to let them know her new destination. They'd worry if she stayed out too late. They might even mount a search party

Funny how a disaster had made fast friends of everyone

who'd waited out the storm. They'd banded like a tribe of lost souls, first sharing nails and plywood to batten down windows as the storm had approached. Those who'd meant to ride out the Category 5 storm had combined shopping lists and argued over how many batteries they were going to need for flashlights, how much water and canned goods to stock up on in case the power stayed off for a few days. They'd offered to pool resources—hand-cranked storm radios and bottles of wine to make the wait more pleasant through the long, dark night.

They'd felt a sense of purpose and courage—and brash recklessness. When the worst of the storm had missed the city altogether, they'd shared premature sighs of relief and toasts to newfound friends.

They hadn't known the big bullet was still coming their way. Not until the storm surge had breached the levees. Then they'd listened in shock as every politician and policeman had urged them to evacuate.

Still they'd held out. All for their own reasons. Some to protect their homes from looters. Others stubbornly refusing to believe things wouldn't turn around quickly.

Miki had stayed to cover the story—to give a resident's bird's-eye view. It wasn't like she'd had anywhere else to go.

When old man Mouton had insisted that they prepare for a long siege, she'd pooled her water, food, and candles with the others and let the Depression-era baby dole out the stores. Residents had shared communal dinners cooked over a Coleman stove, and their friendships had deepened—something she'd never experienced before. Or that she could recall.

She'd found a family at last. For as long as the recovery effort took.

Still, much as she wished she could hit the apartment, she

headed toward Bourbon Street. The compulsion to learn more, to find proof she wasn't nuts, and that Leo wasn't high on something besides lust and blood loss, had her hurrying back the way she'd come.

However, the farther from Leo's apartment she moved, the less plausible and more ridiculous the explanation seemed. She'd been looking for monsters. Looking for the source of her nightmares. But was she really ready to find them?

Police Lieutenant Byron Williams sat at Chessa's old desk, leaning back in her rickety wheeled chair, his shoeless feet crossed on top of a pile of unfinished reports. He was snoring.

Alex crept quietly inside the cubicle, opened the top drawer of his own dented, gray metal desk, pulled out a butterscotch candy, and slammed the drawer shut.

Byron's eyes shot open and his arms uncrossed from his chest to flail for a moment as the chair creaked ominously, teetering before slamming back on all three wheels. His blinking gaze settled on Alex, and a glower deepened the wrinkle bisecting his dark brow.

"Did I wake you?" Alex asked, popping the candy in his mouth to hide his grin.

His boss narrowed his eyes but didn't respond as he rubbed a hand over his close-cropped black hair. "Thought this was the last place I'd be disturbed. Aren't you supposed to be tracking down dog packs?"

"I already did."

"Anything I need to know about?"

Alex grunted, finding it ironic to be asked the same question he'd posed to Simon. Seemed everyone had something to hide. "Probably just what you've been thinking."

Byron's grimace reflected disgust. "Damn weird. Zombies, werewolves . . . demons who think human hearts are snack food. I'll be glad when things get back to normal. Gimme a serial killer any damn day."

"Speaking of which, find any more bodies matching our demon's MO?"

Byron shook his head. "Been quiet. Think you and Nicolas were right about him movin' out of the city."

"Heard from your family?"

Byron grimaced. "Talked to the wife earlier. She's already plannin' on how to spend the insurance check when it comes."

"You had flood insurance?"

"Damn straight. Doesn't mean I still won't take it in the ass. No amount of money's gonna fix what's wrong with my house."

"Have you been out there yet?"

Byron shook his head. "Saw my rooftop on the news. Gonna have to gut the place, if it's even salvageable." His jaws stretched wide around an enormous yawn. "Better get back out there." He bent to slip on his shoes, then stood and cracked his neck side to side.

"I'm leaving the city tonight," Alex announced.

Byron's eyebrows rose. "Plan on comin' back? This section's had a helluva turnover lately."

"Plannin' on it."

"You don't sound so sure."

Since Alex hadn't a clue about what he faced at *Ardeal* or how things would go down in the coming days, he just shrugged. "I'll be back," he said, infusing his tone with determination.

"You've only been part of the team for a few days, but I'd hate to lose you. I need you here."

Alex nodded. He understood why Chessa had clung to her life in New Orleans, fighting tooth and nail not to be drawn into the coven's politics. She knew who she could trust here. Plus life as a homicide investigator was much simpler than navigating through the Underworld.

Byron's heavy footfalls echoed on the linoleum floor as he walked away, but Alex was already straightening his desk, closing folders and filing them away before doing the same to Chessa's desk.

Sitting in her chair, he inhaled her scent. He pulled open drawers, found her slim makeup bag, and held it to his nose. Her soft floral scent, a scent so at odds with her terse, edgy demeanor, clung to the fabric.

The first time he'd met her, she'd worn no makeup, save for black eyeliner. Along with her black hair and black leather jacket, the eyeliner had lent her a ghoulish appearance: armor to warn away anyone meaning to mess with her. Including him. Especially him.

She hadn't wanted a new partner to replace Rene Broussard. Hadn't suspected that the replacement was Rene's son. She'd been slow to trust. Slow to let anyone see beneath the brittle, hard-edged façade she showed the world.

His father had prepared him to be her partner in order to protect her. Simon had encouraged him to get even closer. And Alex had. Now, he wondered whether he'd done the right thing. Chessa had become more to him than just an instrument in the coming conflict.

He missed her. Even loved her. But her heart belonged to Nicolas. Alex had seen to that.

CHAPTER

3

Finding proof of monsters living in the midst of humanity was disgustingly easy. One short walk from the front of Aftermath down a dimly lit corridor, and Miki entered another realm.

A dark realm filled with decadent, wanton delights—if the soft, breathless laughter and throaty moans were any indication. The lack of electric lights and music did nothing to dampen the mood of the people crammed into the small, airless room.

Candles lined the bar and the wooden shelves behind it, casting golden light to the edge of the counter, but not penetrating the gloom beyond. Not that Miki needed illumination to know what was happening in the darkness around her. Bodies writhed together. The musty scent of sex and blood was almost overpowering.

Miki elbowed her way to the long, wooden counter and leaned over it to get the bartender's attention. "Anything on the menu that isn't red?"

Young, blond, and amused, his glance flickered over her. "As long as you take it straight from the bottle. No ice. First time here?"

"Yeah." Her gaze swept past him to roam the room again. Not sure what she was looking for, she came back to him. "Do you know a man named Alex?"

His eyes narrowed. "Maybe."

Was he one of them? A vampire? Or just another groupie trying to get his buzz on? "I know Alex. I'm trying to find him."

The bartender's blue gaze lifted beyond her shoulder, and a smile curved his lips. "Guess it's your lucky night."

Miki shivered when a body pressed against her back. Warm breath feathered the hair skimming her cheek.

"*Sarah*." Alex's rumbling voice vibrated against her skin. "Looking for me? Must have made quite an impression."

"A couple of dents, actually," she said breathlessly, keeping her gaze straight ahead. Her body jerked at his soft laughter. Not from fear. Already she thrilled to his presence, and she realized why she'd really come. She wanted . . . more.

A hand slid around her belly and insinuated itself beneath her jacket. With the bartender's smug smile deepening, Miki shook herself and scowled. "I'm not here to give you seconds."

His hand slid upward, stopping just below the curve of her breast. "Curious, then? Wondered how long it would take until you were ready to nose around for answers. Although part of me hoped you'd play it safe."

"It's your own damn fault. You had to know I'd want answers. Can we talk? Face-to-face, this time. I don't even know what you look like."

"Conversation isn't free," he growled deliciously. "I just stopped for a bite. Maybe we could negotiate payment."

Knowing she was going to cave, she groaned. "Shit."

"Not a flattering reaction to my pass."

"Let me just get this straight. I let you . . . bite me . . . and you'll entertain a question or two?"

"Depends on what you want to know. And you don't have to let me take blood," he whispered into her ear. "I can feed another hunger. Your choice."

She didn't need him to spell out what he meant. His sensual invitation lay simmering among his casually spoken words. She rolled her eyes at the bartender, pretending irritation when her body was already melting inside. "Tell me something," she said, finding it hard to gather a deep breath. "Are you guys always so damn horny?"

The heat of his body against her back and bottom increased as he pressed closer. "Only when inspired, sweetheart."

Feeling quivery, she slowly relaxed against him and leaned her head against his shoulder. "Is it always so easy for you to get what you want?"

"You tell me." His hand cupped her. His thumb scraped her nipple through the thin shirt. "Can you resist . . . now that you've had a glimpse of what it could be like?"

She honestly didn't know, but she hoped she could keep her wits when she surrendered—and she knew she would. She had to know more about this other, darker world. Her curiosity and the desire flooding her body demanded it.

But first she had a choice to make. If she let him take more blood, would she be left weakened, like Leo? Maybe she just wanted an excuse to find the kind of release Alex's voice and playful fingers promised.

She clamped her hand over the one exploring the underside of her breast. "The second choice, I think. But where?"

"Look around you. Does it look like anyone cares what we do? Most people won't remember what they've seen. Not the details."

She would. She planned to get them in her notebook as soon as she had a moment to herself. "I can't do what you want with other people watching," she said, deepening her glare at the blond, who grinned at her dilemma.

"Outside then."

She hesitated, remembering the alleyway where they'd first met and the violence she'd witnessed.

He squeezed her waist. "You'll be safe with me. I promise."

Alex hadn't harmed her before—he'd kept her safe while the battle had raged in front of her. "All right. But we talk afterward."

"Still want that drink?" Blondie asked with a smirk.

She glared at the man, then let Alex lead her through the crowded bodies that seemed to part like water around them, down the corridor again and through a side exit to the street. She caught only glimpses of the back of his head, the thick, wavy brown hair he wore a little long, his broad shoulders and narrow waist. Taut, muscled ass. *Nice.*

Outside, darkness swallowed them again. Shadows deepened.

"Private enough?" he whispered, not letting go of her hand.

"Yeah, but I can't see you."

"Does it matter what I look like?"

"Do you look like Spike with the horny head?"

His soft laughter raised goose bumps on her flesh. "Nothing protruding from my forehead, I promise. I'm handsome. Women find me irresistible."

"I just bet they do," she murmured.

"This alley smells pretty rank. Come with me."

He grabbed her hand and led her to a doorway in a building on the opposite side of the alley. First, he tried the handle, then he set his shoulder against the door and shoved. The wood splintered, and he swept her inside.

Standing in the room, Miki shivered in complete darkness. She reconsidered her options, wondering if she'd been foolish to trust that he wouldn't harm her. No one would hear her, even if she screamed as loudly as she could.

His hand closed around her wrist, and he tugged her deeper inside. "I can't see a thing," she groused as she stumbled after him.

"I can see perfectly. Just follow the sound of my steps." Deeper into the room, he stopped and gripped her waist.

Miki gasped as he lifted her off her feet. A long ledge met the backs of her thighs, and she let him sit her on top of it.

"A counter. It's strong enough. And low enough for what I have in mind."

Nervous now, her body trembled harder. "Do you have a condom?" she asked as she listened to the sounds of clothing rustling.

"If that would make you feel better, I'll use one. But vampires don't need one. They're all sterile."

Factoid number one. But he'd said "they," not "we." She shrugged away his semantics, knowing she was latching onto unimportant details to fight a major case of nerves. "Should I worry about catching something nasty?"

"We don't carry STDs. You're safe." The metal in his buckle thunked on wood, and she knew he'd dropped his trousers.

God, she was really going to do this. Really going to fuck a vampire she'd just met. She collected data like tokens for the favors she allowed. Her teeth began to chatter as fear and sheer sensual tension gripped her body.

He stepped between her thighs and wrapped his arms around her back. "It's going to be okay," he whispered in her ear, nipping the lobe before drawing back. "I won't hurt you. Your pleasure is mine."

With his warm breath gusting just above her mouth, her head tilted back. Why pretend she was only doing this for information? Since her "awakening," she'd yearned to touch and be touched, but she had been so busy learning about her world that she'd allowed little time for relationships.

This wasn't a relationship. Not anywhere close to one. This was fucking in the dark. She didn't know what he looked like. He didn't know her real name. Two complete strangers.

Could anything be more liberating or sexy?

Slowly, she lifted her arms and slid her hands around his naked torso, smoothing them along his sides and around his back. Everywhere she touched, he was hot and hard, his skin soft over tensile muscle.

She couldn't resist trailing her fingers over his face. Nope. No horns or bony protuberances. Then she forgot to be afraid as his lips lapped, dragging hers in circles as he moved closer, rutting the thick column of his cock between her legs. God, it felt divine.

When his hands slipped between them, she murmured, not in protest but encouragement. He grabbed the edges of her jacket and spread them open. His mouth didn't leave hers as he unbuttoned her shirt, flicked the clasp of her bra, and burrowed underneath to cup her naked breasts. He squeezed her, rubbed the flat of his palm over her engorged nipples, then tugged them with his thumbs and forefingers, twisting gently.

Miki moaned into his mouth, slid her tongue along his, sucked his lips, finally bit them—anything to incite him to hurry.

Eager now, impatient to feel his skin on hers, she tugged her cuffs and slipped the jacket and shirt off her shoulders to puddle behind her. He quickly skimmed away the bra.

Their hands met at the top of her jeans, but she let him open them, sighing when the zipper slid down and humid air licked inside.

When his hand thrust down the front of her pants and long, thick fingers slid between her moist folds, her head jerked back, breaking the kiss. "Please, the rest of my clothes, too."

He drew away immediately, tugged off her boots and her jeans, dragging her panties along with them. Before the tiny scrap of material settled to the floor, he pushed her back to lie across the cool counter.

Staring into the darkness, she sighed when his mouth found an aching nipple. His lips closed around it, drawing hard, then releasing it. "Delicious," he muttered, and then he gripped it between his teeth and tongue, delivering a softened bite.

Miki's thighs hugged his hips while he licked his way across her sternum to the other breast and teased it to a point. When the scrape of his beard caressed the areola, she moaned and thrust her hands into his silky, curling hair, pulling it to bring him closer to her feverish skin.

Alex trailed his lips downward, stopping to suckle the soft skin of her belly, tonguing her navel, pausing to rim it over and over again, giving her a delicious glimpse of what he'd do when at last he reached her sex.

As he kissed her lower belly, his fingers combed through her short curls and traced a path along her slit.

Already wet, already pulsing, she moaned as he slid two fingers between her folds and thrust them inside. Her pussy clasped them, drawing them deeper, and he began to pump his fingers in and out while his tongue found the hardening kernel of her clit and flicked it.

With his encouragement, she draped her legs over his shoulders and lay there as he licked and stroked, until her head rolled side to side and her heels dug into his back to leverage her hips up and down, begging him silently not to stop.

"Deeper," she whispered. "More . . ."

His thumb sank into her moisture, then traced a path lower.

Her breath hitched. "Oh God."

Soft laughter vibrated against her sex.

Miki bit her lower lip and squeezed her eyes shut, determined not to let him know just how close she really was, how tightly the heat in her belly curled.

When his thumb rubbed her small forbidden hole, she jerked slightly. "No, no, no . . ."

"Yes," he said softly and growled as he pushed his thumb inside, continuing to swirl his fingers in and out of her pussy.

Miki went still, not knowing how to react to this invasion. The tight ring of muscle constricted around his finger, trying to prevent his entry, but the burning pressure wasn't unpleasant. When he began to work his way out, then back in, along with the stroke of his fingers above, she thought she'd die.

Her whole body convulsed, her pussy squeezing harder on

his fingers, her belly and thighs quivering. Inside, heat coiled tighter around her womb, and she began her ascent.

"Not so quick." He withdrew his fingers, lapped the creases where her outer labia joined her thighs, trailed his lips down her legs, then stood back.

With her whole body shaking, Miki let him ease her up to sit at the edge of the counter. When he snuggled his chest and belly against hers, a thin mewling cry broke through her lips.

The contact was too much. Her nipples dragged across his lightly furred chest, sending darts of electricity straight to her sex. His cock rocked up and down her wet slit. Just a few more lazy slides and she'd be there.

"God, you're lovely," he breathed. His hands closed on her buttocks and slid her closer to him, until she perched on the very edge. Something tearing and a soft pained groan accompanied the sound of latex snapping, and a few moments later he was back.

A vampire didn't need condoms, but he came packing? The thought flitted away as his cock glided downward, and the thick, blunt tip nudged against her slick seam. She reached behind herself to brace her hands on the counter as he slowly slid his cock up inside her.

They both groaned as he stretched her inner walls and more moisture seeped from inside her to ease him deeper still.

Balls-deep now, he halted. "Lie back," he said, his voice thick and strained.

She let herself down, first to her elbows, then with her back pressed flat on the counter. His arms hooked beneath her knees and he pulled her closer, fitting her snug against his groin. "Ready?"

A short, garbled laugh broke from her. "Expect me to talk?" she gasped, so full she thought she'd burst.

Alex pulled out a little and circled his hips, screwing gently back inside her. "You're tight. Really tight. How come?"

What could she say? She couldn't remember the last time she'd made love. *Really*, couldn't remember. "I'm choosy?"

"Sweet, Sarah." He pulled out again and stroked back in, this time stronger, harder. "Let me know if I'm too rough."

"Just move," she begged, her body contracting inside again.

His hips drew back, pulling out slowly, his thickness and the softly ridged texture of his shaft dragging at her walls.

"You're driving me crazy," she said, wriggling, pulsing to bring him back. "Fuck me."

"God," he groaned, then slammed back inside.

Miki's back arched, and a thin, plaintive cry crowded through her tight throat.

"Christ, can't stop," he said, the urgency in his voice driving hers higher.

Miki reached between her legs, her fingertips scraping through the crisp hairs at his groin, then opening to slide around the base of his cock. Thick, turgid—*fuck*, she couldn't believe how good it felt. Her pussy swallowed it up, her channel rippling along its length.

She trailed her fingers up her belly to her breasts. Her nipples were dimpled, the tips spiked and hard. She twirled them and pinched them hard as he stroked back inside.

He gathered up her legs, his hips flexing harder, the strokes sharpening, spearing into her, grinding at the end of each deep thrust. A groan rumbled through him, and he pounded faster, his groin slapping against her moist center.

Miki welcomed his fierce pounding and the heat building inside her, friction crackling between his cock and her inner walls, until more moisture gushed, and he churned in it.

"Play with your clit," he rasped.

Grunting harshly now from his strokes, she slid two fingers into the top of her stretched labia, found the round hard nub and rubbed it. Her breath caught, her belly jumped, trembling on the verge, then suddenly her back bowed and she was flying, her head exploding, a scream ripping through her.

"Fuck!" Alex shouted, and his strokes grew harsh and uncontrolled. He groaned, the sound deepening with his slowing thrusts.

Miki's back relaxed, and she circled her clit gently, drawing out the last rolling convulsions of her orgasm. "Damn," she breathed.

He scooted her back onto the counter and dropped her legs. When he stepped back, she felt a moment's disappointment, but then his tongue began to bathe her as the last pulses faded, soothing her to stillness.

She cupped her breasts, feeling suddenly cold as humid air wafted over her sweaty skin, and she hiccupped softly as her breaths lengthened.

"Fucking amazing, sweetheart," he whispered and kissed her inner thighs.

A laugh that felt suspiciously like a sob racked her. Her first time since she'd woken naked in a ditch without a single memory of her past—and she'd chosen to fuck a vampire in the dark.

What did that say about the person she must have been, that she'd give herself so easily, so recklessly? Was this part of her lost personality she was uncovering?

She must have been a slut. Still, she thought she might want to do it again. "Alex?"

His tongue licked her opening, then disappeared. "Yes, love?"

With tears filling her eyes, she stared into the darkness. "I want another go," she confessed. "Is this part of what a vampire does? I mean, besides causing orgasms with your bite. Do you make us crave you?" God, she hoped that was the reason, rather than her being a nympho, that she felt this insatiable urge.

"We have a special pheromone that lures our prey and enhances pleasure," he responded gently. "We have to feed on the living. It's our special gift for the sacrifice you give us."

"Didn't feel like a sacrifice," she said gruffly, feeling only slightly better about herself.

"It's not supposed to. That's the point. And some of us have stronger pheromones—and can issue an irresistible allure."

"You must be off the scales."

"I didn't need them. You got the straight stuff."

The straight stuff? She already felt as limp as a used dishrag. "It gets kinkier than this?"

He rose up, pulled her off the counter to stand in front of him, and hugged her close. "You really want to know what it's all about, don't you?"

"I have to know."

"I can't dissuade you?"

"Please," she said simply.

A deep sigh whispered over her. "There's a party tonight. If you're hell-bent on satisfying that curiosity of yours, I can make sure you're invited."

"Will more vampires be there?"

"Half a legion. That enough?"

Sounded crowded. "Will you be there?"

"Of course, but I might be a little busy. I'm sure someone else would love to answer your questions."

Feeling disappointed he wouldn't be with her, she sighed and nuzzled his neck. "You're telling me this isn't special. Only par for the course."

"You're special, love," he said, giving her a squeeze, his chin resting on top of her head. "It's why I wish you'd change your mind."

She hadn't known he was so tall. She wished she'd quit finding things about him she liked.

"You're sexy as hell, responsive to my every touch, and lovely, but I already have someone in my life."

Her breath caught, and she stiffened in his arms. "And she doesn't mind?"

"She's vampire, too. She doesn't mind, because she's in love with someone else. Still, eating out is accepted in our world."

She felt only mildly mollified that even a vampire's love life could be screwed up. "*Eating out?* You make me sound like a McDonald's drive-thru."

"Much prettier than that, and you don't smell like onions."

That made her smile. She sniffed, feeling better by the moment with the silly turn of their conversation. "This party. Will I be safe?"

His chest expanded around another deep sigh. "It's always good to be cautious. Not every vamp you'll meet practices moderation. I'd hate to see you hurt. But yeah, you'll be safe—everyone will be on strict orders to play nice tonight."

"Then I'd like to come."

"I can arrange it. You already met Malcolm. I'll place you in his hands. Plan on being there all night."

* * *

After reluctantly leading a sated and trembling "Sarah" through the darkened exit at the back of the bar and depositing her there, Alex found Malcolm and his crew. They'd been roaming the room, still patrolling, by the looks of it.

Malcolm didn't lift an eyebrow when Alex asked him to bring Sarah to *Ardeal*. Alex gritted his teeth at Malcolm's amusement when he mentioned Malcolm was already acquainted with the girl and how.

Then Alex escaped quickly, not wanting Sarah to get a good look at his face. He wasn't sure that Simon's magic would work on a human, and tonight he couldn't afford for anyone to recognize him as a vampire.

Getting himself into *Ardeal* proved easier than he'd expected.

Alex found Erika trolling along Bourbon Street, a crowd of seven young men surrounding her, following in her trail as though she were the Pied Piper.

Where she'd found them didn't matter. The darkness surrounding them didn't put a damper on their high spirits. Alex slid into the back of the entourage unnoticed.

It was a mixed group. Some regulars from the blood bars, a few fresh faces, likely storm groupies looking for a wild ride. Erika's crotch-high red dress promised a hell of a party. He swallowed the contents of Simon's vial, schooled his expression into an appropriately jovial mask, and followed right along.

Stepping down from the back of the panel truck Erika had provided for transport, he noted the added security on the grounds of the estate and felt a moment's trepidation. Most of them were Nicolas's crew— recruits from his band of rogue vampires, there to provide extra security for the council's meeting and to keep an eye out for signs of the demon stalking ever closer to *Ardeal*.

Alex knew all too well that the demon was already inside the estate. He'd found its last victim, its last human host, draped over the iron fence on the night the zombies had attacked—a fact he needed to convey to Nicolas if he could get close enough to speak to him.

Without receiving a single double take, Alex passed several of the *Revenants* he recognized. Feeling more secure, he relaxed.

Simon had told him the spell he cast would only work on the most suggestible of the turned vampires, those more easily led. If Nicolas spied him, he wasn't likely to let anyone know it. His knowledge of what Alex really was had been earned through a close association—sharing Chessa between them. Not something the ancient *Revenant* could comfortably admit to Inanna. Nicolas had invited Alex to make love to Chessa alongside him, allowing him the opportunity, even unknowing, to impregnate her.

No. Nicolas would keep that secret to himself or risk further retribution. A secret of that magnitude couldn't be overlooked. Inanna would see it as one betrayal too many by Nicolas, for whom she still held affection.

As it was, Nic was sitting pretty—a full-fledged council member now, the only male *Revenant* among a coven of female Born vampires.

Alex entered the mansion, passed through the opulent black and white marble-tiled foyer and straight into Inanna's own salon. It was his first time inside, but he recognized it from the memories he'd inherited from his mother, Natalie. This was the room Inanna had used to introduce Natalie to the pleasures of feeding from a willing host.

He smiled as he thought of his mother's shock when Inanna had bared her breast and cunt for one of her favorite *Revenants*, the swarthy Pasqual, to pleasure her while she'd fed.

Natalie had been unable to resist the blood offered by the other male host Inanna had provided her, and she had allowed herself to be drawn into some heavy petting, which had left her feeling guilty. His father had languished upstairs in a bedroom, manacled to a bed, while she'd drowned in the pleasure of her meal.

The same color-drenched furnishings decorated the golden room as the young men Erika had invited entered and were paired at the door with an eager female vampire. Some knew what would be expected, the price they'd pay. No one would complain once the true nature of the party was revealed.

Alex noted the servant circulating with drinks, and he guessed they'd be spiked with a mystical aphrodisiac to ensure the males' compliance. Desire and hunger would rule tonight. The council would feed both lusts before they deliberated.

Determined to slip away into the shadows at the first opportunity to avoid the blood orgy, he stepped past the woman doling out the males.

When a hand slid around his arm and a soft body sidled close, he glanced to his right, startled to find his grandmother, Natalie's mother, Erika, grinning up at him.

CHAPTER

4

Shuddering inwardly, Alex accepted the drink Erika offered and allowed her to pull him deeper into the salon, his mind working fast. He had to slip away before she tried to make a meal of him.

One bite and she'd know he wasn't human. She might be confused, tasting the rich Born blood circulating in his veins. But even as shallow as she was—as selfish as she'd proven to his mother—she wasn't stupid.

So he smiled, taking a small sip of the laced drink. He nodded, murmuring, "Nice. What's your name? I didn't catch it when we talked in New Orleans," he lied.

"I don't remember you. How is that?" she asked, her gaze sliding over him hungrily.

So names weren't important. Only the blood and sex she could seduce from him mattered.

Alex tightened as a wave of desire swept through his body. Erika's allure was strong. No wonder she'd captured so many willing young hosts. With her shining blond hair, puppylike brown eyes, and luscious figure, she seemed a sexy, golden siren.

He wished he could shake her off his arm and put the width of the room between them. This close, the memories she'd bequeathed him strengthened, rushing through his mind. He nearly choked on the next swallow of the drink as the countless faces of the men she'd bedded and bled flashed by. Her life had been one endless search for pleasure.

Best not to linger in conversation or she'd be stuck like glue to his side for the remainder of the evening. "Which way to the bathroom?" he blurted out.

Her lips pouted, but she lifted her chin toward the French doors leading into the library. "Through there. Don't be long."

Alex stepped forward, darting a glance behind him, and sighed with relief when she approached another man. She had the attention span of a gnat—and just about as much loyalty.

He slipped through the doors and hurried to the bathroom. He poured his drink down the sink, flushed the toilet for good measure, and cracked open the door to make sure he hadn't been followed.

With the library still empty and dark and the sound of soft, bluesy music drifting from the salon, he eased out another set of doors and headed up the long, curved staircase to the bedrooms on the second floor. Chessa's door lay unguarded.

He'd known he was risking everything by coming here, but

once inside the house and so close, he had to see for himself that she was safe.

He checked the monitoring room first, knowing they often spied on the occupants of the very special room next door, but the monitors were turned off, thanks to Nicolas's insistence, no doubt. No one would observe him making love to Chessa, or catch other intimate glimpses of his life with the woman he loved.

His father and mother had suffered that exact indignity for days before making their escape from the estate. Every word, every touch and endless stroke had been noted and reported to Inanna so she could be sure Rene served his purpose and impregnated Alex's mother. How it must have grated when they'd escaped before his birth.

Alex slipped inside Chessa's room and closed the door softly behind him.

Water sloshing in the bathroom alerted him to where she was. He hurried to the door, stepped inside, and closed it with a soft snick, enclosing them together for the first time in days.

Chessa glared from a gleaming clawfoot bathtub. "We're not talking."

A smile tugged at one side of his mouth. God, he'd missed her bitchiness. "Good to see you, too," he said, taking a seat on the closed toilet.

Chessa brought up her knees and crossed her arms over her breasts, a blush staining her cheeks.

"Shy now? I've seen every inch of you," he smiled amusedly.

"There are considerably more inches!" she bit out heatedly.

He dropped the smile and leaned forward. "Are you sorry you're outgrowing your clothes?"

Chessa swallowed hard, then shook her head. "You know I'm not."

Chessa's first child, the one she'd conceived during her first and only season, had been murdered as an infant. Her despair afterward had propelled her away from the coven and had made her accessible to him. That and her unusual heritage had made her the perfect candidate to carry his child. She'd guard this one like a lioness would a cub.

"Let me see, Chessa. Please."

She rolled her eyes and pointed to the towel rack. "I was just about to get out anyway."

Alex stood, grabbed the towel, and waited while Chessa let the water out and rose to stand in the center of the tub. He tried valiantly to ignore the fact that she stood naked, her slick skin gleaming. Her hair fell in black tendrils to frame her angular face and large, luminous eyes.

After giving her body one sweeping glance, he wrapped the towel around her shoulders and held out his hand, assisting her over the rim. Then he knelt and placed his hands over her swollen belly.

He'd had her only days ago, but already she looked like she'd carried the baby for five or six months, thanks to Simon's magic—a potion he'd slipped Alex, which he'd drunk before he'd made love to Chessa.

Leaning closer, he ignored her indrawn breath and kissed her belly, giving her soft skin a final caress before standing again. He wrestled the towel from her stiff fingers to blot her dry with efficient strokes, covering her head first to dry her hair despite her sputtering protests, and then moving downward.

When he knelt to dry her legs, he slid the towel along the outside of her thighs, then slowly dragged it up between, halting to gently finger her smooth labia. "I preferred your dark curls," he murmured.

Chessa reached down and clamped her hand over his. "Nic prefers me nude. I can manage the rest on my own," she said, her voice so tight that the words sounded garbled.

He suppressed a smile, withdrew his fingers slowly from between her legs, and released his grip on the towel. So she wasn't unmoved either.

Satisfied, he leaned a shoulder against the wall while she wrapped the thick terry around her body and glowered.

"Are they treating you well?" he asked, his tone casual.

"My meals are served in bed," she quipped.

"Bet Nic loves that."

"Nic hovers." A fierce scowl drew her dark brows together. "No one dares do more than offer me a goddamn wrist."

"Must be nice for him, all that pent-up frustration and only him for you to let it all go with."

Chessa's eyes narrowed. "Nic's . . . *fine*. He's pretty busy, what with the *sabat* arriving. Which, by the way, you shouldn't be anywhere near. What the hell were you thinking?"

Alex pondered quietly, running the question through his mind. "I was thinking that I had to see you." That was only partially true. "You need to reconsider my offer."

"I'm not leaping to the past to cool my heels for centuries while I wait for *my* life to happen again. I'm not Natalie and Rene. I'm not you. I wouldn't do well in a drafty monastery."

"You'd love it there. All those hard-ass men, clashing swords, and isolation would be right up your alley. You just don't want to leave Nic."

Her gaze gathered shadows. "There is that. I love him, Alex. He loves me. Despite the complications *this* brings," she said, staring at her expanding tummy.

"You know you aren't safe here."

"I won't be safe anywhere." Her mouth crimped in a tight smile. "Face it—I'm carrying the child of the only Born male in living history. Don't you think there are covens and nations of Kin out there who would love to carve it out of me, or keep it if they thought the child could give them an advantage?"

He shot her an exasperated glare. "Exactly why you should just say yes."

"No, no, no!" Her hands fisted, but her expression pleaded. "At least here I know who my enemies are."

Alex looked away, knowing that arguing with Chessa was a waste of time. She wouldn't budge as long as Nicolas needed her. "Do you think I'm your enemy?"

"Do you want this child to raise and nurture? To love?" Her voice dropped to a whisper. "Do you even know how?"

His glance swung back. "I will love it," he said fiercely.

"But you want it for something more. Some grand scheme you and Simon have concocted."

Bitterness burned at the back of his throat. "If there is a 'grand scheme,' I haven't figured it out."

"Simon didn't tell you why you had to fuck me?" she taunted.

"Chessa . . ." He raked his fingers through his hair. "Simon doesn't tell me many things. I knew I had to seduce you. I knew I'd impregnate you. That's all I really knew."

"You're just a pawn. No better than me." She pointed a finger and stabbed his chest. "Only you're being led down the rosy garden path by mages. Fucking tricky-dick bastards. Don't you know there's a reason we don't trust them?"

He wrapped his hand around hers and held it above his

heart. "I've lived all my life in their midst. All my life with Simon. I trust he means no harm, that he has a bigger picture of what's coming when he manipulates us."

She gave a contemptuous snort and wrestled her hand from inside his. "You're a goddamn puppet. Prince of nothing."

"I'm a warrior. They've groomed me to lead." He caught her gaze and held it. "Not just this coven but the entire Vampire Nation."

Chessa grew still, her expression guarded. "That's why you're here then? Not to see me. Is something supposed to happen tonight? I wondered why Nic's been scarce."

Alex cocked his head to the side. "He didn't tell you? The *sabat* is meeting here now."

Chessa's indrawn breath answered his question.

"He's probably trying not to worry you." Alex drew a deep breath, fisting his hands. He wanted to shake her. "You shouldn't be here. He knows that. I want you safe when shit hits the wall."

Chessa's eyes narrowed. "Does Simon know you're talking to me?"

"No."

"Has he pushed the issue of my being here?"

Alex didn't answer. Simon hadn't. For his own reasons, of course. "*I'm* pushing the issue."

Chessa stepped closer, sliding her open palm along his cheek.

His heart stilled. He tilted his head, pressing into her touch, grateful for her tenderness, however fleeting.

"Seems like I'm supposed to be here, Alex," she whispered.

"Will you at least promise me something?" he asked, just as softly.

Her nose wrinkled. "Depends."

He pushed a dripping strand of hair behind her ear. "If things get sticky . . . dangerous . . . you'll let me know?"

"This is your child, too. I won't forget that. I can't."

Alex slipped a hand around the back of her neck and leaned into her. "I do love you, you know."

Her smile was gamine, innocent. "As much as any warrior seeing to the dynasty he intends to rule?"

He snorted. "God, you're a bitch."

Her sliding, devious grin was pure, ball-busting Chessa. "Thought you liked that about me."

He slammed his lips on her grinning mouth, forcing his tongue into her.

Chessa stiffened for a moment, then fell limply against his body, relenting beneath the assault of the allure he cast for her, her body pressing closer, her arms wrapping tightly around him.

Dipping inside her mouth, he tasted her, perhaps for the last time. He dragged his mouth away and pressed his forehead against hers again. "Promise you'll let me know."

"I won't let anything happen to our child," she said, her gaze unblinking beneath his. "I'll get word to you if I need help."

"Don't step outside this door tonight. Let Nicolas feed you. Let no one else inside."

Alex stepped back, letting her go. He raked her with one last possessive, all-encompassing glance, then turned on his heels, leaving her shaking in the middle of the bathroom floor.

Miki ran her finger around the top of her crystal glass, making it sing, pretending an indolence she was far from feeling. Since Malcolm had left her in the salon with one last caution about not drinking too deeply, she'd spent the hour watching the party take a darker turn.

Her earlier encounter with Alex had already left her shaken. Raw, intense lust wasn't something she'd experienced before, but that, added to the fact that she didn't know a damn thing about him—not even what he looked like—had her reeling.

It was clear that the sort of reckless abandonment she'd experienced with Alex wasn't out of the ordinary in this other world. That only increased her fear that she was in way over her head. Most of the invited guests were already operating under the influence of whatever spiked the drinks. The bloodletting had begun. So had the lusting.

Feeling a little like a nasty voyeur, she circulated, never pausing long for fear of being drawn into the sexual play.

Clothing was definitely optional.

The crowd inside the salon where the games began slowly thinned as twosomes, threesomes, and larger groups lazily drifted away. Those who stayed didn't seem to mind baring their bodies and appetites to anyone who wanted to watch.

Miki was particularly fascinated with Erika's grouping. The woman who'd tried to draw her into the library alone had lost her dress, and now wore only glittering jewels in her ears and around her neck. She'd also bared her fangs.

The man lying nude beside her writhed as she raked one sharp tooth down his cock, then opened her mouth and deep-throated him, bending over his lap while another man knelt behind her, fingering her pussy.

Miki took another quick sip of her drink before remembering Malcolm's admonition. Her body was tight, her skin hot. Still, she didn't think she was up for the more serious depravity. She wished Malcolm would return, but he'd held the hand of a beautiful, wispy blond when he'd left. They'd looked happy as they'd slipped away. His girlfriend, no doubt. And another vampire.

She'd seen enough, and she didn't think she'd get answers to any questions tonight. Too much mischief stirred the air.

She left the salon and wandered into the richly appointed foyer, just as the teakwood double doors opened and a beautiful russet-haired woman wearing a crystal-studded midnight gown swept inside, escorted by two men in black formal dress. Her gaze swept over Miki, dismissing her. Then she strode directly across the foyer and through a door between the two sides of the curved staircase.

Miki let out a low whistle, her curiosity once again piqued. But with men posted on either side of the door, she didn't think she had a chance in hell of satisfying it by trying a direct route. Remembering the French doors leading into the garden from the library, she headed back to the salon.

She got only a step inside the door when a handsome man approached her. He didn't speak, just snagged her hand and lifted it to his lips for a lingering kiss. "Thank you for your gift," he said, his simple words made more extraordinary by a hint of French inflection.

She knew the formal words, had heard them spoken each time a vampire had raised his or her mouth from a blood host. "I haven't given you a thing."

"But you will."

Rather than feeling angry at his arrogance, a surge of heat flooded her—thick, immediate, so strong she knew she wouldn't resist long. And she didn't want to. Knowing this one ranked off the pheromone scale, she tried halfheartedly one last time. "I'm not into the group thing," she said weakly.

"The library's empty, *ma petite*," he said, without missing a beat. "We'll be alone."

"I know where it is." She walked past Erika, who now rode one of her hosts, straddling him, her knees planted on either side of his hips on a pillowy, wine-colored sofa.

By the time she reached the library, her legs quivered. She kept her back to him, listening as he quietly closed the door and then drew near her, to stand just behind her.

Without attempting another halfhearted demur, she turned and raised her face to his.

His hands cupped her cheeks tenderly, and he bent down to kiss her.

Eyes wide open, Miki threaded her fingers through his thick, dark hair, then traced more along the square curve of his strong jaw. Her mouth opened beneath his, welcoming the spear of his tongue. She sucked on it for a moment, then moaned as liquid heat trickled from inside her.

"So eager," he said, drawing away.

She was. Alex hadn't been wrong about those pheromones. They intoxicated, completely banishing inhibitions. "I've fed one vampire tonight. You can't take much more of my blood."

"A pity," he said, pushing her hair behind her ears and rubbing a thumb across her bottom lip. "Another precious gift then? Or perhaps just one, well-timed bite?"

"Please," she said, surprising herself with her forwardness.

A grin stretched his perfect mouth. "And I thought you a little shy," he replied, his voice teasing.

Miki gave him a small frown. "This is new to me. Not my first time, I mean. What I'm saying is I'm experimenting. But I don't know if I can handle a casual quickie."

"You want romance with your sex?"

Romance? Not something she'd considered or desired before, but with his dark good looks and sensual intensity, she knew she wanted something more. "Will you pretend for me?"

"Will it make it easier for you to say yes? I do need to feed . . ."

"I've already done that, I think. Said yes. I just want some ground rules."

He gave her a slow nod, then took her hand again and drew her to a leather couch with its back facing the garden. As much privacy as they'd be allowed, she guessed.

"You'll be delightful. Your flavors will please my lady."

Startled, Miki frowned. "I don't get it. The way you all are so easy. Your lady won't mind?"

"I didn't say she wouldn't mind. But the jealousy only sparks her fire . . . and it isn't as if I haven't had to stand back and watch her love another." He drew Miki down to the leather couch, then knelt in front of her, drawing her clothes away slowly, piece by piece.

As each one drifted away, he caressed the skin he bared in slow, even strokes that raised goose bumps in his wake and had her blood heating, pooling between her legs. His lady was lucky indeed. . . .

When Miki sat naked in front of him, his gaze locked with hers, and he placed his hands on her knees. He spread them open, and Miki sank back against the soft, buttery leather with a trembling sigh.

"You will do everything I command."

Not a question. Miki's breaths shortened at the firmness of his voice and the quiet, burning sensuality in his expression, knowing her limited knowledge of sex was about to be enhanced. "Tell me what you want," she whispered.

"Watch me. Don't close your eyes. Not once, or I will stop."

That sounded easy enough.

His hands smoothed up the tops of her thighs until they reached the juncture, then his thumbs slid down and spread her lips.

This time she could see what he saw, see the expression of the man as he leaned over her open sex and tongued her. Fierce, hot elation swept through her.

His full, masculine lips mouthed her labia, tugging them, pulling them until they were plump and so sensitive she thought she'd scream.

When he suctioned at the moist, tender flesh between them, her hips rose to press closer, urging him inside.

His tongue stroked out, sinking into her, swirling inside before retreating again. He lifted his head and gave her a sharpened glance. "Alex has been busy."

How could he know? Then she blurted out the question.

"Our senses of taste and scent are far superior to yours. He must have rolled his face between your legs. I can understand— you're delicious and so very responsive. I could swim in your pleasure."

Miki's whole body shuddered. "Fuck me, please?" God, she'd actually said that?

His small, self-satisfied smile irked while at the same time tugging her arousal higher. "When I'm ready."

He bent again, this time licking her with the flat of his tongue—long broad strokes, from the bottom of her pussy to the top, lapping like a dog, the strokes evenly timed, almost soothing, except the longer he plied her with his tongue, the more restless she became. Her hands tightened on the soft leather cushions beneath her. Her breasts hardened, the tips extending as they grew more engorged.

As his tongue stroked lower, she didn't have the breath to protest. When he glanced over her other entrance, she drew in a hissing breath and began to close her eyes.

His tongue halted. His body stilled.

Miki opened her eyes wide.

Firm hands slid beneath her bottom, raising it. Thumbs pressed apart her buttocks.

Bracing on her forearms, Miki lifted her legs into the air, allowing him to tilt her toward his mouth, and she groaned when his tongue laved her tiny asshole.

Over and over again, he teased and prodded, soothing with broader strokes when she began to keen.

Finally, he lowered her and leaned back. "I want you bent over the arm of the sofa."

So much for romance, but the tightness of his voice indicated he might be every bit as turned on as she was. The thought intensified the excitement coiling at her core.

Awkwardly, without much room to maneuver between them, she lowered her legs to the ground and rose up, her pussy inches from him. She blushed when she realized she'd have to push against his face to climb past him.

His slow grin told her he knew her dilemma.

Her knees wobbled as she straightened, brushing her open sex against his nose.

His chest rose as he inhaled; she gasped when he burrowed between her lips and swirled his chin and mouth against her. Then he slid his hands behind her thighs and leaned away, helping her balance.

She stepped sideways to climb past him. He didn't move

from the ground, just stared as she stood at the end of the couch and contemplated the thickly padded leather bolster.

He lifted one eyebrow, giving her a look that said a world about his arrogance and confidence.

She bent slowly over the padded arm of the couch, her face heating at his low chuckle. Still, she liked how vulnerable she felt, her ass raised high in the air, all leverage lost as only her toes touched the floor.

He shoved upward, unbuckled his belt and slid down his zipper, loosening his trousers just enough to reach inside and slowly draw out his cock.

His hand caressed it, sliding up and down its length in one long stroke. Then his gaze rose to meet hers.

Miki's mouth opened automatically, her breaths already panting. She didn't know, didn't care whether the drug had just kicked in or his "special powers" and amazing cock inspired her. Liquid gushed between her legs, trickling down her spread thighs. The way he looked at her, as though he would devour her, as though he meant to take her savagely, had her shaking and her pussy pulsing.

He came to stand beside her, holding his cock in his hand. "Wet it with your tongue."

She leaned toward it, opening her mouth obediently, and swallowed the thick tip. He stroked into her, gliding along her tongue, pressing deeper until she opened her jaws and let him fill her. He tapped the back of her throat twice, gently, then pulsed in and out, more shallowly, before withdrawing completely.

Reluctant to let him go, she followed with her mouth, kissing his cock and rubbing her lips over the soft tip.

His laughter was a deep, sinful rumble. He disappeared

from her sight, but his hands caressed her backside, palms lifting her cheeks, rolling them firmly up and down, then apart, his thumbs sliding between the globes.

Miki's legs trembled, and he laughed again. When his cock nudged between her legs, she groaned, tried to scoot back to take him, but he pushed her forward. Her toes left the ground.

He nudged again, this time sliding along her seam, then he prodded inside, just the tip, just a tease.

"Please, please fuck me," she groaned.

"I want you to caress your breasts. My hands are busy elsewhere."

She quickly brought her hands to her breasts and cupped them, squeezing. Her nipples were tight and scraped her palms.

The man behind her pushed inside again, this time deeper, stroking inward, stretching her inner walls, while his thumbs slid deeper between her buttocks and rubbed her asshole.

Miki couldn't breathe, couldn't think. She wriggled, trying to coax him deeper. She needed more.

When a thick thumb pushed inside her ass, her back arched and she pinched her nipples, loving the painful pressure behind her and needing more. She twisted her fingers.

His cock began to move in and out, his hips gliding side to side to stretch her as he crammed into her. He toggled his thumb in her ass, digging deeper. Then holding it still, he hooked it to pull up. He thrust his cock faster.

Miki's teeth chattered. Her ass burned, her pussy convulsed—welcoming him deeper.

He thrust faster, harder, slapping against her wet juncture as he crashed deeper inside her. She squeezed her inner muscles, discovering it increased the friction building between them.

His low growling moan pleased her, gave her a sense of power, and she squeezed again.

He bent over her, slipped his free hand beneath her body and slid it under her hand to grasp her breast. She arched her back toward him, wanting more contact. His hot skin to hers.

When he nuzzled her neck through her hair, she knew what else he craved, and she shook her head, making her hair fall forward over her face, baring her neck.

His bite stung, his thighs hardened as he pushed and ground his cock deeper, moving them both with his rough, powerful thrusts, forward and back, as he began to draw on the wound he'd made.

Blood rushed from her head. She felt a little dizzy, but elation swept through her at the same time. He pounded her, rocking the sofa so hard that it budged, its legs scraping on the wood floor.

Now, he powered into her, stroking hard, deep, ramming into her channel, churning in the cream he'd drawn from her arousal. Her whole body tightened, arching higher—then she exploded, a long thin wail ripping from her, punctuated noisily by his harsh thrusts. Until at last a stream of hot liquid bathed her womb and hot walls, soothing as he slowed his thrusts.

He disengaged his fangs, licked her neck in tender laps, and slowly pulled away, leaving her slumped over the cushioned arm, unable to move.

A door creaked open. "They're ready for you, Nic," came a low, amused drawl, one she recognized from the alley, when he'd interrupted another sexy bite.

Clothing rustled. A zipper scraped. A hand slid up the back of her thigh and squeezed her bottom. "Now, I thank you for the gift. Be sure to send my greetings to Alex."

As he walked away, Miki scraped the hair from her sweaty face and watched his tall frame disappear into a bright hallway.

A glance at her watch had her wincing. There were still hours until dawn. How many more temptations would she face before this night was done?

CHAPTER

5

Alex returned to the salon, avoiding a path that might take him near his grandmother. He needn't have worried about drawing her attention. Erika was lost in a sensual haze, her gaze unfocused as she bounced on the lap of one of the handsome bucks she'd collected for the evening.

Needing fresh air to clear his head and dampen his disgust, he headed straight for the library, knowing the doors inside that room would lead him to the garden stretching along the side and back of the house.

Behind him a murmur of voices rose, and he looked over his shoulder, his gaze catching on the matriarch of the *Ardeal* coven, Inanna. This was the first time he'd ever seen her in the flesh rather than through time-clouded glimpses of memories in his vast store. And although he knew doing so was dangerous, he couldn't help giving in to the urge to draw closer.

She must have cast an allure over the entire room, so attentive was every gaze, including his own, on her slim body as she swept inside. Long midnight hair, shiny as a raven's wing, brushed past her shoulders to flow down the back of a simple wine-colored sarong. Her slender body was nude beneath it, the silk clinging to the points of her breasts and swirling in the hollow between her thighs. Dark rubies studded the black choker around her neck.

The lids of her almond-shaped eyes were half-closed, like a cat's, as her gaze slowly landed on each man in the room, before seeking the next. Each time her gaze paused, the man sucked in a deep breath, hoping for a nod, a gesture to draw nearer, which she never gave. Until she reached him. Her full lips curved into a slow smile and *she* sauntered toward him.

His body stilled with alarm, as well as a deepening arousal. How the fuck would he keep her from discovering what he was if she decided to take a bite?

She lifted her hand, a graceful, regal movement.

Without hesitating, he slid his beneath hers, bent his head, and raised her soft, slender hand to his mouth. The kiss he gave her smooth skin lingered.

Not by his will.

"So handsome," she said in a lilting voice. "Erika does have an eye."

With her hand still resting on his, Alex swayed imperceptibly on his feet. His face felt hot, then cold. *Shit.* He couldn't stop the rush of memories that swept through him like a torrent.

Searing, suffocating heat. A hot breeze licking over moist skin.

Moonlight silvering the interior of a large, sparsely furnished room. A bed draped in gauze curtains.

A furtive glance down the empty hallway assured privacy, and she entered the room, easing the door closed behind her. She crept closer, her body quivering at the low groans emanating from deeper inside the chamber.

She paused to pinch her nipples through her thin, linen gown, drawing them erect until they scraped deliciously against the fabric.

She approached the bed and swept aside the gauze curtain, staring hungrily at the naked man writhing on the bed, hand fisted around his straining cock. The aphrodisiacal powder the wizard had sprinkled liberally on his food had worked beyond her imaginings.

He would not resist her, however much he respected her father and wished to earn his place at court through his own merits.

"Get out!" he gritted between jaws clenching so hard that his teeth ground loudly.

Inanna's thighs rubbed together, smearing evidence of the desire trickling from her body. She smiled, congratulating herself for choosing so well. The warrior's strong body would pleasure her endlessly and father a ferocious child.

Muscles flexed along his taut abdomen as he rutted into his hand. His thick flanks tensed, carved into relief by moonlight gleaming on sweat as he pulsed helplessly.

That he was handsome—curling dark hair, a strong, masculine jaw, and thin, sensual lips—only added to her delight.

Inanna stepped closer, reaching out to trail her fingertips slowly from his ankle, moving upward.

His powerful leg trembled—but he didn't command her to stop. When she reached his upper thigh, she paused to unfasten the brooch holding her gown at her shoulder. It slithered to the floor.

His ravenous gaze swept her body in an almost physical caress, halt-

ing to examine her distended nipples and her glistening sex. Although the flush staining his cheeks said he was embarrassed by his lack of self-control, his fist ground up and down his cock faster.

"Let me soothe you," she whispered. "Use my body, my woman's furrow, to slake your lust. No one will know."

His lips lifted in a feral snarl.

She took no offense, knowing his show of resistance was false because of the desperation glittering in his eyes.

She smoothed both hands around his fist and knelt on the bed to come over him, her eager lips opening to swallow the tip of his cock.

This time she would use just her mouth for seduction. His respite would be short. When the heat rose again, he'd be forced to accept the relief she offered.

How delicious he was, how glorious would be her satisfaction when her sister cried over the loss of his affections.

With effort, Alex pulled away his hand and opened his eyes.

Inanna gave him a quizzical glance.

"Too much to drink. Forgive me," he said quickly.

Her light, sultry laughter lifted the hairs on the back of his neck.

A tall dark Cajun sidled up beside her, gave Alex a searing glare, and leaned down to whisper in Inanna's ear.

Her glance swept over Alex again, and her lips formed a disappointed pout before she turned and slipped her arm inside the curved elbow of her ever loyal paramour—Pasqual.

Alex let out a deep, relieved breath. He gave himself a stern admonition not to let his arrogance lead him into danger in this court of intrigue.

He slowly circled the room, fighting his own impatience. When he reached the library, he noted a rustling coming from the bathroom, so he headed straight for the French doors and let himself out into the garden, where he breathed in the honeysuckle and rose-scented air, grateful for the respite from the heavy, murky air inside. The scent of sex and blood had become so thick that he thought it would permeate his clothing and his skin. He hated the decadence. Hated the lack of restraint and respect.

Not that he didn't understand the underlying lusts that ruled all vampires or that he didn't seek his own liaisons to satisfy them. But he could measure a creature's strength of character in how he approached assuaging those hungers.

Indiscriminate feeding and sex took no imagination. Taught no lessons.

Perhaps his view had been skewed by spending centuries with a former monk. Lately, however, he'd acted on instincts, on those insidious hungers. Taking Chessa might have been planned, but he'd gloried in the ease with which the act had finally happened.

And then Sarah, whom he'd only meant to protect in that dark alley. What had started as a bite, something to ease her fear and his own hungers, had overwhelmed him. If Malcolm hadn't interrupted, Alex would have taken her right then and there. When she'd found him at the blood bar, he'd finally given way to his lust.

In any case, he was ready to focus on the true business of the evening. He had to know what happened when the *sabat* met. He wouldn't be allowed in the room, couldn't even let anyone know of his interest.

Nicolas was the key. He'd have to approach him afterward. But how would he while away the hours in the meantime?

He wandered through the dark garden, avoiding the pools

of light spilling from the paned windows and French doors, compliments of the generator droning in the distance. Hands clasped behind his back, he pretended boredom in case he was observed, while inside he felt frustrated, impatient, wishing he were anywhere but here.

Here was a dangerous, incestuous cesspool. Yet Chessa wouldn't budge from *Ardeal*. She complicated matters. How would he keep her safe from the *sabat* and Inanna? Chessa knew Inanna was crafty and untrustworthy, but she didn't know the depths to which her *grandmère* would go to get exactly what she wanted.

A door leading from the library creaked quietly open, then closed again. Was someone following him? Alex stepped behind a tall white column to watch.

A woman stepped into a pool of moonlight. She adjusted her clothing, cursing softly under her breath. Disheveled, her long red hair mussed, she raked her fingers through it, wrinkled her nose in disgust, and glanced around.

Dressed in a brown leather bomber jacket and jeans, he recognized her instantly. Malcolm had indeed added her to the last patrol from New Orleans—brought her as food for the straight *Revenants*. By the careful way she walked, he could tell that she'd already indulged in the debauchery. Not that he could blame any man for wanting to take a bite. Her vibrant coloring was like feathers cloaking a luscious little bird. Ripe for plucking.

Alex eased himself closer to her through the shadows, wondering why this woman seemed fated to cross his path again and again.

Her straight back ended in a lush round bottom. Her legs were long and slim. But it was her face that arrested him.

Porcelain-pale skin. A short, blunt nose and rounded, stubborn chin. Although he still couldn't tell their color, her eyes were large and luminous.

She walked deeper into the garden, found a teakwood bench, and settled gingerly down.

Her eyelids fluttered shut for a moment and she inhaled, her shoulders rising, then relaxing visibly. When she opened them again, her expression grew disgruntled. "Damn, I need a bath."

Perhaps here was a bit of distraction to keep him amused as he waited. He quietly approached her from behind. "Enjoying the party?" he asked, deepening his voice so that she wouldn't recognize it.

She jumped, her head swiveling to find him in the shadows. Her eyes widened on him. "I thought I was alone," she said, her tone indicating her preference that he leave. "Besides, I already gave. Twice," she bit out. "So no tricks—keep those damn pheromones and fangs to yourself."

"I'm not a *Revenant*," he said easily, not the least put off by her bristling.

"I don't care what the hell you call yourself, no more 'gifts' are happenin' here."

Despite her prickly demeanor, he settled on the bench beside her, leaning back as though he was oblivious to her annoyance and meant to stay a while. "I *meant*, I'm not one of the turned vampires."

"You're not a vampire?" Her gaze narrowed. "Every vampire I've met has been beyond beautiful. You're too handsome to be a normal guy."

He preferred an indirect response to an outright lie. "I came with a group of guys from New Orleans to attend the party. But thanks for the compliment."

Her expression was no less suspicious. "Did you know it would be like this?"

"Pretty much."

"Then I'm surprised you're out here. Erika seems to have plenty to go around."

He didn't have to pretend a shudder. "She's a slut."

The woman snorted. "Plenty of those here, that's for sure," she said, her voice smaller.

Hearing the soft self-recrimination in her tone, he canted his head and reached over to lift a strand of hair stuck to her sweaty cheek. "Did anyone do something they shouldn't have?" he asked, tucking the strand behind her ear. "Some thing . . . uninvited?"

She glanced away, her lips twisting. "No, but it's not like they play fair."

Alex found her confiding in him as though he were just a harmless stranger—a *human* stranger—amusing, as well as refreshing. "Their allure can be overwhelming," he murmured.

"Exactly," she said, her agreement emphatic. She turned slightly toward him. "I just can't believe—"

"You can't beat yourself up just because a few of them got to you. It's not your fault."

"Not a few," she said hotly, her body stiffening. "What do you take me for?"

He lifted his eyebrows in mock horror. "More, then?"

A scowl drew her dark brows together, and her lips pouted in a bullish moue.

"Sorry. A couple?" He knew even before her curt nod that

Nicolas had fed his hungers; his scent lingered in the air around her body. Made his own tighten with jealousy. Had Nic done it on purpose when he'd scented Alex's musk on her skin?

"I haven't gotten even one bite tonight, but I'm finding it harder to resist them. I think they spiked the drinks. They do that sometimes at these gatherings," he suggested to draw her out even more.

"Not anything I can help you with, buddy. Gonna have to take care of it yourself."

"Will you watch?" he asked innocently.

Her nose wrinkled in disgust. "Uhhh . . . *no!*"

He grinned. "Sorry, I was just teasing. You seem a little tense. Thought I might lighten your mood."

The corners of her lips curved upward, and she ducked her head. When her gaze returned to his, a solemn expression replaced it. "Is it always about sex?"

"Can't help it. I drank too much."

"I don't mean you. Those . . . creatures . . . inside."

Alex waggled his eyebrows. "I hate to break it to you, but when there are men and women in proximity of each other— whatever their species—it's usually about the sex."

"I knew that, in a sort of intellectual way," she said slowly, "but tonight's been damn confusing."

"Get your first bite tonight?"

She nodded, a blush coloring her cheeks. "I kind of wish it had stopped at that." Her legs crossed, then uncrossed. "I met a man tonight. He was my . . . first bite. It blew me away. Which is why I don't get them spiking the drinks."

"The 'drug' they use serves a couple of purposes. It lowers inhibitions—"

Her brows drew low. "They have those special pheromones, why would they need more?"

"It also helps to keep the details of what happens tonight a little fuzzy."

"I only had a sip of a mixed drink. I stuck to the bottled water."

Alex sucked in a breath. "You drank the Perrier?"

"Yeah." She must have seen his wince. "Spiked, too?" she asked, her voice rising. His solemn nod pulled the corners of her mouth downward. "This is so not fair. All I wanted was a little information."

"Curiosity brought you here?" he said, finding it amusing to pretend he didn't already know.

Her head nodded vigorously, flipping hair against her cheeks. "Should have known better. Alex said my questions would be answered here, but Malcolm couldn't disappear fast enough with his girlfriend."

The vehemence in her voice intrigued him. "What questions?"

"About them," she said, pointing toward the house. "Where they come from? What they can do? How they've managed to keep hidden so long?"

"Why the burning interest?" He widened his eyes and dragged in an exaggerated breath. "Are you a groupie? Or here from the *National Enquirer*?"

Her casual shrug contrasted with the way her gaze slid away. The woman wasn't a skilled liar. Something else he found attractive about her.

"I'm just . . . curious."

"'Just curious' made you take some huge risks."

"I need to know . . . things. How the world works. What's in it. You know what I mean?"

"Sure," he said, although his own curiosity was piqued now. "I'm Alexander, by the way," he said, watching her expression closely.

Her gaze sharpened on his face. "Alexander Bytheway? Odd name," she said airily. He could tell she was forcing the lightness, because her breaths were coming faster.

Alex grinned. "Who are you?"

"I'm M—Sarah."

"Mm-Sarah. Nice to meet you," he said, holding out his hand. "Is there anything wrong?"

She winced, then shook her head. "The man I met earlier, his name was Alex."

"Common enough." He couldn't resist needling her a little more. "Does he look anything like me?" he asked, still holding out his hand for her to take.

She bit her lower lip, and moisture welled in her eyes, making her blink. "Not a bit," she whispered. For several seconds, her gaze flicked between his hand and his face, but slowly she raised hers.

When he enclosed her small hand inside his, he squeezed.

Her legs shifted, crossed. Arousal bloomed, the aroma wafting in the air. "I think I need to find a ride home," she said, urgency in her tone.

Her aroma, sweet and crisp, went straight to his cock. "Why did you come to the garden? Escaping?"

"I . . . I thought maybe I could take a walk around."

"Around the back? You curious about the strange goings-on—the other party?"

"Is that what it is? Some awfully high-flying people seem to be gathering back there. I saw one of them. I swear, the crystals on her dress looked like diamonds."

"Probably were. Think about it. Some of them have lived a long time. That's time enough to gather a lot of wealth." Her quickening breaths told him how uncomfortable she was growing. Her palm heated, moistening against his.

She tugged her hand. "You can let go of my hand now."

"Are you feeling all right?" he asked, injecting concern, while inside he felt only a growling satisfaction. Soon, very soon, she'd have to admit defeat. And he wouldn't have to use even a suggestion of his own allure to draw her closer.

"I'm just a little warm."

"Sarah," he said softly, "by now, you know there's only one cure for what ails you."

Her eyes filled with tears she once again quickly blinked away. "You promise you're not a revenuer?"

"*Revenant*. And yes, I swear it. Let me help?"

"I hate this," she said, her voice thickening as her distress grew. "I don't ever act this way. *I don't lust!*"

"No boyfriends?"

"None. I keep to myself. Nose to the grindstone. That's me."

"Sounds a little dull."

Her eyebrows lowered. "My life's full. Not everyone needs to fuck like bunny rabbits to have a good time."

"Fucking has its joys."

"You're a guy. Of course you'd say that." She groaned and bent forward, arms folded over her stomach.

He laid a hand on her back. "Gonna be sick?"

"I'm trying not to jump your bones." She raised her head to glare at him. "Did I mention I think you're really good looking?"

"Getting more so by the minute?" he quipped.

"Uh . . . if we do this . . . if I let you . . ."

"Fuck you?"

Her lips twisted. "God, I hate that word."

"You used it first," he pointed out.

"Are you always such a smart-ass?"

Alex scooted closer to her on the bench and put his arm around her shoulders, bending to look closely into her eyes. "Sarah, I can help you. Why don't you just sit on my lap for a little bit. We don't have to do anything you're uncomfortable with. I'll go slow."

Her eyebrows drew together in a ferocious scowl. "You're not into anything kinky, are you?"

He couldn't help but smile. If she only knew. "Nothing extraordinary," he lied. "Just plain vanilla fucking."

She groaned and shook her head. "God, that word again."

"You said it fir—"

"I know, but when you say it, I get—"

"Hotter?"

"Uh-huh."

"Sit on my lap, love. I promise not to bite."

Sarah straightened, gave him a stricken look, and half rose up.

Alex opened his arms, helped her climb onto his lap sideways, and pressed her head to his shoulder. "It'll be all right," he said, surprised at the twinge of tenderness that swept through him. It hadn't required pretending.

"Touch me, please," she whispered.

"Show me where," he said, lifting his hand and holding it for her to take and guide.

"Sarah" was quick to grab it, slip it under the lapel of her jacket, and press it hard against her warm breast.

He didn't make her ask for more. He shaped her gently in his palm, scraping his thumb across her clothed nipple. He massaged her, knowing his slow, tender movements would build an unbearable fire inside her.

Silently, he cursed Inanna and her minions. There were plenty of willing hosts. The aphrodisiac had been overkill and unusually cruel to someone as confused and inexperienced as this girl.

Still, he couldn't help but be fiercely glad he was here now. To help, of course.

"That's nice, but I'm really hurting now," she said, her voice muffled against his chest.

Alex slid his hand downward, thumbed open her jeans, and slowly drew the zipper down. Then he flattened his hand to slip it inside, gliding down until his fingers met her short curls. He reached lower to slide into delicious, wet heat.

She gasped and pressed her hot face harder into his shirt to muffle a moan.

"Sweetheart, you're going to have to open your legs a bit."

"God, I don't know why I'm so embarrassed. I let both of those neck-biters do much worse without being the least red-cheeked."

"You were under the influence of their allure. Nic's probably knocked you sideways."

"How'd you know it was him? Did you see us in the library?"

Kicking himself mentally for the slip, he murmured his assent.

"You know him?"

"I've met him a time or two." *And fucked his woman with him sitting right beside us.*

She shifted her legs slightly apart. "Is that enough room?"

He toggled his finger on her engorged clit. "You tell me."

"Almost," she said, sounding disgruntled. "Damn."

"How much of that bottle did you drink?"

"All of it." Her thighs tightened, then opened again around his hand. "I was pretty thirsty. Should have known better. The seal was broken. I thought they were being overly helpful."

"Sarah," he said, hugging her body closer to his chest. "It's going to take a while before the effects fade."

"I ache, Alexander," she groaned. "Help me."

He rubbed her clit again, softly scraping the pad of his finger on her tender flesh.

Her hips moved restlessly, scooping upward. "Would you kiss me like you mean it?" she said in a small voice.

Feeling a bit like the wolf teasing Little Red Riding Hood, he nuzzled her cheek until she turned her face upwards. The kiss he pressed against her lips was soft, tentative. She tasted just as sweet as before. Uncomplicated.

She kept her eyes open, staring into his while he ate at her soft lips, as though kissing had been something she'd only newly discovered, or as though she wanted to remember the moment.

He wondered how she'd come to be in that alley. How someone so ill-equipped to maneuver in this world had even found entrance.

His fingers slid deeper, continuing to graze her clit, but

seeking her moist center. He slid inside her, keeping his eyes open too, and he watched while her vision became clouded and her lush mouth rounded beneath his.

"Alexander?" she said, leaning back to break the kiss.

"Yes, Sarah?"

"I can't take any more of this. Make love to me."

CHAPTER
6

Miki wished she'd met Alexander under other circumstances. She might have been attracted to him without any special "help" whatsoever. His handsome face and strong body, so wonderfully complimented by a sense of humor and honor, made him just about perfect.

As it was, she sincerely hoped she never saw him again.

Tonight was an anomaly in her quiet, straightforward little life. She'd been used; her body had been ravished twice already. Before she'd entered the garden she'd shakily roused herself from the end of the sofa to pull her clothing over sticky skin. Standing all alone in the library after being abandoned by a man whose name she would never have known if another hadn't called out to him—she'd been forgotten by him in a moment—had somehow made her feel . . . *less*.

Less herself, less in control, less prideful of all she'd accomplished in such a short time since her "awakening."

And she'd bargained for it all. Sacrificed her blood and her shallow store of memories to fill them with selfish, momentary pleasure and information she didn't think explained away the violent dreams that plagued her.

Yet something about Alexander's playful teasing and surprisingly gentle touch soothed her bruised inner self. For that, she would be forever grateful.

With the drug she'd ingested climbing up her spine, she knew she was still operating under another sort of spell—maybe not the powerful "allure" *Alex* had described, but something else that compromised her values and her natural caution.

She ignored the warnings of her conscience to trust he meant no harm. To trust he might provide her not only relief but also memories to supplant the darker passions she'd experienced this evening.

"Are you sure?" Alexander asked as he held her close. "We can simply wait out each wave and handle it discreetly, just like this."

He made it sound so ordinary, so practical, that she felt slightly less embarrassed that he was talking about her arousal while his fingers swirled inside her. "Why would you do that for me? You don't know me."

"Maybe I like being your knight in shining armor."

She bit her lip when a firm rub shot a jagged bolt of electricity through her, nearly bringing her to orgasm. Miki pressed her face into the crook of his neck and panted. "You don't strike me as the chivalrous sort . . . although you're being very . . ."

"Kind?" he said, amusement and concern intermingled in his tone.

"Helpful," she bit out. Her body tightened on another, stronger wave of heat that plucked her nipples into tight, aching beads. "*Alexander.*"

"Easy there," he said, giving her shallow thrusts of his fingers, the depth of his reach impeded by her clothing.

Frustrated, humiliated . . . but yearning for so much more, she leaned back and cupped his cheek with one palm. "I don't need you to be polite right now. I just need you."

Alexander sighed as though she'd asked him a great, inconvenient favor, but the hint of laughter in his eyes told her he only teased. "How do you want this, Sarah?"

Miki liked the easy way he gave her power—as though they'd been lovers for a very long time and this was part of their own ritual. "I want us both naked," she said without hesitation. "Your skin on mine."

"Sounds rather ordinary."

"I want ordinary. Please? Plain vanilla."

"I'll tell you a secret." He nuzzled her cheek. "Vanilla's my favorite flavor."

"*Quickly?*"

"Vanilla to go, then." He rose from the bench, carrying her in his arms. "I know just the place," he said and headed deeper into the garden, toward a gazebo.

Moonlight brightened as clouds thinned momentarily, illuminating the whitewashed, latticed structure. He climbed the steps, set her on her feet in the center of the planked floor, then pulled the cushions from the benches lining the outer walls to fashion a makeshift bed.

Miki wrapped her arms around her belly, shivering as she waited. When he'd arranged everything to his satisfaction, he finally looked back at her.

A frisson of alarm quickened her pulse. Gone was the teasing man. Now she noted just how large he was, how his height loomed over her, casting a long shadow. The breadth of his shoulders stretched the white buttoned shirt he wore, which couldn't disguise the thick muscles of his arms. Below, his legs, spread and braced on the wooden floor, were encased in dark trousers that hugged thickly hewn thighs.

She wondered who he really was. His hair was a little too long to be a businessman's. His body was too well built, too honed for a desk job. The dark intensity of his gaze had her guessing he had a more dangerous profession. Bodyguard, professional wrestler, fireman, cop.

She wondered why she was wasting time guessing. Running would be the smart thing to do right about now. Right before he stepped in front of her, framed her face with his large hands, and bent to kiss her.

Miki moaned against his mouth, giving up on any thoughts of a rational course of action—surrendering to the pressure of his firm lips.

His arms moved slowly around her, as though he didn't want to spook her, or perhaps to give her one last chance to change her mind.

But Miki couldn't break the delicious kiss. Alexander rubbed his lips on hers in drugging circles, coaxing her to part them with soft thrusts of his tongue against the seam of her closed lips. She smiled for a moment and felt his mouth tighten with an answering grin, then she opened to let him inside.

As his tongue stroked inward, he shifted on his feet, widening his legs. He gripped her hips and pulled her closer, close enough for her to feel the column of flesh rising against his belly. His mouth trailed from her lips to her ear. "See what you do to me?"

She shivered at the tight, growling quality of his voice. "I impress myself," she teased, almost feeling sorry for him. His cock was a thick, long ridge straining against the fly of his trousers. Her pussy tightened, ready to grasp it, ready to swallow him whole. She undulated against him, rocking to cup his length against her belly.

Then because she thought he might take his own sweet time, trying to go slowly for her sake, she tucked her hand between their bodies and reached down to touch him—first his balls, giving them a gentle, but firm, squeeze. Then she traced his length with her fingers, rubbing up and down the thick column through his pants until he rutted into her hand.

Lord help her, she wanted to feel his cock rutting inside her, churning in the cream seeping from her depths.

Miki wrestled out of her jacket—a chore since his arms still held her close. She leaned away and let her fingers fly down the row of buttons at the front of her shirt. It too landed somewhere behind her on the floor. The bra nearly defeated her, because by now her hands shook too hard.

Alexander pushed her fingers away, slipped his thumb under the band, and opened it with a deft twist.

When warm, humid air licked at her nipples, Miki's eyes fluttered closed. The relief, the teasing softness filled her with urgent despair.

Her lover released her and knelt on one knee in front of her, going for the gaping waist of her jeans.

Fearing she might crumple to the ground, she clasped his shoulders to steady herself as he slid her pants down her legs until they bunched around her ankles.

"Should have thought about the boots first," he grumbled.

"Please hurry," she said, scissoring her thighs shallowly to ease the ache flaring between them.

"Let me do something for you. Afterwards, I'll give you vanilla, baby." He didn't wait for her assent, just pressed on her thighs until she made a space, and he put his face between her legs.

Without preamble, his mouth latched onto her swollen clitoris.

Relief was immediate, exploding through her, wrenching a cry from her as she trembled against him. He continued to suckle long after the tremors subsided, then he lapped softly at her, soothing her.

"That happened absurdly fast," she gasped.

"Glad I could be of service. Now, let's get the rest of your clothes off before it starts again." He struggled with her boots, then tugged her narrow jeans down the rest of the way until she stepped out of them and was completely nude.

"No fair," she said shakily.

"I won't ask you to help me. Just lie down and get comfortable."

His clothes hit the ground so quickly that she almost smiled, but already the ache was building, slamming through her fast. She spread her legs and eased her fingers into her pussy, trying to assuage the burning tension.

Naked at last, Alexander knelt at her feet, and she opened wider, waiting impatiently as he settled between her splayed thighs, stretching his body slowly over hers, giving her time to adjust to the feel of his warm skin and weight against her. When he stopped moving, his body, so broad-shouldered and heavy, pushed her deep into the soft cushions.

Breathless and trembling with uncertainty and anticipation, Miki closed her eyes briefly, then brought up her knees on either side of his hips, inviting him without words to slide inside her.

His face, partially lit by a stripe of moonlight, betrayed his inner tension. His lower jaw ground upward, his nostrils flared. However, he didn't move his hips, didn't attempt to take her, although she'd issued a clear invitation. Instead, one hand smoothed over her hair, then cupped her chin, his thumb curving to rub her bottom lip as he stared.

"You don't have to go slow," she said, feeling painfully taut. "You don't have to be careful with me. I promise I want this. I won't change my mind."

His gaze swept over her face, settling on her mouth. Then he aligned his nose with hers and kissed her softly, quickly. "You're sure about this?"

"Absolutely," she gasped with more certainty than she actually felt. All she knew for absolute-fucking sure was that her body was on fire. He was here, cocked and ready to go, and she couldn't wait a second longer for him to stroke the itch rippling up her cunt.

When he lifted his head, he planted both hands on either side of her shoulders and raised his chest from hers. He flexed his hips, prodding her opening with the blunt tip of his cock.

Almost there. Almost inside me. Miki measured the moments by the number of heartbeats it took for him to find her opening.

When at last he started pushing inside, his eyes squeezed

shut and a look of rapture crossed his strong face. "You're so damn wet . . . *so fucking hot* . . ."

Then he halted, abruptly pulling away and expelling a deep breath. "*Shit*. Wait, almost forgot." He reached for his pants, slipped his wallet from a pocket with one hand, and extricated a foil packet.

Miki smiled with relief. Not a sterile, disease-free vampire— Alexander was what he'd claimed to be. An ordinary Joe. Just a man with a massive hard-on.

After he rolled the latex down his cock and resumed his position, pushing between her labia, Miki circled her hips, helping him find her entrance again. When he did, they both held their breath.

He adjusted his weight on his arms, spread his feet wider on the ground, then stared down at her, letting her know she was still in charge.

Miki smoothed her hands down his lean, slick back, glided over the curve of his firm buttocks, then clasped them, urging him closer. She raised her hips and tensed her pussy around the head of his cock to emphasize her terrific need.

Slowly, he stroked in and out, delivering strong but shallow thrusts that coaxed moisture from inside her to coat him and ease him deeper inside.

Miki's inner walls already felt hot, sensitive from previous rough usage. His gentle strokes grazed the swollen flesh but didn't abrade; he took his time, easing deeper only after her channel filled with creamy welcome and her body began to undulate helplessly beneath him.

Miki couldn't help staring down the space between their bodies, watching the long, dark column of his sex sink between her legs, watching the way his chest and belly flexed and shuddered as he thrust.

She couldn't resist reaching between them, once again sliding her hand down to ring a man's cock. She found Alexander every bit as imposing as Alex, and she was relieved a man didn't have to be a vampire to be so well endowed.

A man could be ordinary, funny, kind—and still fuck like a god.

Alexander seemed to know exactly what she wanted, exactly how much and how fast she could take it. He stroked smoothly into her overheated pussy and gently prodded side to side, then circled, seeking that special spot.

When he found it, breath hissed between her teeth.

"Did that hurt, or have I found it?" he asked, his voice silky and just a bit wicked.

"You're there," she bit out. "Just do it again."

"Bossy!"

Her gaze finally rose from where their bodies connected. "Do you take orders?"

He grunted, and she couldn't tell if he was laughing at her or hurting. "Depends."

"On what?" she panted as he slid deeper.

"Depends on how badly in need my partner is."

"Otherwise?"

The corners of his lips lifted in a wicked smile. "I like to be in charge. On top."

"You're already on top."

"Baby, you're in complete control of me. Haven't you noticed how I've waited politely for your cues? I've been a complete gentleman." He thrust inside her again, this time stroking so deep, so fast, that he pushed the air from her lungs.

"You say that," she gasped, "as though you're surprising yourself."

"I am. I'm always selfish. By now, I should be saying, 'God, I can't hold back a second longer,' making myself sound desperate, then coming in a flurry all over you."

"I rather like the idea of you 'flurrying.'"

"Your cunt's awfully hot, sweetheart. I can tell you're chafed. You sure?"

"In for a penny, in for a pound," she said tightly, wondering how she managed to keep talking when every nerve ending in her pussy was firing electric jolts of pleasure straight to her core.

"That's a very British saying," he said, not the least out of breath as he continued to stroke evenly inside her. "Never understood what the hell it meant exactly."

She wrapped her arms around his torso and tried to pull him closer. "It means fuck me. I don't care how much it hurts. I'll face consequences later."

At last, he relented and came down on top of her. His weight provided comfort while at the same time ratcheting up her excitement, because she knew he was about to let loose. "Enough of the English lesson?" she asked, her words sounding breathy rather than glib.

"I think I like you tense and needy. Makes me feel like I'm a god."

Since she'd just had a similar thought, she moaned. "Play like you're Thor, then, and give me some thunder."

His hips rolled to give her an easy, but insistent, inner nudge. "Do you want the lightning bolts, too?"

"Only if they last longer than a quick flash in the sky."

Alexander kissed her cheek, her nose and swept her lips

with a hot, quick kiss. "Do me a favor then. I don't want you in the way."

"I'm in the way? My being in the way of something is the point, right?"

"Don't get bitchy. I'm only saying I can be faster, stroke you harder, if you're completely open. Ease your thighs from around my waist and raise your legs high and wide."

She did it quickly, opening completely beneath him, pointing her toes like a ballerina.

"Now let your legs relax outward, just a little more."

When she'd opened as wide as she could without doing a gymnast's split, she locked her gaze with his.

"Now, when I start, all you have to do is grab something to keep from moving up our moveable bed. Got it?"

"You trying to impress me?"

His hips rolled in the saddle she'd made for him, his cock digging deeper, stroking toward her womb. "Have I so far?"

Miki bit back a groan, not ready to let him know she was already mighty amazed. "I'm withholding judgment. Have to see how far you move me."

A small, tense smile quirked up one side of his mouth. "What do you need to render judgment in my favor?"

"You shutting up and fucking me so hard I forget any other men I've had tonight."

"Tall order. Those guys were vampires."

"I think they were too full of themselves and their super-powers. They cheated. You're doing just fine."

"Am I?" he drawled, circling, scuffing her clitoris with his pubic hair.

At that moment, with her pussy contracting, clamping hard around his dick, she realized he was teasing her. She leaned up and nipped his chin. "I'm getting ready to crawl all over you in a second if you don't start moving. That's pretty damn good."

"You're just under the influence."

"I'm hornier than I should be, but I'm not delusional. I know this is good."

He came up on his arms again despite her moan of protest, then lifted his hips to drop them sharply down on hers, slapping her open crotch. He did it again and again, until the moisture inside her leaked out and they were both quickly soaked.

His strokes quickened, shortened, sharpening at the end of each thrust.

And even though she wished she could wrap herself around him and hug his body close, she reveled in how open, how exposed she was. She could see his cock glide in and out . . . watch her vulva sink with each inward stroke and stretch outward when he rose . . . could feel the powerful hardness of his lower belly and upper thighs as he pounded at her.

Because she couldn't aid him in any way, she had to accept everything he gave—every stroke, every slap, every swirling, circling dip as he screwed into her.

He could have sought his own unimpeded pleasure quickly, but he watched her, looking for those telltale cues she didn't know she was giving. And when her pussy began to ripple and tremble, and her breaths shortened to sobs, he lifted her buttocks in his palms and slammed harder into her, shoving her onto his cock as he stroked inward.

Shorter strokes, faster . . . until at the end he worked her up and down his shaft so fast that her cries lengthened into an endless, broken wail.

When she came back to herself, dragging in gulps of air, she rolled her head and stared at him. He shuddered, his chest glistening with sweat. His firm, strong cock was still buried deep inside her. "You didn't come."

"Impressed now?" he gritted out.

"Wordless," she whispered.

He rolled, taking her over him.

"Thought you liked to be on top," she grumbled, sure her shaking limbs would have her collapsing in a limp heap any moment now.

"I do, but I'm too tempted to flurry some more. This way, you can take what you need. Get yourself worked up for the next round."

"I'm already quite happy. Boneless, actually."

"It won't last long."

Sure enough, her channel pulsed around him, giving his shaft a sexy caress. "This is so not fair."

"You said that before."

She lifted one eyebrow. "Am I boring you?"

Both his eyebrows rose, and she blushed, glad it was dark. His lack of boredom had her bolted to his hips.

Miki leaned over him, bracing her hands on his shoulders. She began to move, tentatively, testing the way this position felt, experimenting with a roll and a little bounce to see how her movements made him react.

Gazing down her body to where they joined, she lifted high enough to watch his thick glistening shaft disappear inside her as she swallowed him again. Up and down, forward and back, churning, and then finally grinding in tight circles while sweat broke on her skin, trickling from her temples and between her breasts.

She leaned closer, liking the way the sweat eased the glides.

Her body felt fluid, graceful, strong. Her thighs gripped his hips harder and she plunged down on him, crashing her hips against his. Growing breathless again, she lay closer and flexed her bottom up and down, mimicking a man's movements to fuck him.

Alexander groaned and slid his hands over her buttocks, gripping them hard as he gave her a sexy little roll that ground his cock deeper, touching the spot again, raking it with his veined shaft and the ridge encircling his crown.

With the slow grinding movement, she could feel it all. She rubbed her nipples on his chest, rubbed her belly against his, couldn't get enough of his skin and hers, moving together. The soft hairs covering his body were a gentle loofah scouring her hypersensitive flesh.

"I don't want to be on top anymore," she said in a little voice, her bottom flexing faster.

"Want more flurry?"

"Please."

"Thank God." He slid her off his cock. When she began to roll to her back, he stopped her, flipped her to her belly, snaked an arm beneath her waist, and lifted her hips high.

Miki rested on her elbows, her breath rasping as he arranged her body for his pleasure. Behind her now, his hands gently guided her knees apart, then scooped up her hips to form a sharper angle.

With her legs spread wide open and her sex swollen, she knew how she must look. Wet and open, her pussy clasping around air. He could see everything.

She expected to feel his fingers open her right before he plunged his cock inside. The hardness she'd teased and pumped upon was ripe, ready for release.

Instead, she felt his fingers pause to trace the tattoo that stretched across her lower back. "Naughty girl, you have a tramp stamp."

"It's just a bird."

"Why'd you choose it?"

She shrugged, as though it had been unimportant, when in truth she didn't know why it was there. Why that particular design had appealed to her former self.

He trailed his fingers lower, following the crease between her buttocks downward. He halted at her anus and circled it.

Sarah drew a ragged breath as her anxiety elevated.

"Ever been fucked here, Sarah?" he said, his voice deepening.

She jerked as he used that name, wishing she'd told him the truth to begin with. "No."

"But it's been touched?"

She nodded quickly, wishing he'd move along and stop rubbing her there.

"Probed?"

The way he said it, a little drawn out and rasping, the way he touched it, softly, reverently, made her shiver. She drew another deep breath and nodded again.

"I'd love to do more. Will you let me?"

"Alexander, I don't know . . ." Why did he ask? Why didn't he just do what he wanted? How could she tell him, "Yes, you can fuck my ass?"

"Does it embarrass you for me to play with it?"

"Yes," she hissed when his fingers rimmed her again.

"Good. You've given up so much tonight, without thinking, without giving permission. I think I'd like to see what you will allow. I think you'll let me do anything I want."

Would he ever stop talking? Her whole body was trembling, burning, and he wanted to tease her? He could have her any way he wanted, and she'd be kissing his feet in gratitude so long as he did something quick. *Now!* "God, you're sounding as arrogant as them now."

"But you like it?"

She rocked shallowly, forward and back, trying to tempt him to enter her, any damn place he wanted, trying to ease her own tension with the soothing motion. "Please, don't tease me."

His lips pressed against one buttock, trailed wetly from one to the other while her heart hammered against her chest.

Fingers tucked inside her pussy, burning her. At her indrawn breath, they pulled free.

She felt the cushions dip beside her. He bent down, his gaze looking into hers.

Miki had the thought that anyone spying on them would see twin moons aligning. She almost smiled.

Alexander's lips pursed a moment, as though he was thinking. "You're a bit raw. I think you'd better rest your juicy cunt."

Miki closed her eyes, wrinkling her nose. "Never thought I'd hear it described quite like that."

Alexander's eyes danced with mischief. "Prefer moist, gooey center?"

"Don't! My ass is in the air. Laughing now would be too undignified."

"More undignified than we already are? Well, we have options," he said, his voice trailing off in a sexy slide while his hand glided over her bottom.

"Options? Like a menu?"

"Menu? Now I'll be fixated on food."

"Mention hot dogs and buns, and I'm out of here," she growled.

"I was going to say . . . you have options. Entirely up to you." He pressed a finger on her lips when she opened her mouth for another retort. "I could suck your clit, again."

She moaned against his finger and stuck out her tongue to lap along the sides.

This time he moaned, then cleared his throat. "Maybe later. I deserve a reward. Second option: I could give your little asshole a test drive."

She bit his finger. "You won't fit."

"You'll be amazed how much your body can take when properly inspired."

"The clit thing, I think."

"Coward," he whispered.

Miki groaned. "I just can't say it. How about you do the whole take-charge thing? Be the caveman to my damsel in distress."

"You're mixing metaphors."

"What if the damsel prefers the caveman to a rusty old knight?"

"You can cry uncle any time you're not comfortable."

"Alexander?"

"Yes, sweetheart?"

She forgot what she'd been about to say. "You shouldn't call me that. *Sweetheart*. I might think you really like me."

His smile, which looked just a little sad, made her heart ache. "Funny enough, that doesn't scare me."

CHAPTER

7

Alex watched as Sarah's tongue swept out to wet her lips. When she looked ready to say something more, he suddenly felt a chill caress his spine. Perhaps it was a subconscious warning that he was falling too deeply into the fantasy.

After all, he wasn't an average kind of guy. The complications he'd bring to an ordinary sort of relationship could bring grave consequences. As much as he might have liked to continue the teasing, to follow the path this intriguing little bit of romance might have led him down, he wasn't truly free to pursue it.

Already, her gaze spoke of her blossoming feelings. The trust in her eyes and the poignancy of her softening features pulled at emotions he hadn't the luxury to enjoy.

In all fairness to her and himself, he couldn't allow the connection between them to deepen.

Tonight was just an interlude, regardless of how much part of him wished he'd been free to pursue her. Her misconception of his true nature entranced him. She believed him kind, honorable. An average guy. A *good-looking* average guy.

She amused him, seemed able to draw out a whimsical side to his nature he'd never before discovered.

But she was only a distraction.

Drawing away, he knelt behind her again, ignoring her as she lifted her head to glance behind her, her expression questioning, as though she sensed the change in him.

He ignored her confusion, instead concentrating on the ferocious ache tightening his balls. "So caveman it is," he murmured.

Again, because he couldn't resist, he swirled his fingers in her liquid heat, coating them in cream, tunneling a little deeper to remind her why he'd offered options in the first place.

Her wince gave him a pang of regret, but he reminded himself she wasn't exactly Little Miss Innocent. She'd entered the vampire's den with her eyes wide open. Her bite in the alleyway should have been warning enough.

So her morning-after regrets had begun to weigh on her before the night was even through. So she'd drunk a potion that took some of the decision out of her hands.

She'd been the one to accept *Alex's* invitation.

She'd lost a little blood, given up ownership of her body for one night. Maybe she'd learn a lesson. This world wasn't kind to humans. Better she learn with him than with some of the others, who'd discard her as soon as she'd fulfilled their purpose, without worrying too much about whether she'd survive the guilt and nightmares afterward.

He hadn't coerced her into doing a damn thing. She'd squirmed on his lap, gotten him hard with her lush peach perfume and the heady scent of her arousal—had *begged* him to help her.

Playing a rescuer wasn't anything new to him, only he usually charged in to save humans from ravaging demons and vampires—not from their own lust.

Now that he'd renewed his priorities, he could take care of the business of feeding his own appetites. That she would find relief from her relentless arousal was the benefit she'd receive for her gift. He'd never have to see her again.

If he handled this right, she'd never again be tempted to enter this world.

Still, when she glanced back, her wide, glistening gaze reflecting alarm, he felt an irresistible urge to gather her close and reassure her that all would be well. Her heart-shaped face and luminous eyes were growing on him. If he spent too much more time with her, he'd be convinced a relationship with her was possible.

He dragged his gaze from her face and stared instead at what his hands closed around: her lush round ass, her plump sex, and the little hole above it that would no doubt chew his dick to pieces. The thought of how tight her virgin asshole would feel closing around him had a dangerous, growling hunger building inside him.

"I take it back," she said, her head swiveling to look straight ahead.

"What? Control?" he drawled. "Too late." To emphasize his

point, he clamped a hand around her hip to hold her still.

She wriggled slightly, as though testing the strength of his embrace and will. "Actually," she said after she'd stilled, "I think the drug's wearing off. We can stop now."

"You forget one thing," he said slowly and precisely, careful not to give her the warmth of gentle teasing. Letting her hear the natural tone of his voice. "I've seen to all your needs. Don't you think I deserve a little consideration?"

Her brows furrowed in confusion. "I'm sorry about this. Truly," she said in a small voice.

"You will be." He bent over to blanket her back, sliding his hands down her arms to clasp her hands firmly. "Tomorrow, when you wake up," he whispered in her ear, "you'll want a bath, but there isn't any water for a long soak. You'll feel dizzy and wonder just how much blood was taken and how long it will be before you feel like yourself again." He lapped her neck, tongued her earlobe, then squeezed her hands hard as he nestled closer to continue in a rougher tone. "It will take a long time for the memories to fade, for you to feel you're the one in charge of your own life, because now that you've tasted and been tasted, you'll crave it."

A shuddering breath made her whole body quiver. "Is that how it is for you? Why you're here?"

He'd expected her to resist, to try to pull away her hands and head. Instead, she'd offered him empathy. "I don't have a conscience when it comes to my pleasure or my needs, *Sarah*. You needed me. I was amused. A few hours of mutual enjoyment isn't such a bad trade, is it?"

"Why are you acting this way?" she said, her voice growing gruff, as though she was fighting the urge to cry.

"Because you want more than I can give you." That was as much of the truth as he could offer her.

"I only asked for help." This time her voice broke.

The sound nearly made him reconsider his path. Alex tamped down the regret and pity welling up inside him. "You asked me to fuck you, but you want more, don't you?"

"I already decided I never want to see you again. As nice as I *thought* you were, I still never want to be reminded of what happened here."

Alex swallowed, closing his eyes for a second. "Let's make sure you don't forget the lesson," he rasped. Then he thumbed her clit, pressing it hard, following with a flick of his fingernail.

Her bottom jerked, and she gasped. Her shoulders bunched, and she tried to crawl forward from beneath him.

He tightened his hold on the notch of her hip, not letting her budge, and leaned away. With his free hand he continued to torture her clit, while he slid fingers deep inside her. Her cunt was hot and soaked, her lips parting to welcome him inside.

Only he'd already been there. Another opening, one un-breached beyond a little fondling by Nicolas and himself, drew his attention.

At that moment, he realized he might be a little jealous. Was that the real reason he pulled away from the feelings she tugged from him? He'd never been jealous of a lover. They were so easily found, so easily replaced once they bored him or clung too tightly. He wasn't a promiscuous vamp, but he had lived centuries and had had more lovers than he could count or remember. But he didn't think he'd ever been jealous before.

Besides, his destiny precluded anything but political matches.

Yearning for something he couldn't have, something he could never be, was a waste of time and a drain on his emotions.

He sensed Sarah would be a huge drain. A colossal disaster. A vulnerable human would have to be made a vampire. Even then his enemies would be so many that she would never be safe.

Political matches wouldn't require an investment of affection.

So sex was all this could ever be. And only tonight. Whether she thought she was ready for this or not, he had to have her. He bent close, anticipating her shock, and licked the seam bisecting her buttocks.

She dropped to her elbows. Her ragged breaths shook her shoulders and back. Still, she uttered no protest, giving him silent permission to continue.

A wash of possessive lust swept through him, gripping his balls hard, jerking his cock. Anticipation had his own breaths shortening, the muscles of his chest and thighs tightening. He gently dipped a finger into her vagina and withdrew it, then used her silken cream to rim her little puckering hole, circling round and round before pushing slowly inside.

The tight ring of muscle contracted, squeezing him, and his dick jerked again. *Sweet Jesus*, he could hardly wait to feel its hot clasp.

Although he'd decided to steel himself against her charms, he didn't want to be cruel. He dropped more moisture from his mouth into her crack and used it to ease another finger inside her.

Her entrance squeezed hard around him, resisting his intrusion. Sarah's long "uhhhhhn" stretched out as he slowly rotated his fingers to ease the tightness.

"Breathe, love," he whispered. "Relax."

She shook her head. Her body quivered. But she didn't try to pull away.

Alex slipped his free hand beneath her and palmed her pussy, heating it up, massaging it and her clit as he worked his fingers deeper inside.

Finally, he felt the tension ease around him, and he pulled out his fingers, ignoring her sigh of relief before thrusting three fingers quickly inside her ass.

Sarah's back arched. "*God, Alexander . . .* too much!"

"Easy baby," he crooned. "I haven't even begun."

He might have relented if the hand cupping her pussy hadn't instantly been drenched. Her cunt spasmed, clenching, opening, clenching again. Similarly, her asshole pulsed.

If he'd been the average guy she thought he was, he might have given her time, days perhaps, to ease her into this sort of play. Instead, he withdrew his fingers, ground his palm against her pussy one last time, then transferred the moisture to the latex sheath covering his cock.

He stroked himself up and down, gritting his teeth, squeezing the base of his cock for a moment—a warning to himself not to let go, not until he felt the first sexy convulsions of her body when she came.

And he knew she would, despite the discomfort, and because of the burning pressure he'd exert against her virgin entrance.

He grasped his cock just below the head, placed himself at her back entrance, and flexed his hips.

She jerked forward. He followed, this time gripping her hips before he pressed again. Her breath hitched, and a tight moan gurgled at the back of her throat as he continued to push. At last the ring relented, and he slid just inside.

Her forehead rolled on the cushioned seats, but she held her body perfectly still, as though afraid to jar him. They both struggled to breathe for a long moment.

Then the heat surrounding him, filling him, became too much to resist. Alex flexed, pushing forward, cramming further inside, his jaws grinding together because it felt so damn good. Her ass cinched his cock. He dropped more spit into her crease, brought his cock out and rolled the tip in the moisture before reinserting it gently. This time the resistance was much weaker. He gave her a tentative thrust—shallow, controlled.

Sarah shifted her trembling knees, widening her stance. Because she thought she might crumble at any moment? Or was she bracing for a "flurry"?

"How are you feeling, Sarah?" he asked tightly.

"I burn," came her small voice.

"Want me to stop?" he asked, without any intention of doing so even if she did say yes. "Am I hurting you?"

"Not . . . exactly."

"You feel pressure?"

"Yes."

"Heat?"

"God, yes," she sobbed softly.

"Do you want more of me?"

"Please . . ."

If she'd looked over her shoulder at that moment, she might have grown afraid again. His lips were drawn back in a feral snarl. His body tensed, muscles bulging as he finally let his blood flow through him, pumping him up, readying him to come unglued.

With Sarah braced, he thrust forward, easing deeper,

stretching her, filling her until she gulped for air. He pulled back and thrust again, another steady glide. When he came at her a third time, he stroked faster, and then pulsed in and out, increasing the tempo of his thrusts, working his hips in circular motions to stretch her further.

When her back began its sensual arch, he gripped her ass hard and powered into her, pummeling her soft bottom as he moved faster and faster until he hammered her, shoving her forward, shoving her across the pillows until they slid away and she scraped her knees on wood.

Still, he didn't relent, didn't slow down. He followed her across the floor, his knees grinding into the planks.

She reached out to grip the edge of a seat and held herself steady for his assault, her body stretching forward, back bowing, her buttocks rippling with his powerful thrusts until she cried out.

When she crumbled toward the floor, he scooped up her hips and continued to hammer. Her ass was hot, tight, burning through the latex as it clamped hard around him, restricting the blood flowing away so that his erection didn't flag, his orgasm couldn't explode.

Finally, he pulled out, wrapped his hand around his cock, and masturbated himself, shoving his cock through his fingers, fiercely pumping up and down his shaft. When he came, he shouted, stroking through the explosion that shot cum against the saggy tip of his condom and emptied his balls.

After his release finally waned, he opened his eyes. His knees were splayed, his fist still clutching himself, stroking more gently up and down to draw out the last dying ripples of his orgasm.

Sarah had fallen to the floor of the gazebo and rolled to her side. Her large eyes watched the motion of his hand. Her liquid gaze stared in rapt fascination.

He let go of himself and rested his hands on his thighs while he dragged air into his starving lungs.

When the last deep shudders racking his body eased, he rolled the condom off his dick and tossed it away. Sarah's gaze remained glued to him. He ringed the base of his cock to keep himself engorged and hard, then lifted his hand toward her.

She placed hers on top of his palm and he pulled her across the floor, pulled her down until her head was even with his cock. Holding her gaze, he lifted his buttocks and speared into her mouth.

Sarah opened automatically, closing her lips around him to suck the crown, mouthing him gently, then sucking hard to draw him inside.

Alex threaded his fingers through her auburn hair and tugged her head closer, forcing more of his length into the warm, moist cavern of her mouth.

Her head jerked backward, but she didn't release him, didn't try to deny his silent command. She swirled around the head, licking under the ridge surrounding his glans, dipping the tip of her tongue into the slit at the center. She enclosed him again, sucking hard, drawing him inside. He flexed, shoving along her tongue, stroking toward the back of her throat.

Her jaws widened and she swallowed, the back of her throat clasping him as it opened and closed, caressing him, opening again until she took him deeper still and bobbed her head on him, following the tug of the fingers tightening in her hair.

She murmured and groaned as though she couldn't get her fill, couldn't take him deep enough. She planted her hands on his thighs and slid one up to cup his balls, rolling them in her palm, wrapping her fingers around them to squeeze and pull with just enough force that he no longer needed to hold his cock.

Blood pooled again between his legs, strengthening his erection, filling it, stretching it until her mouth couldn't hold all of him without her teeth raking his shaft. He didn't care, couldn't stop spearing into her, bucking against her as she caressed his balls and sucked him hard.

Her groans swelled around his cock, vibrating against the crown, trembling down the shaft, and he had to pull away, had to bury himself inside her again.

Fighting the hands reaching for his cock, pushing her face away, he turned her body and plunged into her hot cunt, bucking hard, ramming deep, glorying in her ragged howls as he pumped his cock into her tight pussy, faster, harder—harder, sharper, following her when her knees gave out and her body flattened on the floor.

He shoved apart her thighs to root as deep as he could reach, her buttocks cushioning his belly and his balls raking painfully against the floor.

Alex squeezed her buttocks, pushing them apart, trying to get deeper, needing to tunnel until he tapped her womb, and then he exploded, cum gushing until he wallowed in her dripping cunt, stroking, thrusting still.

"Stop," she sobbed. "No more."

Alex's balls contracted at the misery in her voice. He halted his motions, but he couldn't bring himself to leave her. He lay over her, crushing her to the hard floor, burying his face at the back of her sweaty neck as his body spasmed and his cock twitched inside her.

He'd never been so out of control. Never wanted to punish, to mark a woman with his scent and fluids. Like a goddamn dog. He'd been a rutting, mindless animal.

Where was the guilt? Why didn't he feel remorse as she shook beneath him? Instead, all he felt was satisfaction—*bone-deep*, *primal* satisfaction. As though he'd claimed her for his own. Never would another man touch her without sensing he trespassed.

Which was nuts. He wouldn't keep her. Couldn't let her be a part of his life. Even if she wanted to, begged him to let her stay—which wasn't likely now.

He licked the back of her neck, drank in the scent of her—peaches and sex—and felt his fangs slide from the roof of his mouth. He could taste her and she'd never know, never remember.

He could do that. A special talent only he possessed. He could wipe the whole evening from her mind. He could give her peace.

Only then she wouldn't learn the lesson. Wouldn't remember him. He was selfish enough to want to be part of her dreams for a long, long time. So he concentrated only on robbing the memory of this last, furtive bite and raked the razor edge of his teeth along her neck, seeking the pulse hammering against the shallow vein.

He bit harshly, sinking quickly, loving the way her body tightened beneath him, her cunt clamping on his dick as he began to draw, sucking her essence down like it was nectar.

Hot, salty-sweet and metallic—the flavors coated his tongue while her blood slid down his throat to warm his belly, slowly seeping outward to fill his body with a powerful, lustful surge of pure energy.

Her thin cries filled the air around him as another, last orgasm swept through her body. Then suddenly she slackened beneath him.

He withdrew his fangs, licked closed the wounds, and slowly climbed off her unconscious body, surveying what he'd done. She lay spread-eagled on the hard floor. Her fingers curled into the wood.

He found his shirt and used the tails to wipe cum and streaks of pink from between her thighs, then he dressed himself and gathered her clothes. He approached her cautiously, reaching out to squeeze her shoulder.

"Sarah," he said quietly.

She moaned and rolled her head, pressing her forehead to the floor. "No more," she repeated.

"Help me get you dressed."

Her arms slid closer to her body and she raised herself up on her elbows, turning her head to look over her shoulder, her gaze not meeting his eyes. "I want to go home," she said, her voice hoarse and ragged.

"Get dressed. I'll find you a ride."

He left her alone in the gazebo, his steps heavy while she stayed behind, shrugging into her crumpled clothing like an old woman. At the front of the house, he sought one of half a dozen black limos lined up in a row along the pebbled, circular driveway; he arranged her transportation, then headed back into the garden. He found her sitting on the bench once again, her jacket zipped to her neck, her body hunched over.

He knelt beside her feet and cupped her cheek. "Time to go, love."

Her gaze seemed hollow, listless. Her mouth was swollen from kisses and the damage her own teeth had done as she'd bitten down to still her cries. Her face was mottled, as though she'd been crying.

He'd done that. Nicolas hadn't touched her deeply. He'd used her body, fed from her, but he hadn't broken her spirit. Alex had done it for her own good—to keep her out of reach of the demon, to keep her out of reach of those who would tempt her curiosity, then drain her of will and spirit.

She wouldn't forget the lesson. He hoped like hell she'd never seek entrance into the dark realm again.

CHAPTER

8

Nicolas Montfaucon drummed his fingers on the polished ebony table, trying to ignore the stares from the rest of the council ringing the round table. While he hadn't expected a warm and friendly welcome, he'd thought the *sabat* had at least received a little forewarning that he'd joined their ranks.

For whatever reason, Inanna hadn't bothered to tell anyone she'd unilaterally decided he would take Chessa's reserved seat.

Not that Nicolas worried too much about his reception, or that the females around him would reject his new status. Not while the grounds were surrounded by his men. The unleashed rogues he'd recruited to force his way onto the council were crawling over the estate, working side by side with the turned vampires who'd never broken their masters' tethers.

His men had made sure they didn't blend well. They didn't wear the black SWAT uniforms of the Security Force, choosing instead to emphasize their individuality. A mixed bag of army camouflage, blue jeans, and Kevlar had to be jarring to the women who liked everything and everyone to be in their place and tidy.

Controlled, bridled . . . subservient to the rule of the women who'd created them.

Nicolas had shielded his plans from the coven's matriarch, Inanna, who had shared his siring with his wife, not realizing that the blood-bond would be diluted and his love and loyalty would be his own to give where *he* chose. For long centuries he'd bided his time, learning everything he could about the dark world he'd entered, trying to find his place. Trying to discover the purpose God had given him when he'd offered him the gift of eternity while destroying the family he'd cherished.

One vow had remained unbroken, almost from the beginning of his Undead existence: his promise to avenge his brother's and wife's loss by ensuring that their murderer, an ancient beast called The Devourer, never roamed free. Nicolas had watched over his sarcophagus since the day the monster had ravaged his wife and stolen his brother's body—until The Storm had interceded and swept the beast to freedom.

Now more than ever, Inanna needed his help to recapture the beast. With his ability to skip bodies upon the death of his host, Nicolas could only wait for the bastard to grow cocky and make a mistake. One thing they all knew: The Devourer hadn't left the area and was likely to infiltrate *Ardeal*. He had a score to settle with his ancient foe, Inanna.

Nicolas observed Inanna sitting among her council—not

quite her peers, because she was their matriarch and related to most of them. They'd called her *Grandmère* when they'd greeted her with kisses that hadn't quite touched her cheeks. Once the niceties had been dispensed with, they'd stood on one side of the room waiting for the signal that the meeting would begin, while Inanna had stood with him, her hand tucked inside his elbow. The women had eyed him suspiciously, probably wondering whether she'd elevated a paramour to wait on her during the session.

At last, Inanna had made the announcement that they should begin, and that Nicolas should take Chessa's seat. Silence had greeted her suggestion.

Until one woman, her lips pressing into a thin line, had remarked, "We have matters to discuss that should remain cloaked."

"If they are matters that concern the *sabat*, then it is entirely appropriate that Nico attend."

The woman's eyebrows had risen. "You say that as though he will preside with us."

"Have I not made my intention clear by allowing him among us?"

The affect had been like a small incendiary explosive going off. Shocked silence, followed in moments by a chorus of shrill voices.

Inanna had simply smiled her catlike smile and taken her chair, waving him to his new seat while the others had fussed. Finally, they'd quietly taken their seats, realizing Inanna had had no intention of explaining or defending her decision. It had been made. Nothing they could do about it now.

However, the stares aimed his way did not abate.

Some were openly lustful, wondering just what he might

have done to earn his unprecedented seat. Some were resentful. Some were so cold that he knew himself a marked man.

In fact, he was the only man sitting at the table, and the only one allowed admittance to a meeting of the *sabat*. Ever.

The council disliked change of any kind. Yet another change had been made before his inclusion had even been announced to the body—*she* had arrived just after they had seated themselves.

A member of the Wolfen Nation, from the South-Central clan, now sat beside him. Her scent wafted softly over him, feminine, light, a little minty for his tastes—not a hint of dog.

Still, Nicolas tightened, finding his gaze drawn to her time and again. Scenting a natural adversary. Her dark brown hair glinted red in the candlelight shining from the chandelier above the table. Her deep navy gown clung to every curve of her tall, statuesque figure, the crystals studding the gown reflecting prisms of light against the damask tablecloth. Beautiful and powerful, her regal status was stamped on her handsome features.

Inanna bristled in her seat, eying the *were* as though she expected her to bare her canines and lunge across the table at any time—not that her expression reflected any fear. Pure unadulterated revulsion and fury shone in her trembling body and narrowed eyes.

Her momentary triumph had been trumped by the other member's audacious move.

Nicolas had to hand it to the wolf. She sat cool as a cucumber, appearing oblivious to Inanna's rage. But then she hadn't been invited by their host, the matriarch and oldest living vampire on the continent.

"What is she doing here?" Inanna demanded, her normally singsong voice sounding tight and bitten.

"Her presence is required, *Grandmère*," murmured the woman beside Inanna, her tension evident in the way her hand played with the pendant dangling between her small breasts. Brunette with flawless skin and tilted, almond-shaped eyes, Cecily was closest to Inanna's age, having been born into the Dacian era, when vampires had moved freely through that ancient kingdom's court.

"Required?" Inanna kept her tone even and her gaze glued to the nightmare sitting across the table from her. "Then why was I not included in the conversation? As your hostess, I would have liked to prepare for our guest."

"As council members, why were we not included in the conversation that granted Nicolas a seat among us?" Apparently Cecily had been chosen the spokesperson, because none of the remaining eleven members so much as twitched.

"What I do as your leader should not be questioned. Nico has earned his seat. We have need of his skills."

"The way I heard it, he usurped his place at this table through insurrection."

"An impressive show of force," Inanna said, a small, tight smile curving her lips. Her gaze locked with his. "Nico can be trusted. He is bonded to me. As to that little insurrection, he acted in our best interests, no harm or foul intended. Sometimes, we are too intransigent, too married to our customs to see that times change. The *Revenants* demanded a voice for their gift of loyalty. Nico will be their voice."

"We should have been consulted," Cecily said, red seeping into her cheeks.

"Cecily," Inanna said, the lilt more prominent now. "Are you upset because he's *Revenant*, or because he's male?"

A chirping laugh followed Inanna's cutting remark. It came from Madrigal, who'd also arrived from Miami with Cecily. Their long-standing affair was no secret, but bringing attention to Cecily's preference for the company of women had scored a direct hit.

The vain and vapid Madrigal didn't understand the set down.

Cecily gave Madrigal a quelling glare. "Nico's insurrection and your solution to his defiance cause us concern, but it is not the only reason we're here."

"To say I was surprised at your summons would be an understatement of my concern," Inanna said softly.

Nicolas settled back into his chair, already bored with the proceedings. The women talked in circles, chose their words as a warrior might his weapons. He wished the bloody hell they'd get to the point.

"There is concern your control over this vital region is slipping. Nico's revolt is only one incident. Rogues continue to thumb their noses at our authority here, roaming openly, choosing when to sire a mate, choosing to sire companions—without thought to consequences, because there are none. They continue to hunt our breeders and kill them to force our extinction." She took a deep breath and locked gazes with Inanna. "Then there is the matter of the *Grizashiat*."

Inanna reached for the wineglass in front of her and curled her fingers around its base. "You would hold me responsible for the act of nature that released him from his sarcophagus?"

"Of course not, but you have proven ineffective in recapturing him."

"We cannot find him until he makes a move against us. He

will try to infiltrate *Ardeal*. We have plans in place to trap him."

Cecily drew a deep breath, her gaze narrowing. "And what about the daywalker?"

"A daywalker?" Inanna sounded bored. "There is no proof. Perhaps it is an urban myth."

"How can you know for sure? Do you even know what your vampires breed? Born females residing outside your purview, coming into season uncontrolled, their mates unknown to us. It was bad enough when a mage intermarried with one of your own."

Nicolas stiffened at this last charge. She spoke of Chessa; her father had been a natural mage, and both her parents had been sentenced to death for crossing that boundary.

Cecily's eyes glittered with malice. "Can you tell us a male Born does not exist?"

Inanna's chin rose. Her glance swept each member inside the chamber, resting at last on Nicolas. "If a male exists, we shall find him."

"Not without help," Cecily bit out.

"Yours?" Inanna scoffed. "I assure you we do not need to augment our force."

Cecily's smile held a hint of triumph. "Who better than a wolf to track down an abomination?"

Alex slipped back into the salon, giving one quick, wary glance to the wine-colored sofa where Erika had cavorted earlier with her studs. When he didn't find her, he heaved a sigh of relief. The salon was much quieter, the murmurings less heated. Most had sated their appetites and now simply cuddled in various stages of undress.

Alex hovered near the entrance to the foyer, keeping an eye on the guarded door at the center of the twin staircases. When the *sabat* adjourned, he'd grab Nicolas. The sooner he gathered the information he needed, the sooner he could get out of here. Each moment he lingered, he increased his risk of detection.

He couldn't wait to get home. To slide back into surroundings that didn't hide a thousand intrigues. Home was the unpretentious one-room apartment his mother had first rented from Simon when she'd arrived in New Orleans. When she'd slipped through the portal into ancient Scotland, the apartment had waited for him. He'd claimed it the day after she'd left; that seven hundred years had passed was only a relative thing for the Broussards.

From the corner of his eye, he noted the door opening. A woman wearing a dark blue dress exited. The door shut behind her and he relaxed, until she drew nearer the salon doorway. Something in the way she moved, her head held high, her tall, stately body carried with a warrior's confidence, struck a familiar chord. . . .

Gabriella! Too late to escape, he knew the exact moment she caught his scent—her head jerked to the left, then the right, as her nostrils flared.

Alex stepped into the foyer, directly into her path, and slid his arm around her waist, turning her toward the salon.

Gabriella's back stiffened, and she struggled against his hold. "Just one shout," she whispered furiously, "and they'll fall on you like ravening beasts."

"So why aren't you screaming?" he murmured close to her ear. "Are you too proud to be found caught off guard? Or are you curious why I'm here in plain sight?"

Her gaze narrowed. "You were always an arrogant bastard. It's why I had you killed." She leaned close and sniffed along his neck and face—as if unable to control her *were*-instinct to fill her senses with her prey's scent. "Why aren't you dead, by the way?"

"That assassin you sicced on me with the lousy aim?" He *tsk*ed and nuzzled her neck in return. "Gabi, couldn't you have done better? Once I pulled the arrow from my chest, I bit him. *You know how good my bite is*—he simply forgot I walked away."

Changeable as the Louisiana weather, Gabriella leaned back, her lips pouting. "But you never returned. How did you know I was responsible?"

Alex lifted one brow. "You aren't the only one with a keen nose, Gabi. You made love to him before you set him on me."

"A silly, selfish mistake, but how could I resist? I was already missing you in my bed." She paused, then threw back her head to laugh. "How galling it will be when they discover you're here right beneath their noses! The bitches."

"Your amusement is doomed to a short life. You won't reveal me."

"But you're the very reason I'm here. Of course, I didn't know it would be you, exactly, but I did feel rather nostalgic when I was offered the opportunity to hunt again. It's been so long since I've tasted Born flesh."

"Sorry to disappoint, my dear. You will not reveal me, Gabi. I won't let you."

She glanced around the room. "You and who else? I assure you there isn't a vamp in sight who won't give chase."

"They'll never get the chance." He reached into his pocket for his key chain and the crystal dangling from the fob. He warmed it in his hand inside his pocket, then pulled Gabriella close, pressing his lips to hers.

Light flared around them, and then blinked out.

Alex opened his eyes to stare into Gabriella's face. He was waiting for her to stop blinking against the momentary blindness.

Her scowl was something else he remembered about her. It was not a feminine expression; her face grew surly and dark. Her lips lifted from her white teeth. She jerked out of his arms. "What the hell did you just do, *vampire*?"

"I brought you someplace special. My own private bolt-hole. Feel privileged—I haven't brought a woman here in centuries."

Her head swiveled, taking in the small, cozy cavern. Fine Persian rugs covered the floor, and silk tapestries swathed much of the cool, natural stone walls. Candelabras flared bright, lending a golden glow to what was essentially a cave.

"Where am I, Alex?"

"Somewhere quiet, where we won't be disturbed." He wandered to a small bureau set against one wall and lifted a bottle of wine from his collection. He glanced into the mirror above the bureau. "A drink?" One corner of his mouth lifted. By turning his back, he told her he didn't consider her a threat.

Gabriella's hands fisted at her sides. "Take me back this instant! Do you realize the trouble you will cause?"

He poured two glasses, turned, and walked to where she stood in the center of the room next to a small smokeless fire burning in a circular pit. "I take it you are in New Orleans under some immunity accord granted by the *sabat*?" he said coolly as he handed her one of the glasses.

"Of course," she spat. "By invitation, which apparently is

something you'll never receive. I was promised safe passage. If I'm harmed in any way, my nation will go to war."

"You won't be missed. I promise." He handed her a glass, half-expecting her to fling it in his face.

Instead, she lifted it to her lips and poured it down her throat in a single gulp. "Someone will have seen us 'pop out.' Your coven will not be able to keep this a secret for long. I didn't come to New Orleans alone."

"Not my coven. Yet." Alex stepped closer, close enough to feel the brush of her chest as she inhaled. He lifted his hand to stroke her hair, seeking now to calm her, knowing he had to play to her primal proclivities. "Be assured," he said softly. "The coven will never know you went missing. This place isn't in New Orleans; it isn't even in the same dimension or time. When we are done here, we will return to the exact place from which we exited."

She pulled away from his stroking hand. "Is that supposed to make me feel better?"

"Darling," Alex drawled, knowing he was getting to her. Her nipples sprouted against the heavy silk covering her. "You might as well have a seat. We'll talk. Get reacquainted. We'll come to an agreement."

"Take me back, and I won't tell them you were there. I'll let you have time to flee, for old time's sake, for what we once were to each other."

"Just what were we?" he asked, pretending confusion.

Her full lips pushed into a moue of disappointment. "Was I really so easy to forget?"

Alex snorted. Not likely. She'd scored his back countless times, left him spent, legless with exhaustion. A more energetic lover he'd never had. That her loyalties could not be swayed from her pack was at the center of what had killed their relationship.

God, he was going to have to fuck her. Alex didn't have to force a smile. His arousal stirred, thick and urgent. "I promise I won't bite unless you want me to."

A low, feral growl reverberated from her throat.

Without looking up from the glass he'd poured for himself, he said, "Turn and I'll collar you, bitch."

"I'd like to see you try." The sound of her gown slithering to the floor had his body tightening, readying.

For the second time that night, a wolf carried him to the ground.

CHAPTER
9

He rolled with her, coming over her thickly muscled, lupine body. Her jaws, with their long, jagged rows of teeth, gaped but didn't snap. Her claws, however, shredded his shirt, drawing blood as they raked his chest.

Alex wrestled her, flipping her onto her paws, then straddling her body to pin her beneath him as he worked the silver linked collar he'd palmed before leaving the bureau around her thrashing snout. Finally, he dragged it over her head and cinched it tight, strangling her.

Gabriella gurgled momentarily, then her body transformed, melting beneath him into her naked human form, the silver chain working like the charmed object it was.

She panted rapidly, her face and body pressed against the carpet, completely at his mercy now. Just as he remembered she liked it.

Arousal flared hotter in his groin as he stretched over her, his hands reaching to manacle her wrists. "Will you obey me now?" he whispered into her ear.

Her body shuddered. "Uhnnn . . . Alex," she said breathily, her legs parting to display her willingness to submit.

Ignoring her invitation, he smoothed her hair off her neck, inhaling her scent—warm spice and wild wolf. He pressed a kiss to the chain, noting the delicious shiver that racked her shoulders. He fingered the choker's clasp, locking it to ensure her continued cooperation, then quickly climbed off her, surreptitiously adjusting his cock.

"You can't leave me this way," she said plaintively, glancing over her shoulder.

Because he needed her calm and because he couldn't resist reacquainting himself with her strong, lithe body, he ran his hands along her back and sides, gliding down her quivering flanks to pet and gentle her. "Am I ever cruel?" he drawled, careful not to stroke between her thighs.

Her bottom lifted, and then undulated down. "Only when it's needed, darling. *And I need, now.*" She came up on her hands and knees, arching her back to tilt her pussy upward, her submission clear. "I remember how well you liked our ways, Alex," she said, tossing back her head and giving him a direct stare—challenge, as always, reflected in her expression.

Alex suppressed a smile. The woman always led with defiance, but he knew secretly she craved his mastery. He lifted his hand and swatted her ass.

Her indrawn breath was quickly followed by a low, throaty laugh.

He glided his hand over one firm, fleshy globe. "That wasn't meant as foreplay, love. We're talking."

"First?" At his even stare, she huffed, "Fine. Talk away. But afterward, I really do have to scratch an itch." She rolled to her back and sat up, shaking out her long brown hair behind her.

"Would you feel more comfortable clothed?" he asked, handing her the crumpled gown. Watching the flex of her toned ass and thighs was wreaking havoc on his libido, and he needed to conclude their business before this encounter took its natural course. He'd only whetted his appetite for sex with sweet Sarah. With Gabriella, he could unleash the wildness inside himself without fear of harming her.

"Alex," she said, giving him a reproving look, "you should know I'm always most comfortable in my own skin." She dropped the dress again and strode to a low-backed sofa, sitting languidly, then slowly raising her long legs to tuck them beneath her on the plush cushion. She draped an arm across the back of the sofa, her breasts lifting with each deep inhalation, waiting like the predator she was as he took his seat at the opposite end. "Now who's afraid of a little nibble?"

Giving her ample bosom a quick, regretful glance, he stared at his wineglass. "How about we speak plainly, Gabi. About my situation, about yours?"

"Let's," she said, her voice deepening again as her greedy gaze swept his body. "Why are those women jonesing for you, darling?"

"They want me dead because I threaten their balance of power."

"One little vampire?" she drawled.

He raised one dark eyebrow.

Gabriella scooted closer on the sofa, stretching her fingers to comb through his hair. "They don't know you as well as I do, otherwise they'd know you're an *honorable* man." Her gaze hardened as she pulled his hair.

Unhurried, he reached up and grabbed her hand, bending back her wrist until she gasped. "Stop being a bitch."

Her eyes widened in mock innocence. "You mean you're not honorable? Is there something you're not telling me?"

Alex fought the urge to roll his eyes. The woman wasn't going to let him get straight to business without rehashing the past. "All right. So I wasn't completely open about the reason I romanced you to begin with. I apologize."

"Please," she said, her lips pouting, "if discovering I was only a means for you to get your hands on your precious *lilum* stone wasn't bad enough, to find out you were boning that bi-sexed demon whore at the same time really cut it."

He lifted one brow. "Is that why you decided to do away with me? You were jealous?"

Her masculine snort made him smile. "That and the bounty on your head. Even back then your womenfolk wanted your hide nailed to the floor in the sunshine—only that won't work on you, will it?"

Alex had always liked the way Gabriella talked. Like a man. If she'd been a man, they might have been great friends. "Again, I apologize. Tell me, Gabi, are you really so eager to see me dead? Aren't you the least bit curious about why I'd bother my ass to hang around New Orleans, where I'm obvi-ously not welcome?"

"Oh, I don't know," she said airily. "The need to rule? The need to control everyone around you . . ." She slid her finger along the edge of her collar. "We both know how much you enjoy being in control."

Alex's eyelids drifted down as he eyed the collar, then dropped his gaze to follow the flush of heat ripening her breasts. Her rose-colored nipples darkened, the tips beading.

She snuggled closer, pressing herself against his arm, and he turned his head to let her nuzzle his neck. "Does anyone in your clan know how much you love to be dominated?" he asked.

"Of course not. I'm very careful, usually, about whom I allow to cover me. Can't let any of those alpha males think they can be my master."

When her teeth nibbled his earlobe, he shuddered and murmured, "Wouldn't do at all to let a man be on top, hmmm?"

"Like I said, I'm choosy . . . and discreet. I have my position in my clan to consider." Her tongue trailed along the edge of his jaw. "Alex . . . ?"

"Yes, love?" He waited, knowing what she'd ask, knowing he couldn't refuse, but also honest enough to admit he was so damned aroused after their tussle that he needed the explosive release she'd offer.

"Remind me why I couldn't get enough of you . . . for old time's sake?" The amused curve of her lips was at odds with the need reflected in her intense gaze.

"A chase, then?"

Her breath hitched, lifting her chest. Her nipples dimpled. The musk of her honeyed arousal wafted in the air around them. "Loosen the collar?" she asked in a deepening contralto.

The collar was only for expedience. They both knew he was powerful enough to tame her, even in her lupine form. "Have you learned any new tricks?" he asked, narrowing his eyes.

Her chin dipped, her eyes rounding innocently. "Alex, do you really think I want to kill you here? I'd be stuck here with only your sad carcass to feed me for a day or two." She leaned closer and nipped his chin. "And we both know I have a ravenous appetite."

Alex fingered the clasp on her collar, loosening it.

Gabriella tugged it off and tossed it aside, then relaxed against the cushions as though she hadn't been so horny that her belly and thighs quivered. "I'll wait until you've stripped. I don't want you handicapped."

Alex set aside the glass he hadn't touched and rose from the sofa. Glancing down at his shredded shirt, he ripped it off and mopped the drying blood from his chest. When he glanced up, Gabriella's expression showed not a hint of remorse for the damage she'd done. Her pink tongue stroked over her top lip.

After he stripped the rest of his clothing away, she kicked out her legs and stood.

Wearing only his amulet, Alex braced his legs, readying to lunge, but she strode slowly toward him, her hips swaying, moisture gleaming on her inner thighs. As she drew near, she reached out to trace one long, angry scratch on his chest. She tracked it down his abdomen, then slowly walked around him, scraping her nail along his shoulders, his arm, before she finished the circle and lifted her brown gaze to his. "Nice, Alex. The years have been kind to you."

"As they have to you, love," he responded with a slight cant of his head.

She knew how beautiful she was, told him so with the intensifying flex of her thighs and feminine roll of her round hips. Powerful, so sensual she made his teeth ache—her confidence was just one more thing he liked about her.

Tossing back her head again, she paused in front of him to rake his body with her gaze, head to toe. Then she backed up to stare at his rising cock. Standing so close that her nipples grazed his chest, she held his gaze while her hand lifted and cupped his balls, hefting them softly on her palm as though assessing their weight.

Her nose lifted and she sniffed. "You stink of human, Alex," she said softly. "Who'd you do before me?"

Alex gave her a steady glare. "A girl. A blood host."

"You dared to take a bite, right there with the coven all around you?"

"Good thing, wasn't it?" he growled. "I'm going to need my strength."

"Hmmm . . . The question you need to ask yourself, vampire, is do you trust me?" Her smile, feminine and challenging, stretched across her lush lips as she stepped backward, shaking out her hair again.

Gabriella drew a deep breath and held it, her head falling back. Then she shook out her arms and legs, as though preparing for a sprint. Her shoulders lifted, her legs spread, then she sank her head toward her chest while locking with his gaze.

Alex's skin prickled at the wild, primal expression entering her regal features.

Her eyes flared gold for a moment. Then her back and shoulders slumped forward, and she fell to the ground, her hands landing flat in front of her, knees resting there only a split second. Hair sprouted to cover her face and flanks, then her whole body began to tremble and contort.

Her face jutted outward, stretching into a snout. Her back lengthened, legs and arms shortening, the joints crackling as they changed orientation.

When her transformation ended, Alex smiled, having never grown inured to the miracle of her true nature. Her pelt was lush and thick—black at the roots, blending to brown, then golden at the tips; a reddish ruff shone beneath her chin.

He held out his hand to the wolf, waiting with his breath held to see what she would do.

A low growl rumbled through her, not deep or sonorous enough to give him pause. He thought she might be laughing at him, giving him a growl to remind him he should be on his toes.

Her head sank toward the floor, her eyes never leaving him, and she crept toward him, her shoulders loose, relaxed. When she reached his outstretched fingers, she licked the tips, then scooted her head beneath his palm.

Alex chuckled and scratched behind her ears, digging into the thick fur until her growling became a thin whine.

She moved closer, sliding her shoulder against his thigh, leaning into him as though she only meant to rub against him.

Alex knew better than to relax. He grabbed a handful of the hair at the back of her neck and shook her gently. "Remember who has to take you home," he reminded her.

Her jaws opened, her tongue lolling out as her mouth stretched into a lycan smile.

He let her go. "You've been warned. Now, I'll show you how much I trust you." He let go of her and clasped his hands behind his back.

Gabriella leaned into his thigh again, resting her considerable weight against him. Then she nuzzled his belly with her nose, sticking out her tongue to swipe him there once.

"Ready to stop playing?"

The wolf snorted, then stepped directly in front of him, sitting on her haunches while she looked into his face.

Alex held her gaze, unafraid, knowing she would test him.

She lifted her nose, rubbing her finely furred snout along the inside of his thigh, rubbing up, then down, then up again.

"Gabi . . . ," he warned.

Her snout glided up again until her wet nose nudged his balls.

Alex's breath hissed between his teeth, but he didn't unclasp his hands.

When her soft, warm tongue laved one testicle, Alex forced his legs farther apart. If she took a bite, he'd kill her. Even Gabriella on a tear wouldn't be that stupid. He closed his eyes and let her lap him with her long tongue, over and over, until his toes curled into the thick carpet under his feet and his cock jutted straight up from his crotch. Her low-pitched growl vibrated against him, driving his arousal upward.

How long he stood there with his eyes closed as she licked his balls, then ventured up along his shaft, he didn't know. This wasn't something he'd have permitted in their previous relationship, but back then, he'd held all the power. Now, he needed a favor.

When the laps shortened, the tongue feeling a little less slippery, he gazed down to find the woman kneeling between his parted legs, mischief in her eyes and finely arched brows.

Alex thrust his fingers through her hair, pulling hard until her mouth opened around a gasp. With his other hand he pushed his cock downward, between her open lips.

Her gaze narrowed, and her bared teeth closed around his crown.

Alex wiped all trepidation from his mind and his features. He tightened his jaws, lowering his brows and daring her to attempt a bite. For a long, charged moment they froze, gazes locked, then Gabriella slowly opened her mouth wider.

Alex didn't even think about pulling away. Without hesitation he stroked into her mouth, straight toward the back of her throat.

Gabriella gurgled, then swallowed, the action giving his head a strong caress.

He slipped both hands around her head and held her just where he wanted her, pulling her close as he stroked forward, shoving her back when he withdrew.

Gabriella didn't fight his hold, didn't murmur a single protest, just groaned as he continued to fuck her generous mouth until he thrust her off him with enough force that she tumbled to the floor behind her.

Before she got her elbows beneath her, he came over her, flipping her to her knees, clamping his teeth at the corner of her shoulder and piercing her skin as he forced her forward on her hands, then spread her thighs wide with rough nudges from his knees.

With his cock tucked between her legs as he stroked along her lower belly, he had her wriggling, trying to scoot forward to capture him with her moist pussy.

Instead, Alex held her trapped, his belly blanketing her back, his cock gliding along her seam while his hands raked over her breasts and belly like the marauder he'd been when they'd first met.

As he began to suckle her skin, drawing her rich, lycan blood into his mouth, Gabriella quivered, the strength of her tremors shivering through him. She raised one arm and hooked it behind his neck, holding him there.

Alex gentled his touches, caressing the breast stretched by her raised arm, thumbing the nipple until it spiked hard, the velvet skin around it contracting, dimpling.

"Please, Alex," she murmured. "*God*, fuck me."

Alex glided his hands down her belly until he reached his cock. He closed his fingers around his shaft and stroked, pushing his belly hard against her round ass.

"My pussy'll fuck you better than your hand. Fuck *me*, Alex."

Alex opened his jaws, disengaging his teeth.

Gabriella moaned in protest.

"I haven't told you to speak," he said, keeping his tone flat, emotionless.

"Alex," she sobbed, her hips wriggling to glide her lips along his shaft as he continued to stroke into his fist. "I won't speak. Tell me what you want. I'll do it."

"I don't want anything from you, Gabi. Just a hole to stick my cock inside."

"Use mine, please," she whispered.

Alex smiled against her hair. "Perfect answer," he replied softly. "Put your face against the carpet."

Gabriella dropped to her elbows and placed her forehead against the carpet.

Alex backed away from her body, not touching her, letting her wait for a touch or a command.

Her body trembled. Her inner thighs grew slick with her arousal.

He crawled beside her and cupped the back of her head. "You know I only do this because I care for your pleasure."

Her head scraped the carpet as she nodded, afraid to reply out loud.

Alex remembered his amazement all those years ago, when he'd discovered the secret cravings of this proud *were*. He'd lay money she'd never let a single member of her pack know what really got her off. Likely she played with humans, visiting anonymous lovers who wielded whips and bound her with ropes, never realizing they teased a powerful predator.

Alex almost pitied her. To be naturally submissive, yet never able to seek a mate among her own kind for fear of losing status—she had an eternity of loneliness ahead of her.

Maybe he was the answer to her dilemma. A marriage between the Wolfen Nation and the Vampires—the political marriage he needed. He'd satisfy every yearning she ever had, and she would never demand his love.

Something to mull over in the coming days.

The thought sent a chill through him and his thoughts went back to Sarah. Sweet Sarah. She too had presented her ass to him, and he'd breached it and her trust. At least she'd be safe now.

Then because it was expected, and because he needed to lose the edgy anger he'd accumulated since bundling "Sarah" into the limo, he bent below Gabriella's upraised bottom and lapped at her cunt, then rubbed his nose, chin, and mouth in the wetness trickling from inside her.

Her back sank lower, tilting her ass higher, giving him access and permission to do whatever he wanted.

Alex placed kisses on each fleshy globe, then lifted the top off a woven basket beside the sofa. He pulled out a knife and a length of silk rope. He cut the knot from one end of the rope and frayed the edges with his fingers. He wound the rope around both fists and pulled it taut with a snap.

Gabriella didn't make a sound, but her pussy clenched, then opened.

Although he knew he shouldn't touch a woman when anger and frustration rode him, he let the passions warring inside him guide his actions.

He trailed the soft frayed end between her buttocks and along her slit, wetting it. Then feeding two feet of the rope's length through his fist, he raised it high and flicked it at her ass.

The snap made a thin, but satisfying, crack and left a reddened mark on her pale skin. "You can tell me to stop at any time, Gabi, but know that if you do, I'll dress and we'll be finished here."

Her breaths rasped, but she stayed silent.

He flicked the rope again, hitting the opposite cheek. Then he popped her in a different spot. He worked the fringed tip faster and faster, until small red welts rose on her skin and her bottom trembled.

When he flicked her clit with one precise strike, she whimpered.

Again he bent over her. He tongued the reddened clit, peeking from beneath its thin, stretched hood. "Sweet, sweet Gabi," he groaned, pressing her lips apart to lap at her creamy folds.

Soft, rasping sobs shook her body.

Alex marveled over how such a powerful woman could be made into a mass of quivering nerves by simple, empty commands and a little physical punishment. How the hell had she managed to remain unchallenged by any of the alphas in her widespread clan?

He knelt behind her, cupping her pussy in his palm, toggling her clit with just one finger. "I want to hear you now, love. Tell me what you want."

A long, *human* howl erupted from her.

How long had she needed his brand of loving that she could be brought in minutes to this peak—trembling, incoherent— her pussy clasping on his hand? "Tell me, sweetheart. Want more?" he asked, swatting her pussy with his palm, then rubbing it, then swatting again.

"Uhnnn . . . *Alex* . . . fuck me hard," she gritted out, gasping when he slapped her wet cunt particularly hard. Her thighs tightened. Fresh, heated pre-cum gushed to soak his palm, and he knew she was close.

"Like this?" he asked, thrusting three fingers into her passage, purposely dragging out her agony.

"Fuck no! Your cock, you goddamn bastard."

Alex *tsk*ed, pulled out his fingers, and sat back on his haunches.

Gabriella's head jerked up, swiveling to stab him with a lethal glare.

"You didn't say please," he said.

A furious cry ripping from her, Gabriella launched herself at him, slamming him against the ground, her thighs straddling his hips and grinding on his cock.

Alex slid a hand between their bodies, covering her cunt. Another slid around her hip to anchor her there, unable to take him inside, unable to even rut her way to orgasm.

Her breasts heaved; her belly jumped. She leaned forward and clasped his shoulders, then bent closer and ground her lips against his until both their mouths were bloodied.

When the salt of tears mixed with the taste of their blood, Alex relented, bringing his hands to her cheeks to force her to gentle the kiss.

As her lips softened and trembled, he wiped away her tears

with his thumbs. "Easy there," he murmured as she slid her mouth along his cheek and jaw.

"Fuck me like I matter, Alex," she whispered in his ear.

His eyes squeezed closed, his stomach clenching at the raw need in her feminine plea.

She raised her head and gave him one of her direct stares, the effect spoiled somewhat by her glassy, glistening eyes. "Don't go thinking I love you," she rasped, her gaze sliding away. "It's just been a long damn time since I've wanted to be taken . . . mastered."

Alex studied her glittering eyes. Did she love him? Is that why she'd tried to kill him all those years ago? Deciding he didn't really want to know, he accepted her words at face value.

His hands glided up her back, massaging her strong shoulders, then came around her rib cage to gently cup her large, round breasts. "Roll over, baby. I'll give you what you need."

CHAPTER
10

Gabriella climbed off his hips and lay on her back on the plush red carpet, her gaze hungry, her face taut with need.

Alex came over her, knowing she wanted him to be the one in charge, but also suspecting that this time her need was for the human connection he'd always brought—the tenderness he rewarded her with after the battle had been won.

He shaped her cheeks between his palms, cautioning himself to take his time. The seconds ticking by didn't really count in this realm. Their separate quests, waiting back at *Ardeal* for them to fulfill, wouldn't be delayed or changed unless they consciously decided to carry the strands of passion that bound them here back into that world.

Resting on his side, his body snuggled close to hers,

he bent to kiss her mouth, inhaling her soft, ragged sigh. Her lips molded to his, following his languid lapping motions as his hands caressed her face and his fingers slid into her thick, warm hair.

The kiss was staid for them, innocently binding them for the moment—a promise that however their passions might move them, this moment was precious, a mutual gift of solace.

Alex felt his heart slow, his body and his mind renewing. He kept his eyes open, waiting for her body or a fleeting change of expression to tell him when she was ready for more.

Her eyelids drifted open, and her lips curved beneath his. When he lifted his mouth, she whispered, "Do you remember the first time we met?"

Alex's glance slid away.

Germany. A dark, moonless night. An inn at the side of a lonely, rutted dirt trail, leading from Heidelberg to Worms. After the rain-freshened wind of the open trail, the air in the inn was nearly unbreathable due to the smoke wafting from a poorly vented hearth.

He rested his head on his hand and pretended to search hard for the memory. "You wore a dark cape," he said slowly, "and swept into the inn like you were royalty, two retainers following in your wake. You captured the gazes of every patron while you eyed them back . . . until you came to me." He narrowed his gaze and lifted one brow. "You said, 'He'll do.'"

Her smile widened, a dimple appearing in one cheek, giving her a youthful, mischievous air. "I've always had an unerring instinct when it comes to choosing lovers. However, that time, I seriously underestimated your 'suitability.'"

His answering grin stretched his lips. "You won't convince me you were anything but thrilled with that miscalculation."

Her nose wrinkled. "I must admit, when I found myself tied to the bedposts, spread-eagled for your pleasure, I didn't mind at all that you'd tricked me. The things you did to me . . ." She shivered deliciously.

He cupped her chin and rubbed her lower lip with his thumb. "Tell me. Was it your first time?"

One finely arched brow rose high. "The first time that I wasn't the alpha in bed? Yes. You punished me for my arrogance." Her eyes widened. "I couldn't believe I allowed it. Still can't. Did you use your allure? I never felt it."

"I didn't have to," he drawled.

"Think it was your manly charms alone?"

Alex chuckled softly. "That and my firm hand on your backside."

"Must have been that," she said breathlessly. "Alex?"

"Ready for another go?"

"Please."

Only too willing to oblige—since a compliant Gabriella was so much easier to deal with than the snarling wolf—he slid his leg over hers and nudged his hard cock against her hip while he trailed his hand down her throat, pausing to gauge her rising excitement by the quickening thud of her pulse.

Her eyes grew unfocused, the pupils dilating. She stirred restlessly, her breasts lifting, an unspoken invitation to ease what ached.

He glided lower, capturing a breast, lifting it, massaging it, tormenting the rigid point at the center of her dusky nipple. He leaned over her, latching onto it, sliding the flat of his tongue over the sensitive tip until she mewled.

"A very kittenish sound, coming from a wolf," he teased when he let it go.

She played with the unclaimed breast, squeezing it, tugging

on the nipple. "I can become a tiger, if you don't kiss the other one quick."

An urgent but pleasurable heaviness settled in his balls and cock. Rising over her, he straddled her thighs and scooted down her body, bending his head directly over the opposite breast.

She dragged away her hand, smoothing it over her ribs, and lower, creeping toward the juncture of her thighs.

Alex allowed her foraging and stuck out his tongue to flick her nipple, over and over. Then he lapped harder, dragging it upward with each lap.

"I love to have my breasts fondled and sucked," she murmured, fingers spearing through his hair to bring him closer. "Did you like me licking your balls?"

"I loved it, my sweet bitch." Then he opened his jaws wide and worked his lips around her breast, drawing as much of the ample globe into his mouth as he could hold.

Her body rolled restlessly beneath him; she began to pant. "I wondered how far you'd let me go . . . never dreamed you'd allow that much. I could have licked you until you came, you tasted that good to me."

Alex growled and suckled harder, using his swirling tongue and lips to excite her while starting to rut his cock against her hip.

Gabriella untucked her fingers from her pussy and pressed against the top of his head to encourage him to move downward.

And because he was ready, he allowed her to guide him past her soft, quivering belly to the base of her mound until her richly scented musk drew his tongue to her pussy.

With her legs still closed, he delved between her tight lips, turning sideways and slowly shaking his head back and forth to work up and down her slit, until he felt her jerk as he grazed her swollen clit.

When Gabriella's fingers pulled up her folds to bare her clitoris, Alex curved his tongue around it, and laved, flicked, and sucked it until her breaths rasped harshly.

Kneeling on one knee, he nudged apart her legs, smiling at her eagerness as she slammed them open and planted her feet on the carpet to tilt her cunt toward his mouth.

Needing no further hints, he leaned over her, parting her with his thumbs. He laved her inner lips, drinking the fragrant, salty-sweet essence that slid like warmed honey from her body to greet his tongue.

Gabriella's soft, rounded belly trembled wildly. Her thighs hugged his shoulders.

He speared into her, swirling his tongue to capture more of the silky fluid from her inner walls, groaning as her flavors exploded on his tongue.

Gabriella grew more restless, her hips softly undulating against him.

He left her channel and licked upward, pressed against the top of her hood to expose her clitoris, and flicked it with rapid, butterfly lashes. A ragged moan broke from her, and he took the cue, inserting two fingers into her vagina as he continued to torment her clit. He slid them in and out, slowly at first, then pumped them faster as her pussy clasped him in rhythmic, sucking kisses.

A third finger thrusting inside had her back arching off the ground. "Alex!"

He withdrew abruptly, not wanting to finish her this way;

besides, his own arousal throbbed hard, impossible to ignore. As he came up her body, her arms slid around his torso, dragging him strongly up her length, her hips curving to align her cunt with the cock scraping up her thigh.

When she'd captured him, letting him rest the blunt head at her entrance, she swallowed, then drew a long, jagged breath. "I don't want this over too quickly. I know I always seem to be hurrying you along—"

"I understand, love. You want *me* to show restraint." Alex gave her a lopsided smile. "You must think I'm Superman."

"Have I exceeded your capabilities?" she asked, giving the tip of his cock a sexy "kiss" with her pussy.

Alex ran his hand down her side and back up, then cupped her full breast. "How is it you can make a man feel like a god and a boy at the same time?"

Her nipples beaded against his palm. "Don't all women know how?"

"Not many wield that power as well as you."

"Aren't you lucky, then?" Her cunt tightened, trying to draw him inside. "Alex, come inside me, quickly now."

Alex braced apart his knees and began to push inward, then he halted, groaning. "Wait. Forgot . . . *fuck!*" He pulled out and reached blindly for his trousers, shoving his fingers into a pocket to extricate his wallet.

"You and your bloody damn sheaths," Gabriella moaned. "Do you really think you can impregnate me? We aren't even the same species."

"I'm a Born male. Don't ever underestimate that fact." Finding another foil packet in a side pocket of his wallet, he tossed the wallet away and tore the foil with his teeth.

Before he could remove the latex circle, Gabriella took it from his hand. "Let me."

Alex once again rolled onto his side, half sitting as Gabriella came to her knees beside him. She placed the circle in her mouth, gave him a sexy wink, and bent over his lap. Her mouth opened around the tip of his cock, her tongue doing extraordinary things as she maneuvered the condom over the head, then rolled it down his shaft with her lips.

"Nice trick," Alex said, cupping the back of her head as she drew off him.

She gazed up from his lap, one brow arching. "I like to impress my human lovers."

"You make them wear a condom, even though the chances of your getting pregnant by a human are slim to none?"

She smoothed her cheek along his cock. "You never know, and I never leave a thing to chance."

Holding his dick, he tapped her lips with it. "So you know where I'm coming from."

"I wouldn't really mind . . . with you, that is." She pursed her lips and gave his crown a soft, lingering kiss.

"Gabi . . ."

"I know." She rolled her eyes, but her lips straightened into a pained line. "You have bigger plans than siring a litter with a wolf."

Since his thoughts hadn't been so far from that train of thought earlier, he remained silent rather than lie for the sake of expedience. He had to think, to strategize, before he ever broached the topic, because once he committed to her, there'd be no going back. She'd kill him before she allowed him to jilt her; her clan would hunt him like a dog.

Gabriella lay on her side, facing him. She slowly lifted one firmly muscled thigh over his hip. "I hope this hasn't put you off. I know how baby talk can wilt the proudest man."

"I'll try not to wither away," he said dryly.

"Where were we?"

"You were just about to be fucked."

"Love that word. The verb form, in particular."

His hand rubbed over her thigh, then clutched her ass. "I prefer my women incoherent," he growled.

"I'm mumbling already."

Holding her ass still, he plunged into her cunt, forcing a groan from them both.

Gabriella adjusted her thigh higher along his hip.

Alex lay down, stretching out his arm for her to lay her head upon. Side by side on the carpet, they shared a slow smile.

"We're doing this like old lovers," Gabriella said. "Like a couple of centuries never passed."

"Don't you remember? It was always like this for us. Fiery at first, then lazy, lingering. We knew each other's bodies and preferences so well."

"You make us sound boring."

"Never. Just comfortable . . ."

". . . in our own skins?"

Another smile and Alex leaned close to press a quick kiss to her lips. "We still have to talk."

"I know. We will. And I think . . . I'll listen this time."

"Do me a favor, then. Stop thinking. My balls are ready to burst."

Her breath huffed. "Thought you were going to do me slowly."

"Think my cock's reached its limit for restraint. You keep squeezing it."

"Like that?" she said slyly, giving him another inner caress.

He dragged in a deep, slow breath. "*Goddamn*, you have the strongest cunt muscles."

"Oooh, you really know how to make a woman feel special."

He thrust his free hand into her hair and gently cupped her head. "I'm no player. I'm choosy too. And I never told you I wasn't sleeping with someone else."

"I know. It's a vampire thing. You're all whores. You just a little less so. Why's that? Afraid to populate the world with your super-sperm?"

Alex shrugged. "That, and I can't make promises."

"Few women these days hope for anything beyond a great lay."

"I want more."

"So you deprive yourself of this?" Her eyes darkened. "I'm sad for you."

"Don't be. I'm too busy to be preoccupied with my cock."

Her nose wrinkled. "Now you sound like a eunuch. You know . . . anytime you want some uncomplicated, no-strings sex—"

"Promise not to send any more assassins my way?" he growled.

"Sorry about that," she said softly. "I regretted it for a long time afterward. I rarely lose my temper like that these days."

"Helpful to know. Can we do a little less talking?"

"I think I'm having my *after*glow before."

"You were always a contrary woman." Alex lifted her thigh from his hip and pressed it toward her breast. Leaning slightly toward her, he stroked deeper.

Gabriella touched his lips with a finger, and he opened his mouth for her. She poked it in and he sucked, wetting it.

Then, reaching around her raised thigh, Gabriella circled her engorged clit as he thrust steadily, until her face flushed and her lips rounded.

"Ride me, Gabi." Alex fell to his back, taking Gabriella over him, but he halted her from moving. "Backwards, love."

Without demur, she rose on her knees and faced away, then waited while he held his cock straight up for her slide down. Alex raised his knees and flexed upward to impale her as she fell. She leaned over, stretching his cock away, clamping her hands on his knees as she began to glide forward and back.

Alex grasped her buttocks, massaging them in circular, opposing motions. Her movements gained momentum and her pussy tightened, her inner walls rippling all along his shaft as she dragged at him. Gabriella drew slowly off his cock, rocking forward, then scooting back to envelop him.

The slow downward drag enflamed him, but it frustrated him as well. Alex continued to massage her lush ass, gripping her tighter, trying to encourage her to make shorter strokes, but she wriggled, jerking shallowly, shaking off his guiding hands.

Alex traced the crevice between her cheeks, pausing to finger her tiny hole.

Gabriella tossed her hair back and growled, lunging forward, then bouncing back harder. She forced his legs wider, repositioning her knees for better balance, then she thrust one hand down to grab his balls.

When she squeezed him hard, his body shuddered, and he flexed his buttocks, spearing harder into her.

She rolled his balls in her palm, encircled them with her fingers, then began to tug them, gently at first, slowly increasing the pressure, until the angle of her strokes and the tightening around his balls arrested his spiraling orgasm.

"Fuck. Gabi. *Bitch*."

Her laughter, low and sultry, washed over him, leaving him sweating, shaking, grinding helplessly.

Her long straight back arched, her hair brushed her waist in soughing waves, her bottom shivered as she bounced harder.

Then her hand released his balls, slid higher, ringing the base of his cock, forcing it to swell harder as blood was restricted.

Alex roared, bucking under her, lifting her with his upward lunges as he bounced her on his cock, taking control of the rhythm of their mating.

Her hips rolled, riding his cock and groin like a saddle, accepting his wild bucking as she brought her knees more securely beneath her and simply poised above him to take his thrusts.

Alex pounded into her pussy, stroking endlessly, enduring the heat of another lapping wave of moisture spilling from inside her.

Past restraint, past the point he could let her take her own pleasure from his body, he sat up, forced her forward, and brought his knees beneath him.

She let go of his cock, braced her weight on her hands, and arched her back to press her ass snug against his groin.

Alex breathed deeply, placed a restraining hand on her shoulder and another on her hip, then slammed his cock into her rippling passage, cramming deep, slamming his hips and belly against her body, the jolts shoving air from her lungs as he powered into her.

When the pressure in his balls exploded, he thrust like a jackhammer—shallow, fast, harsh.

Gabriella let loose a long, aching howl, and then her arms quivered and folded.

Alex wouldn't let her fall away; he thrust and thrust, not slowing until his balls were emptied and his cock throbbing—drenched, spent, caressed by the slackening convulsions of her inner walls.

He pulled her upward, into his arms, brushing her hair backward, tilting her mouth to his.

The kiss he gave her was hard, a branding of lips that softened to a gentler molding as her trembling slowed.

"I'm shattered. Utterly wiped," she said, smiling tiredly when at last he lifted his lips.

Their bodies still connected, Alex didn't respond. Instead, he slid his hands down her damp belly, past the moist curls, raised the thin hood over the bulging, engorged knot of her clitoris, and circled it with two fingers.

Gabriella groaned. "No more. Can't breathe."

He rubbed harder, and her pussy clasped around his cock, a reflexive contraction of muscle—a sexy little caress that encouraged him to continue to slowly circle. "Let's talk now."

Gabriella gasped. "You're insane . . . Can't think."

"Then don't. Go with your instinct, instead of weighing all the outcomes." He tapped her clit, then toggled it again.

She wriggled, trying to grind down on his cock. "We have all the time in the world here. You said so yourself."

"This doesn't have to be the end of us, Gabi. But we do need to conclude our bargain."

Gabriella's head fell back against his shoulder. "The only bargain I've made was to capture or kill you. They aren't fussy how you're rendered to them."

"Do they know what I am?"

"Only that you're a daywalking vampire. I'm sure that bitch Inanna has her suspicions. The others are less sure."

"So they don't know for sure that I'm Born. Only that I'm not confined to roaming at night."

"That's what I said," she bit out. She cupped his balls again, tugging with just enough strength that he wasn't alarmed but rather grew aroused again.

He cupped her breasts and squeezed them hard.

Gabriella's breath hissed between her teeth. "What do you want from me? Time to escape?"

"For you to turn a blind eye."

"I can't do that. My clan agreed to this hunt. They have no more love of a daywalker than your coven-sisters."

"There is more at stake than just my continued existence."

"All I have is your word on that."

"I can give you a glimpse into our future. Show you a window into the darkness."

Her head slid along his shoulder as she tilted her face to meet his gaze. Her expression was open, hopeful for a reprieve in their private battle.

He could use that.

Gabriella nuzzled his cheek. "Show me."

CHAPTER

II

Alex kissed her shoulder, then gently lifted her from his lap. They both drew deep, ragged breaths as his cock slid free from her hot, silken sheath. He stood and grabbed a napkin from the bureau, then handed it to Gabriella, who grimaced but quickly wiped away the moisture gleaming on her thighs.

"Are you taking me somewhere else? Should I dress?"

Alex shook his head and held out his hand.

Gabriella approached him warily, but she slid her hand inside his, not hesitating when he pulled her close and turned them both toward the bureau and the mirror hanging above it.

She glanced up, a question in her eyes.

"When I was very little, still a boy," he began softly, "before I came into my powers, Simon gave me a crystal and told me that if ever I was in danger, I should hold it in my hand and wish myself away."

Her head tilted, her gaze sliding slyly toward his abandoned pants.

Alex lifted her chin with a finger to bring her gaze back to his. "The spell he used to craft the key to this room answers only to my touch."

She wrinkled her nose, then smiled innocently. "Of course it does. Tell me the rest of your fairy tale."

"I came here often, bringing things for my comfort. Weapons and games. Food and drink. One day, Simon asked for me to bring him here. He brought that mirror and hung it. He told me if ever I wanted to see my future, I was to touch the frame—never the glass—and wait. It would appear."

"No 'Mirror, mirror on the wall' incantation?" she asked, her tone lazy and amused.

Alex lifted an eyebrow. "It has its own enchantment. Mirrors are a specialty of Simon's." He turned her face back toward the glass. "Touch the frame."

Alex kept his attention on Gabi's face, watching the mirror from the corner of his eye. He knew well enough what she would see and preferred reading her reactions so that he might gauge the impact of what she saw.

She lifted her hand slowly, gave him a darting, narrowed glance, then touched her fingers to the bottom of the frame.

The mirror's surface began to shimmer, their reflections blurring, darkening, then disappearing.

Gabi gasped and jerked back her hand.

The mirror blinked, and then returned their reflections again.

"Don't be afraid. Touch only the frame and you'll be fine."

"What happens if I touch the glass?" she asked, tension creeping into her voice.

Alex shrugged. "I don't know. I never tried."

Gabi shook her head. "How does a kid with a magic mirror never give it a try?"

Alex met her gaze in the mirror. "Because I've seen what's on the other side."

She blinked, her expression sharpening. "It's that scary?"

"If you'd summon your courage, you can find out for yourself."

Gabi's eyebrows furrowed. "I'm not afraid. Just cautious. Why should I trust you?"

"If I'd wanted to harm you, I'd have tightened that collar 'til you choked," he growled.

Gabi rubbed her back against his chest. "Alex, I'm a sick little wolf cub. The way you just said that made me wet."

He rolled his eyes. "Gabi. Touch the frame."

Her chin came up, and she reached to grip the bottom edge of the gilt frame.

The shimmering cleared, the surface appearing liquid.

Gabi leaned close to peer into it, but she jerked back when her breaths rippled the surface. Their reflections darkened, becoming vague shadows as the window opened into another room.

Golden candles from heavy chandeliers and wall sconces barely pierced the dark corners of the large hall stretching before them. The walls of the room were made of precisely hewn gray stone, with keyhole windows that opened into darkness. Wooden tables laden with mounds of food stretched the length of the hall. Benches flanked the tables and were filled with people—women dressed in lavish gowns and jewels, men wearing medieval chausses and tunics. They'd sat down to dinner, but their faces turned time and again toward a dais, where a single gilded table rested. They bent their heads together, talking.

"They can't see us?"

"They don't even know we observe. And we can't hear them."

"But it's beautiful," Gabriella said. "Everyone's beautiful."

"Beautifully garbed, love. A gilded cage. Keep watching." He'd seen this ritual play out hundreds of times. His belly tightened, and he placed his hands on her shoulders, gripping her firmly.

Gabriella stiffened, but she kept her gaze locked on the room.

"Watch the woman in the wine-colored gown," Alex said softly. "Look closely."

The woman sat at the end of one of the tables nearest their "window." Her dark gown was edged with shimmering embroidery. A bloodred stone hanging from a heavy gold necklace lay between her breasts. The man beside her turned toward her, slipped his finger into the top of her gown, and pulled it down to expose a puckered nipple.

The woman's mouth opened around a silent scream. She leaned backward, trying to escape his touch, but he thrust a brawny arm around her back and bent to capture her breast between his teeth. He bit, blood seeping downward to disappear against her dark gown. Although she shoved and pulled at his coarse, black hair, he didn't budge from her breast.

Her lips drew back, and then her teeth elongated, every one of them growing, interlocking from top to bottom, until her mouth was overfilled, and she snapped and gnashed ineffectively as the man held her upper body in his strong grip.

Her body stretched, her back losing its stiffness, falling toward the floor, but he climbed off the bench to follow her there. Her arms reached outward, then waved as though boneless. They began to change colors, from pale, creamy white, to green, to dull, ashy gray. She cupped her hands, fusing the fingers together, forming two heads that resembled cobras. The heads stabbed toward the man's back and face, sinking long fangs into his neck as he continued to savage her breast.

Gabriella's body shuddered, but her horrified gaze didn't veer from the couple. As though their struggle was a cue, all around them others began to claw at clothing. Men swept women onto the tables, lifted their skirts, and began to rape. Knives and forks struck flesh, and blood began to spill across the floor.

Gabi shivered in front of him, her gaze widening.

"Step a little to the left, love," Alex whispered. "Watch the door."

Reluctantly, she shuffled to the side, her knuckles whitening on the frame she still grasped. Her head turned slowly, her gaze dragging reluctantly from the carnage.

At this angle the entrance to the hall could be observed. Two short, burly men flanked either side of a set of large wooden doors.

"Stare at the guards, let your gaze blur just a little and find their auras," Alex said close to her ear. He did the same, staring at the two men whose frames seemed to waver, a dark shadow detaching from each of them to slump forward to the ground on all fours.

Their dark, shadowy outlines grew darker, their forms more substantive. Deep, slavering muzzles protruded. Canines the length of daggers curved from their jaws.

"They're dogs?" she whispered.

"Hellhounds. Their screams can drive a man mad. Or so Simon has told me."

The door opened, and the dogs leaped around, their bodies tensing and quivering in their excitement, their jaws opening and shutting around silent howls. Wind gusted inside from pitch darkness, carrying leaves and small branches.

A man entered, so tall he dwarfed the hounds, who tucked their tails between their legs as he held out his hands to them. Grabbing them by the scruffs of their necks, he walked the length of the hall while all gazes turned toward him—except for the first couple, still writhing on the floor.

He halted beside them, lifted one hound off his front legs, and then released it.

The hound lunged toward the couple; its jaws opened wide and snapped around the back of the man's neck, cutting it in two. The man's head rolled away as his body grew slack above the demon woman.

Gabi flinched, but she didn't release her grip.

Alex admired her courage. He'd been in his teens before he'd grown inured to this endless feast.

"Who is he?" she whispered.

Alex glanced back to the tall, powerful warrior, who continued with one hound toward the dais, where he took his seat and slumped in his chair, his hands gripping the arms of his throne, his expression wiped of any emotion. "The Master of the Demons."

"Are they all demons?"

"No. The man never changed his form when he attacked the demon woman. He's a human, forced to relive his own sins and torture again and again. Watch long enough and you'll learn a lot. Demons and humans meet in the hall, fornicate, and feed off each other."

"And the Demon Master?"

"Never moves from his throne until the meal is complete. Then he leaves, the servants sweep away the carnage, and it starts again. Look for his aura, Gabi."

He knew the moment she'd found it by her sharp indrawn gasp.

The Master's aura surrounded him in a large black cloud that slowly firmed, so immense it stretched the length of the dais. His spiked tail swept up and down, then curved toward his body as it settled. But it was the crenellated ridges atop his snout and the golden, glowing eyes, with their lizardlike, slitted pupils, that identified his inner demon.

"He's a dragon? They exist?"

"You're a werewolf," he said dryly. "Why are you so surprised?"

"Because I've never seen one in this realm. Alex?" Her head swiveled, her gaze locking with his. "Is this happening now, or is this the future?"

"The answer's more complicated than that. And simpler."

"I don't understand. That sounds like mage talk."

Alex couldn't help smiling. How many times had he railed at Simon for his ambiguous pronouncements? "Let me try to explain. The same way this cavern doesn't occupy the same place or time as our reality back home, neither does that place. *When* doesn't matter so much, but Simon believes the *how* will occur soon. In our realm and time."

"The 'how' to accomplish what?"

"For them to escape. To breach a portal and enter our realm."

"Why do you think that will happen?"

"When I started watching this feast, centuries ago, there weren't as many tables. They weren't situated as close together as they are now. So close—"

"You feel like you could reach through and touch them?"

"Right. Fewer demons, fewer humans. The hall is filling. One day there will be no more room."

"Are there no other rooms in that keep?"

"There are an infinite number, but Simon believes that if we opened windows into each of them, we would find the same thing. Not enough room, and so many demons and unfortunates that the carnage of each night's punishments stretches longer every meal."

"What is that place? Does it have a name?"

"You know what it is, Gabi."

She withdrew her fingers from the mirror. She waited until it blinked and returned their pale reflections, then she turned to wrap her arms around his waist, snuggling her face against his chest. "It's Hell. Isn't it, Alex?"

He tightened his arms around her, felt the faint shivers, and knew that she'd realized she'd glimpsed her own future.

Miki gave the driver a haggard smile as she stepped out of the limo with his assistance. She'd fallen asleep in the backseat.

Her body felt stiff, her movements forced. She was tired and bruised, inside and out. And dirty.

She longed for a hot bath. One she could lie inside and never leave, just emptying and reopening the taps to fill her tub long past the time her skin pruned.

But there was no running water in the building. Not even a light over the entrance as she fumbled in a pocket for her key.

As the limo pulled away from the curb, she held out her keys, seeking enough moonlight to find the building key.

The lock turned behind her. The shadow in the doorway was stooped and thick. Old Man Mouton stood in the opening, a shotgun resting across his folded arms. "Thought we were gonna have to mount a patrol of our own, missy."

"Sorry I didn't tell you I'd be late. Something came up." If only she'd stopped by when she'd thought about it earlier. She might have hesitated, might have decided it was wiser to stay inside.

Light blinded her for a moment as he pointed a flashlight at her and scanned her body. "Best get off the doorstep. Not safe out there, *fille*."

The gruffness of his tone, deeper than usual, had Miki's throat tightening.

"That man from the magazine come by earlier. Dropped off an envelope. Bet it's cash. And notes for you."

"Emile was here?"

"Just said that," he snapped.

Miki took no offense, knowing his gruffness hid a soft heart.

"You get on up to your room. Keep your door and windows locked."

Miki blinked tiredly. Windows, too? She lived on the second

floor. Well above reach of any criminals looking for an easy target.

But the way his gaze bored into hers told her there was more to his warning. His lips firmed. "There's craziness on them streets. Crazy people. Crazy *t'ings*. I don't have ta tell you 'bout it, now."

His whispered words sent a chill down her spine. He knew. Knew what she'd found. What she'd done. Miki's gaze slid away from his. "Thanks for looking out for me. I'm heading to bed."

"Remember, keep those windows closed."

The air inside the stairwell was thick, humid, and starting to stink with garbage piling up outside the building and in the occupied apartments. Her room would be stifling. "I'll remember," she replied and started the climb to her apartment.

"Need my flashlight?" he called after her.

Wanting to get away, to be alone and lick her wounds, she didn't answer; she just lifted her key chain in the air, hit the end of the small flashlight hanging from the fob, and began the slow climb.

Once inside her one-room apartment, she stripped, dropping her clothes and letting them lie on the ground as she moved toward the bathroom. Inside, she lit candles, stoppered the sink, and filled the basin with bottled water. She started with her face, working suds into a cloth, then scouring her skin in circles.

Watching her own reflection in the mirror, she concentrated on working methodically—scouring, rinsing, before moving on to another area to clean. She paused at her neck, turning her head to find the faint indentions where Alex and Nic had taken their bites and healed her wounds with their tongues. She scrubbed extra hard on the corner of her neck.

The last place *Alexander* had bitten her.

The liar. He'd said he wasn't a vampire. A *Revenant*, as he'd called them. But she recalled the savage bite he'd given her at the last when she'd been too overcome with misery and enervating pleasure to throw his words back at him.

Alexander was the man in the alley. And she'd been fool enough, desperate enough, to want to believe he was human and good.

She scrubbed behind her ear, circling over the tattoo Alex had remarked upon. The one she'd chosen in this new life as a symbol of her rebirth.

She rinsed the cloth, soaped it again, and rubbed lower, over her aching breasts, welcoming the discomfort, washing her skin as though she could wash the memories of what she'd allowed—no, invited—them to do. Her nipples flared, raw and red, too tender for even a soft touch, but she scoured them anyway.

Working steadily, she reached the apex of her thighs. She lifted a foot and placed it on top of the closed lid of her toilet. The first touch of the cool, wet cloth to her inflamed pussy had air hissing between her lips.

She began to shake. She knew she was suffering from a mild case of shock and needed to lie down, but she couldn't until she was done. Until she was clean.

Tonight, she'd learned a lesson. One she would never forget. Despite the strides she'd made in repairing her damaged, hollow life, she was still vulnerable to monsters, human and inhuman. Regardless of whether or not she kept her eyes wide open, she could be seduced into lowering her reserve, could be tempted to enter dangerous waters.

She'd nearly drowned tonight. Nearly begged Alex to take her, to make her one of them, because for a moment, she'd felt whole, desired, complete. An illusion. One fostered by his allure and her loneliness.

She'd never forget. But what she feared most was that she wouldn't be able to resist seeking him out again.

Miki finished washing herself, then found a soft, shapeless nightgown. She slipped it on and lay down on top of her sheets. She closed her eyes, tried to clear her mind of everything she'd learned and experienced. So much had happened, so much that made sense of things she'd already known instinctively.

Vampires weren't just cool kitsch for Halloween. An underworld filled with creatures of the night preyed on humans, feasted on their blood and sexual appetites, manipulated their emotions, toyed with their vulnerabilities.

Okay, so maybe she was just superimposing her beef with Alex on the whole species, but damn if he hadn't made her trust him.

How he must have laughed up his sleeve at how naïve she'd been. She'd thought him an average guy. She'd spilled her confusion and self-disgust, then pleaded with him to help her assuage the hunger the vamps' *Spanish Fly* had caused in her.

And like the Spider to the Fly, he'd waited, while she'd writhed and cursed and finally begged him to make love to her.

He'd even used a condom. Pretended he'd had the need for one to reassure her. Only he'd forgotten the farce that last time, hadn't he?

She'd assumed he'd been overcome with lust—until he'd

taken that wicked bite. Alex hadn't been a hero, hadn't been her knight in shining armor. He'd been after the same things as Nic and the vampires who'd attacked Leo in the alleyway. Blood and sex.

Because he'd built her trust first, the lovemaking had transcended her first two experiences. Not until he'd sunk his fangs gum-deep had she suspected the lie. Why he'd bothered at all with the subterfuge, she didn't understand.

Perhaps he liked a little mind-fuck with his side of pussy.

Miki rolled to her side, tucked a pillow against her belly, brought up her knees, and wrapped her arms around it. She didn't need a man in her life, didn't need romance . . . didn't need to connect with another person.

She'd awoken alone, crawled out of the ditch naked, and flagged down a passing car all on her own.

She relaxed her grip on the pillow and stretched out her legs. Tonight had been an anomaly, nothing more. *A lesson*. Not to be forgotten.

With so few memories to fill her thoughts, she wondered if she'd ever be able to let it go. Before tonight, she'd only had her nightmares to review like an endlessly looping tape. Perhaps she should be grateful to Alex after all.

The monster whose teeth had gnashed at her burning flesh wasn't nearly as preoccupying now as the memory of Alex's handsome face, flushed with desire as his cock and his warmth slipped inside her soul.

CHAPTER
12

Alex "flashed" with Gabi back into the exact moment they'd departed from Inanna's salon, his lips still smothering hers. He broke the kiss and cast a quick glance around the room to assure himself no one had noticed anything.

And they hadn't—not the flash of light that had engulfed them or the fact that he now wore a different shirt.

"Bastard!" she spat, as soon as she shook free of his embrace. "A little warning that time wouldn't have been amiss."

Alex smothered his grin at her predictable annoyance. Gabi didn't like surprises or feeling out of control—except, of course, during sex. "You looked lovely. I saw no reason to delay."

"As soon as that condom rolled off," she hissed, "you couldn't get me back into my gown fast enough."

"Did I rush that last bit?" he drawled.

"Shut up, Alex," she said, her lips crimping into a straight line.

Ignoring her protests, Alex slid his arms around her again and bent toward her.

Gabi's face tilted slightly, the glinting anger in her eyes warring with the softness of her pouting lips.

"Can you really stay mad at me?" he whispered. "After everything we've shared?"

Her mouth curved despite her will to cling to her irritation. "Maybe I rushed you," she admitted sulkily. "I was just a bit aggressive."

"Lady, I have the scratches to prove it," he growled.

Gabi's gaze broke with his, and a flush bloomed on her cheeks. Her glance swept the room. "I can't help thinking how amusing it would be to shout out, 'I've found him!'—just to see them push their lovers off their bodies and scramble into their clothes for a chase."

Alex bit her earlobe. "But you won't."

Her smile dimmed. "You knew that was a foregone conclusion. Even before you showed me your magical mirror."

"Because you regretted killing me and have lived with the guilt for two centuries?"

"No, because there isn't a vamp here who can match my sexual appetites." She gave him a smoldering glance from beneath her thick eyelashes and slid a hand down his abdomen to cup his sex. "How dull my life here would be for me . . . without you."

Alex's eyelids dipped. "Planning on staying long?"

"As long as I'm amused."

He tilted his head, narrowing his eyes. Something in her shifting gaze alerted him. "Why am I not buying that?"

"Because you know me so well?"

"I know you well enough to be sure a simple hunt was never the only reason you came. Are you scoping out Inanna's territory?"

Gabi's fingers trailed along the tops of his shoulders. "And if I am?"

"I would tell you to pull your pack from New Orleans. You won't get whatever it is you want by stealth."

"Then how will we get it?"

"By treaty. By my promise to you."

"You don't even know what I'll demand."

"Will it be more than I can give?"

She hid her gaze beneath another sweep of sable lashes. "You really think you have a chance to knock Inanna off her throne?"

"She sits on sand," he ground out. "She'll die choking on it."

"Such bitterness. You sound as though you know her, but I bet you've never even met the woman."

"I know what she is. I know what she's done."

"I wish I could be around to see her fall."

Alex backed her up against a wall, his body flush with hers. Her tightening nipples stabbed at his chest. "Then help me avoid detection. Let me continue to operate out in the open."

She caressed his cheek and rubbed a finger over his lips. "I'll give you some time, but you can't leave me waiting long. I want to see you."

Alex stroked her fingers with his tongue, gauging her arousal by her quickening heartbeats and breaths. "Think I can resist finding you, and soon?" Alex slipped his hand beneath her hair. The kiss he gave her lingered, tasted, supped. When he drew away, her face glowed.

Alex felt a twinge of remorse for the game he played. Gabriella, for all her bluster, was a sensitive, loving creature. When her fierce heart was engaged, there was no holding back. The woman didn't do anything by halves. He might hurt her again.

Once had been devastating. Twice, and the consequences might prove fatal for him.

Voices from the foyer drifted inside the salon. Alex went still at the sound of Nicolas's deep timbre. He raised his head. "Sorry, love. I have to go."

She turned her ear toward the door. "The *sabat* must have concluded this night's meeting. Anyone in particular you don't want to meet?"

Alex didn't answer. Instead, he kissed her lips hard, thrust her away, and turned, striding toward the library again to escape through the garden.

Just as he opened the French doors, a gust of air brushed against his back. "Hello, Nic," Alex said, turning slowly.

Nicolas stood in shadows, his tall frame bristling with anger. "Give me one good reason why I shouldn't raise the alarm now and let the coven know their *daywalker* is here."

Alex breathed a sigh of relief. If Nic was taking the time to have a conversation with him, he might actually listen to what he had to say. "Let's take this outside."

"And give you a chance to escape into the sky?"

Alex blinked. "You know I'm Born?"

Nic closed in, his lips stretching into a mirthless smile. "Not until you just said it."

"I'm not trying to keep it a secret from you, but it's interesting Chessa didn't give me away."

"Chessa's emotions are complex right now. She's hormonal. Something to do with her *pregnancy*, you bastard."

Alex folded his arms over his chest, pretending he wasn't already shifting his balance to bolt through the door. "Are you really unhappy about that? Unhappy for her? Or jealous you couldn't be the one to plant it in her womb?"

Nic's eyebrows lowered and his hands tightened into fists. "I'm going to kick your ass."

Not *kill* him. Alex took note. "Again, let's take this outside, where we'll draw less attention. I promise the wings will stay folded until we're done."

Nicolas stuck his fists on his hips; his scowl was brutal, his gaze penetrating.

Alex turned again to the door, giving Nicolas his back, trusting the core of honor he knew still resided inside the former warrior monk.

"Out to the grounds behind the barracks," Nicolas growled behind him.

Without glancing back, Alex nodded, striding through the door and straight past the flower garden and the bench where he'd seduced Sarah, past the gazebo where he'd fucked her, ravaged her, tasted her rich human blood. He'd thought to teach her a lesson and hoped to never see her again. But he'd made a grave mistake. An oversight that further complicated his already muddled life.

Later, after he bested Nicolas, he'd seek the information he needed to track her down.

If he bested Nicolas. Nic wasn't your average vampire. He'd trained as a warrior all his life and long *after*life. Strong and skilled, he also had righteous anger bulking out his muscles and his resolve.

Alex had no doubts that Nic wanted to hurt him. Badly. Adrenaline had to be slamming through his body as they approached the barracks and took the path to the arena behind it.

Perhaps he'd let Nicolas get a few licks in to help assuage his anger and self-recrimination. Nicolas had his own guilt to deal with. He'd manipulated Chessa's emotions and her sensuality to burrow beneath her gruff façade and stake a claim on her heart. He'd invited Alex's participation in her seduction, thus enabling him to impregnate her.

He'd betrayed Inanna and the Born he'd served for centuries in a bid to earn if not equality, then at least respect and a voice on the ruling council. His means had been questionable, nearly earning him a death sentence. But he'd prevailed.

Because the time was nigh.

Inanna sensed it. Knew she needed all the allies she could amass. Alex needed to turn Nicolas from his devotion to the woman who'd been responsible for his induction into the Underworld.

But first, he had to let Nicolas come to terms with his anger.

With Nicolas at his back, Alex followed the pathway from the whitewashed barracks through a thin stand of oak trees to the training field. The scent of freshly mowed grass and heavy, humid air filled his nose and lungs. Lights on motion detectors flared as they stepped onto the field.

At the center of the training arena, Alex faced Nicolas, who already prowled around him, tension radiating from his body in hot waves.

"How do you want to do this?" Alex asked, keeping his tone casual as he deepened his breaths and summoned his own inner demon to the surface. Forcing his gaze away from his adversary, he calmly rolled up his sleeves.

A gust of air whooshed ahead of the fist rising to collide with his jaw.

Alex took the blow, letting the force drive him back a step. He raised a hand to rub the side of his face and glared at Nicolas, whose fangs curved beneath a feral snarl. "Nice," Alex murmured. "Do you even know why you're so angry with me?" He cocked his head left, then right, and shook out his arms, sinking into a fighter's stance, with his hands raised and balled into fists.

Air whipped around him. A kick landed against his knee, but Alex resisted, standing firm, thinking it better to let Nicolas spend some of his rage early. Perhaps then he'd be ready to listen.

Nicolas flashed past him again, his forearm clouting Alex across the shoulders. "Fight me, bastard!"

"I'm just letting you take a few practice blows, Nicolas. Just to be fair."

"I don't need your handicapping me in any fight," Nicolas roared. "This isn't a game."

Knowing he was taunting the man into a fury, Alex still couldn't help tweaking his anger a notch higher. "I don't want you totally demoralized," he said, his voice calm and sympathetic. "I'd rather you still feel strong, secure in your own power."

"Again, I don't need any favors from you."

"If you're ready, then . . ." Alex didn't give him any more warning than that. He sank, gathering power in his thighs, then launched himself from the ground, springing high above Nicolas's head, turning midair to land directly behind him. He swept out a foot, catching Nicolas below the knees and shoving him forward.

Nicolas rolled, then quickly regained his footing to face Alex. His gaze narrowed. "You're fast. I'll grant you that. Faster than your womenfolk."

Alex lunged forward, clamping his hands on Nicolas's shoulders, squeezing as he pressed him down to his knees.

They wrestled a moment, Nicolas resisting the hold, his hands coming up beneath Alex's arms to pummel his ribs and his chest with several solid, breath-stealing blows.

Still, Alex held on, pushing to the point where bone popped and crackled.

Nicolas must have sensed how close he was to defeat; he sank to his knees. "You're stronger. But not invulnerable." He slammed his fist between Alex's legs.

When Alex's breath left him in a pained wheeze, Nicolas brought up his arms and swept Alex's hands outward, knocking them away. Alex took a step back, his hands planted on his thighs as he bent, dragging in tight breaths. "I . . . underestimated . . . your venom."

"What? You thought I'd fight fair?" Nicolas swung his leg in an arcing roundhouse kick, aiming straight for Alex's head.

Alex dropped and rolled beneath the kick, coming up in a crouch, his groin still throbbing hard. "Won't make that mistake again," he gritted out.

"You think you can cow me with your superior speed, your power. . . . Your showboating is wasted on me. I've fought demons a hundred times more intimidating than you and lived."

Alex grimaced and straightened. "If I intended to cause you serious harm, I would. What I prefer is a conversation. We have mutual interests—"

"You won't ever have Chessa again. She chose me."

"She's the mother of my child. There will always be a bond between us."

Alex dug his heels into the grass and pressed forward at the exact moment Nicolas launched, his expression a mask of fury. Their bodies slammed together, their hands wrapping around each others' throats as thighs and buttocks bunched to propel them forward.

Alex had weight and superior strength on his side; Nicolas, blazing anger that shot adrenaline through his body.

Alex dug his toes deeper in the grass, feeling his face heat and his expression tighten as a growl of frustration ripped from his throat. He strained the muscles of his neck, bulking them beneath the powerful, tightening grip of Nicolas's large hands.

Nicolas's feet slipped in the grass, enabling Alex to shove him backward, momentum allowing him to take another step and another, until he plowed forward, carrying Nicolas to the ground.

Nicolas's thighs strained, bucking beneath him, hammering his knees into Alex's. Then he planted his feet and thrust upward, attempting to roll with Alex.

Alex had had enough of the match, feeling frustrated and more than a little foolish for expending energy on a battle neither was really willing to win because victory could only mean the death of one of them.

But how to end the match? They could battle like this for

hours. Alex almost smiled as he stared down into Nicolas's face, which was growing purple from his stranglehold.

Alex was brawnier, heavier. Without leverage, Nicolas would have to concede.

Alex stretched out on top of Nicolas, pinning his ankles with his feet, his chest with the weight of his own. Letting go of Nic's neck, he clamped his hands around his wrists and stretched them above his head.

"What the fuck do you think you're doing?" Nicolas spat, his lips curling in disgust.

"Ending this," Alex said glibly, relaxing now that he had Nicolas pinned and off-balance from the intimacy of their position. The humor of their situation had Alex fighting the urge to chuckle, which would only further enrage the vampire already trembling with rage beneath him.

Nicolas slammed his head upward, but Alex drew back from the head butt. "Easy now," he whispered.

"Alex . . . ," Nicolas's voice rose in warning.

"Relax. I'm not after your cock. And I know you haven't the slightest interest in mine. Let's have that little talk."

"I can't think with you plastered to me. This is . . . *unseemly.*"

"But effective," Alex said smoothly. "You have to concede that."

"Are we going to just lie here? Are you so cowardly you won't fight me like a man?"

"That's the key phrase, you know. Like a man. I'm not really. Never have been. I'm demon-spawn. A Born vampire. You, my friend, came into this world a man."

"The point of your lesson being?" Nicolas said, gritting his teeth.

"Chessa is Born. Also, *never a woman*, although she is human in her heart."

"We're back to the subject of her child."

"My daughter."

"You can't be certain it won't be a son, since I now understand males can be born."

"One every generation," Alex murmured agreeably.

"Alex, get the fuck off me. This isn't comfortable."

"Because you're growing aroused? Don't worry about it. It's natural. The pressure of another groin pressed to yours. Instinctive, really. Nothing to do with your manliness."

"I'm worried about yours."

"Don't be. Also perfectly natural." Alex couldn't help teasing him just a bit more. Nicolas's growing panic nearly had him chortling. "Let me shift a bit." He lifted his hips, aligning his cock alongside rather than directly on top of Nicolas's. "Better now?"

"Alex! *Get off!*"

"Not until you give me your word we'll talk. No more fisticuffs. Civilized conversation."

"Not possible," Nicolas ground out, his face red and contorted with fury. "Chessa is undone. Weeping all the time. Your little package has shaken her."

"I gave her a gift. One to replace the hole in her heart. One you could never fill no matter how many decades you tried."

Nicolas stopped struggling, and his expression grew stark. "What do you want from us? What must we do for you to go away?"

"That won't ever happen," Alex said slowly, wanting the message to finally sink in. "For better or worse, I'm part of your lives now. *Forever.*"

"I don't accept that."

"You think exposing me to the coven, delivering my body, will end this?"

Nicolas's lips twisted. "I think it will be one problem removed."

"Would you think for a minute with your mind instead of your pride? Who will stand between Chessa and Inanna once the baby is born?"

The last traces of anger finally faded from Nicolas's dark eyes. "I would have you take the child . . . but Chessa would be inconsolable."

"Then we must protect her together."

Nicolas's internal struggle played out in the tightening of his mouth, the fierce flex of his grinding jaw. But at last he turned aside. "What do you want from me?"

Alex shut his eyes, knowing that what he said would be binding. "Your acceptance that I am a part of your lives . . . the father to her child. And I'll agree never to seek intimacy with Chessa again."

"You saw her tonight, didn't you?" Nicolas whispered.

Alex thought it wise not to mention the fact that she'd been nude and that he'd touched and kissed her. He nodded slowly. "I needed to know she was safe for the moment and healthy."

"How did she receive you?"

"She was angry . . . at first. She refused my offer to help her escape. She won't abandon you."

Nicolas closed his eyes for a moment. "If I were stronger, I'd force her away from me. For now."

"But you love her."

Nicolas's stark, haunted eyes said it all.

Alex let out a slow breath. "You can't reveal me to Inanna. Not yet."

Nicolas gave him a sharp nod. "Agreed."

"Not going to ask why?"

"I had already decided I would protect you. For Chessa's sake."

Alex gave Nicolas a mock scowl. "Then what was all this about, Nic? Missing me?"

"Like a toothache," Nicolas said, raising his upper lip to give him a little fang.

"I've worked up quite an appetite," Alex murmured, not quite done tormenting the man beneath him.

Nicolas leveled a lethal glare. "Sink *anything* of yours into me, and you will die."

Alex drew a deep breath and closed his eyes. "You smell divine. Are you sure?"

"Alex . . ."

Alex leaned forward and planted a kiss on Nicolas's forehead, laughing as his face screwed up in disgust. Then Alex rolled to the side, kicked out his legs, and flipped upward on his feet in one fluid movement, ignoring the throb between his legs.

From Nicolas's kick, of course.

Nicolas rose more slowly, his eyebrows lowered in a deadly scowl. "If you ever mention this to anyone . . ."

"Embarrassed that I pinned you? Or that you enjoyed it?" Alex ducked beneath the blow Nicolas swung toward his face, then bobbed up, grinning.

Shaking his head, Nicolas glared. "I have to get back. The *sabat* members are mingling with the guests. You'd better leave."

Alex began rolling down his sleeves, then clicked his tongue in disgust when he found a tear along the seam. "Was I the only topic of interest during the meeting?"

"A wolf has been hired to track you."

"Met her. Delicious woman."

Nicolas shook his head. "Do you have a death wish?"

"Gabi and I go way back."

Nicolas's mouth opened, then snapped shut. "Figures." He turned toward the house and began walking away.

Alex's long strides quickly ate up the distance between them. "Communication between us will be difficult."

"Won't be a problem at all," Nicolas said, flashing his teeth. "Since we won't be talking."

"If you need help, you're to contact Simon."

Nicolas snorted. "Simon is the last person I would ask for help."

"Still upset he kept me a secret from you?"

"I'm upset that he manipulates all of us. Our friendship is over."

"You need all the friends you can get now."

Nicolas aimed a sharp glare. "I will protect what's mine."

Alex grinned. "You know if anyone sees us walking back through the garden together, looking mussed, they're going to jump to some embarrassing conclusions."

Nicolas's smile was tight and didn't reach his eyes. "I dare them to say a word."

They passed the barracks. At the edge of the garden, Alex planned to peel away into the darkness and find a secluded spot to take to the air.

Instead, a long, feminine scream pierced the quiet. Alex and Nicolas shared a charged glance.

"Leave now!" Nicolas barked.

"Not a chance."

"Then stay out of sight."

They loped toward the garden, slowing as they spied the crowd gathering around the flagstone patio.

Nicolas shoved his way inside the circle, disappearing as he knelt at the center.

Alex followed in his wake, feeling certain no one would notice him because all gazes were turned to the body lying crumpled beside the garden bench.

CHAPTER
13

Nicolas knelt in the blood that was seeping slug-gishly from Erika's nude body. Horror held him mute and immobile. For all her selfish, hedonis-tic ways, Erika was still one of them. Family. And a member of the coven's Security Force, which he'd personally trained.

The agony of her final moments was etched in her expression—eyes wide with fright, her mouth open-ing around a silent scream. But still so beautiful. Golden blond hair in disarray, smooth, pale flesh, pink nipples, long, muscular legs . . .

The memory of her beauty would be forever marred by the sight of the bloody, ragged hole at the center of her soft belly.

For a moment, the raised voices around him

blended into a hum that seemed to quiet as his focus narrowed on the gaping wound just beneath her ribs.

Then something brushed against him, and soft sobs beside him drew his gaze upward, breaking through his frozen fascination.

Madrigal's shoulders shook with her ragged cries as she stood beside him, wringing her hands. "I only left for a moment," she whispered. "To clean up a bit. We'd shared a host . . ."

A glance at Madrigal's mussed hair and clothing said how well she'd enjoyed her snack. Nicolas wondered with grim amusement how Cecily would react once she realized her girlfriend hadn't been able to resist Erika's formidable allure.

"How could he do this with so many people around?" Madrigal asked, a hint of rising hysteria entering her voice. "How did he get past the guards?"

"He's been here all along," Nicolas said tonelessly, pushing the words past his tightening throat. Then he turned his gaze back to the ground and forced himself to examine Erika—to push past the horror and look for clues.

The wound below the center of her chest was consistent with the ones he'd already seen in all The Devourer's recent victims. With his fingers clamped together, the monster plunged his hand through flesh, thrusting deep under the sternum, straight into the chest cavity to rip out the heart.

A quick, efficient death for human as well as Born. But messy.

His gaze whipped around the pavement. Splashes of Erika's blood were being smeared beneath the many feet stepping through the trail. So much for following it to the killer. Again his gaze fell on the body.

"Get everyone inside," he said over his shoulder, not caring who might act on his order. He couldn't drag his gaze from Erika's mutilated body.

Apparently, neither could anyone else, because they continued to press closer.

Nicolas aimed a sharp glance at Pasqual, who hovered at the edge of the growing, murmuring crowd. "Get them into the salon."

Pasqual gave a sharp, tight-lipped nod and began to corral the shocked partyers inside.

Gradually, the crowd thinned. Only members of his merged Security Force remained in the garden, taking positions to cover them, although it was far too late. "I knew he was near," he whispered to no one in particular, "but I just didn't think he'd plot something like this . . ."

Alex pressed a hand on Nicolas's bruised shoulder, which made him wince. "Sorry," Alex said, his voice gruff. He squatted beside Nicolas, his gaze sweeping Erika's body.

Right, this was Alex's case. His alone now that Chessa had left the police force. *Temporarily*, so she insisted. Nicolas's stomach churned. "The bastard's probably inside the house now, laughing up his sleeve at the panic he's caused."

A muscle along Alex's jaw flexed. "Chessa—"

"Will be fine for now. He wouldn't dare try something else so soon. He'll want our nerves stretched taut, waiting for him to strike again. He thrives on the anticipation."

"Why Erika?"

"Because she made a spectacle of herself tonight. Fucked everything with a dick. Fucked him, too, I'd bet." Nicolas knelt closer and breathed in the many scents clinging to her skin. Too many blended to be helpful.

Alex stood and circled Erika's body. "She was straddling

him on the bench when he struck her. She fell backwards. Dead before she hit the ground."

Nicolas nodded. Naked with her legs splayed open, she hadn't tried to break her fall with her arms, which lay across her stomach.

"So, we're looking for a man?"

Again, Nicolas nodded. It was happening again. The dread seeping through him, chilling him to the bone. "We have to wait until he strikes again."

"Perhaps someone saw who she was last with."

Feeling stupid, like his mind was stuck in slow motion, Nicolas shook himself and came slowly to his feet. There were questions he should ask, people he should examine before they scattered.

"Nico." Inanna's ragged, tear-filled voice came from directly behind him.

Nicolas turned slowly, lowering his gaze to meet hers. Her eyes shimmered with tears in her ashen face. He opened his arms, and she sobbed, stepping close so he could wrap his arms around her. They'd been here before—sharing their misery, their helplessness over the death of one of their own.

"She might have been a vapid whore," Inanna choked out, "but she was one of us. My *damu*."

Nicolas raised his gaze, searching for Alex over the top of Inanna's head. Alex had backed away, to stand in the shadows cast by a tall oak. His gaze was fixed on Inanna, his expression blank and dull. Something odd was happening here.

Nicolas kissed the top of Inanna's head and nodded to Pasqual, who glared daggers his way. "Take her inside. Let no one near her."

As Nicolas held open his arms to release her, Inanna snuggled closer, murmuring a protest, clinging to his body still.

Pasqual bent close and whispered to her, cooing softly, pulling her gently from Nicolas. His last searing glance spoke volumes. Pasqual had thought he alone owned Inanna's affections since Nicolas's betrayal. As Pasqual led Inanna inside, he draped his arm possessively around her narrow waist.

Nicolas strode to Alex, who stood blinking, his face reanimating. Color rose in his cheeks, and his features tightened as he met Nicolas's gaze.

"What's with you?" Nicolas bit out. "Did you just remember my men might recognize you from the other night?"

Alex shook his head. "Simon cast a spell. Most *Revenants* won't give me a second glance."

"I wondered how you managed to mingle and not cause someone to question your being here." Nicolas dragged a hand through his hair. "I'll get my people to start taking statements concerning anything odd they may have seen, then have the guests removed to New Orleans."

"And the *sabat*?"

"They're staying here. Guests of Inanna."

Alex grabbed his forearm. "Nicolas, you know Chessa isn't safe here."

Nicolas's jaw ground closed. "I know it. But do you really think she'll budge from this house now?"

"She's so damn stubborn . . ." Alex studied Nicolas for a moment; Nicolas's body slowly stiffened under the scrutiny. He knew he wasn't going to like what the other vamp had to say.

"Would you consider removing her against her will?" Alex said slowly.

Nicolas released a deep, slow breath. "Even if I could spirit her out of the house without anyone noticing, she won't step through any portal. She won't leave me." *And I won't let her*, he left unspoken.

"I have a place," Alex said quietly. "A bolt-hole. I can take her there and leave her. She'll be safe, and we can retrieve her later."

Nicolas wanted to slam his fist into Alex's face again. Was Alex using this as a ploy to take her away from him? It's what he'd been pushing all along. "I don't like it."

"Nic, I give you my word. No harm will come to her, and she'll be returned—to you—as soon as this is over."

"She won't go."

The corners of Alex's mouth curved. "Then let's not give her a chance to protest."

Nicolas didn't like it, but as he glanced back at Erika, he knew he didn't have any real choices. Chessa and the child had to be protected—even against Chessa's own indomitable will. "You can do it that quickly?"

"I can. You know there isn't another option."

"If something happens to you, how will I find her?"

"Simon will know." At Nicolas's instant scowl, Alex shrugged. "Dude, you're gonna have to get over your beef with him. He prepared this escape for me centuries ago. It's the only thing I've got."

Nicolas felt a cold, hard knot settle in his stomach. He'd lost one woman he'd loved to the monster when he'd arrogantly believed he could hold back the evil around him. His arrogance had cost Anaïs her life. It had taken centuries to find another woman who moved him as she had. He couldn't lose Chessa now. Couldn't risk her life, no matter how much he hated putting her in Alex's care. Or how much he distrusted Simon. "You've already been up to see her," Nicolas said softly, his shoulders slumping. "You know the way."

Alex hesitated, his expression somber, his eyes reflecting empathy. "Will you come with me? We can see her there and be back in a moment. I'd rather have you at ease with the arrangement."

Nicolas didn't want to be grateful to Alex for a damn thing, but he couldn't help the relief that washed over him. He led the way inside the house, taking care to avoid the salon, where a loud rumble of voices erupted, swirling around the mansion. He sped up the staircase, down the hallway, and entered their room with Alex on his heels.

Chessa spun toward the door, her eyes widening when she saw the two of them enter together. "Oh hell no!"

"You don't even know the question yet," Alex said, grinning.

"What's going on down there? I heard a scream. No one's come up to fill me in."

"Erika's dead," Nicolas stated without inflection.

Color drained away from her face. Chessa glanced toward Alex. "I'm sorry about your grandmother."

Alex shrugged, his expression shuttering. "She wasn't anything to me."

"Was it The Devourer? He's here?"

Chessa was quick as ever. Alex's gaze locked with hers. "He's among us."

"Which is why you can't stay here any longer," Nicolas broke in quietly.

Chessa shook her head, her gaze pleading with his. "You can't send me away. Not alone. Come with me?"

Nicolas cupped her cheek. "Alex will take you someplace safe."

"Again, *hell no*!" She clutched his forearms. "I'm not leaving you."

"Only until we've captured him."

"He'll use one of Simon's portals, and I'll be cooling my heels forever before I see you again. I won't do it."

Nicolas let his gaze slide away rather than let her see how much this was killing him. If he showed a moment's weakness, she'd use any chink in his armor she could find. "We've already decided it," he said, keeping his tone flat.

Her breath caught, and she lifted one dark eyebrow. "You two are in accord? I thought you said you were gonna kill him the next time you saw him. What the hell happened with that? Wait a second." She leaned close and drew in a sharp breath. "His scent's all over you. What have you two been doing?"

Nicolas felt his face heat and shot Alex a glare.

Alex, the bastard, only grinned. He walked toward them. "Enough with the reunion. Let's do this." He put his arms around them both, and Nicolas hugged a wriggling Chessa close to his chest.

Bright, white light engulfed them, and Nicolas blinked for several moments before he could see where Alex had brought them. "A cave?"

"Are you burying me inside a goddamn mountain?" Chessa said, her voice rising.

"A few rules, Chessa," Alex continued as though she hadn't spoken. "My domain is yours. Make yourself comfortable while you're here. When I come back to bring you food, do not try to kill me, or you'll be stuck here an eternity. I'm your key out, so be nice."

Chessa's blistering glare should have fried Alex where he stood. Nicolas felt better at the angry heat radiating from her body. She wasn't loving Alex now.

Her hot gaze whipped back to him. "Nicolas, are you really going to let him do this?"

Nicolas brought her as close as her burgeoning belly would allow. He smoothed his hands down her back, memorizing the feel of her curves. "Chessa, I need to know you're safe. Protected from the beast and the *sabat*. Give me this peace of mind to do what I must. Please."

Chessa's lips worked, pressing into a thin line, then crimping downward as her shoulders and chin lowered in surrender. "Anything more I need to know, Alex?" she said without looking toward him. Her gaze remained on Nicolas, as though wanting to commit his face to memory.

"The mirror is enchanted," Alex said. "You may touch the frame, but never, ever touch the glass."

"I'll keep away from the mirror," she mumbled. "I'm gonna look like hell in a few days anyway."

"There's bottled water in the bureau, and wine."

"How will I feed?"

"I'll return to you," Alex replied.

Nicolas drew in a deep breath. Chessa's lack of self-control when she grew hungry was what had landed her in her current predicament.

"I'll offer her blood only, Nic," Alex added wryly.

Nicolas nodded, not having any choice other than trusting Alex for now. "I fed tonight," Nicolas murmured.

"Go ahead and let her take her fill. We have time."

A blessed reprieve. Before Alex could change his mind, Nicolas pulled Chessa to the sofa and sat down, helping her straddle his lap to lean over him—her preferred position for feeding. He canted his head and sighed as her lips trailed along his neck, then her fangs sank deep, piercing his jugular. Her hot mouth suctioned against his skin, pulling blood toward the wound. Arousal spiked instantly between them.

If he'd been alone with her, he'd have dragged away their clothing and made love to her while she'd fed, but Alex watched, and Nicolas wasn't willing to share another intimate encounter with the Born vampire now that he understood the power he possessed. He wouldn't risk the bond of loving he shared with Chessa. Wouldn't expand it willingly to include the Born who'd already sired her child.

Call him selfish, but he'd also decided he never wanted another man to serve her sex with her meals.

Nicolas felt a moment's remorse, remembering the sweet woman he'd taken before the *sabat* had met. If he was going to place strictures on Chessa, he'd have to be willing to make his own sacrifices.

Chessa rubbed her open crotch against the ridge firming beneath his trousers, moaning while she drank deeply.

"I know," he whispered. "It's gonna be hell."

Her hands slipped down his chest, molding the curves, sinking into the hollows beneath, then trailing lower.

Nicolas's body shuddered as she sucked particularly hard, sending blood rushing toward her mouth in a dizzying rush. His cock swelled thicker against the rub of her hand.

"Go ahead, Nic. She'll be here a while," Alex said softly as he lifted a bottle of wine from a cabinet and poured himself a drink.

Nicolas groaned, trying to hold onto his resolve, but he

slipped his hands beneath Chessa's blouse, clasping her full breasts with his open palms. Chessa whimpered against his neck, and her thighs trembled around his hips. And because Nicolas couldn't stand the thought of not having her one last time, he pulled down the elastic band at the top of her stretchy pants and slipped them over her hips.

After a few awkward moments of Chessa trying to aid him but not wanting to come off his neck, he had her lower body stripped and his pants opened at last.

She knelt above him, letting him guide his cock toward her entrance. When the tip slid between her wet folds, they both groaned and she sank, taking him inside her in one long, shuddering downward thrust.

They rocked together, gently at first. Chessa withdrew her fangs, lapping desperately against his skin to close the wounds. Then she lifted her head, pressing her forehead to his. "How can you leave me here? Alone?"

"It will kill me, *ma petite.*"

"I almost hate you for this." She rocked, grinding on his cock and tugging her shirt over her head.

Nicolas wished he could let her take him however she craved, but the need to leave his mark, to remind her who spurred her lust to unimagined heights, had him cradling her body against his and turning her to settle her back against the seat of the sofa.

He placed one foot on the carpet, a knee deep in the soft cushions, and hooked his arms beneath her knees, bringing her sex higher to fit more snugly against his. Then, holding her gaze, he pulled her knees toward him and, at the same time, thrust hard toward her womb. He began to stroke into her—

slow, hard strokes that circled and slipped side to side, caressing every inch of her channel, drawing honey from her depths that bathed them both in liquid heat.

Footsteps shuffled beside them, and Nicolas snarled a warning. But Alex sat down on the carpet beside the couch and lifted an arm over his shoulder, his cuff rolled up as he offered his wrist. With his back to them both, he settled beside them, sipping wine while Chessa sank her teeth and fed, her eyes never leaving Nicolas as he fucked hard into her moist cunt.

Nicolas drew out the moment as long as he could, savoring a slow, rising tension that had Chessa's torso writhing, her legs tensing over his bent arms. When her orgasm peaked, she clamped hard on Alex's wrist, forcing a sharp exhalation from him. Nicolas knew it could have been pain, but knowing the bastard, it had to be his own release sweeping through him. Nicolas was beyond caring whether the other vampire found his pleasure—a wave of primal triumph expanded his chest, gripped his balls, and tightened his thighs and buttocks until cum squeezed through his cock in scalding jets of relief.

He pumped through his orgasm, long past the last ripples of pleasure from Chessa's honeyed walls, until his breath rasped and his whole body trembled. Only then did he lean over her, kissing her forehead while she finished feeding from Alex. Then Nicolas kissed her lips, taking the blood pooled inside her mouth, swallowing it as she smeared her mouth against his, sharing the flavor of her meal.

When their lips tightened in a shared smile, they turned their faces toward Alex, who watched them with a lazy, satisfied smile of his own.

"Think that might last you a while, Chessa?" he asked silkily.

↳ Her soft snort was followed by a delicate wrinkling of her nose. "Why does this place smell like wet dog?"

Nicolas felt a grin stretch his lips.

Alex's expression turned a little chagrined. "I brought a friend here. She's into dogs."

Nicolas narrowed his gaze. Alex and the *were*-princess, here? Nicolas didn't remark on the strong scent of sex in the air, but he knew Chessa couldn't miss it either. Let her think about that. Vampires had a natural aversion to *weres*, which made Alex a rather kinky bastard.

"Better say your good-byes," Alex said softly, getting up and returning his glass to the bureau.

Nicolas pulled Chessa up and slipped pillows behind her back, settling her legs along the sofa. "You should rest."

She raised her face, panic flaring in her widening eyes.

Pain lanced through his chest—swift and sharp. "I'll see you soon," he said, his voice gruff.

"Don't you let anything happen to you. I'll cut out your heart myself if you do."

"Nothing will happen, *ma petite*," he said, framing her cheeks with his palms. "You're my whole world, everything I want. I'll be back for you."

Her dark eyes glistened with unshed tears, but one corner of her mouth lifted. "I'll be waiting."

Nicolas sealed their lips with a hot, hard kiss, then stepped back.

Chessa offered him a teary smile. Nicolas felt Alex's touch on his arm, and she disappeared in blinding light.

Back in the bedroom once more, Nicolas squared his shoulders. "They're probably wondering what's keeping me."

"We weren't gone for longer than a moment."

Nicolas nodded, then narrowed his eyes. "Don't forget to feed her. Often." He drew a deep breath. "Pleasure her if you must, but don't fuck her, Alex."

Rather than the sly grin he expected, Alex's solemn gaze met his. "I'll take care of Chessa. Not myself."

Without replying, Nicolas swallowed and turned to the door. The sooner he trapped the beast, the sooner he could kick Alex the hell out of his life again.

No matter that he was really beginning to like him.

Alex took the stairs up to his apartment, treading slowly, his thoughts turning inward. Foremost on his mind now was the fact that he had to tell his mother, Natalie, that her birth mother was dead.

With daylight a couple of hours away, he meant only to make a quick stop to change his rumpled, dirty clothes and apprise Simon of all that had happened since they'd last spoken. He wasn't sure what he'd tell him about his brushes with Inanna. The encounters had left him disturbed, raising questions about the memories he'd unearthed.

He'd been glad for Nicolas's presence when Erika's body had been discovered. Had Inanna come upon him without the buffer of Nicolas, he might have given himself away.

As it was, as soon as Inanna had entered the garden, he'd felt that same odd feeling—his body clammy and cold, his mind pulling away into the past.

He recalled the first memory that had come unbidden when he'd touched Inanna's hand. The ancient ones occasionally bobbed to the surface of his mind, offering indistinct, blurred images and fragments of conversations. Useless for the most part.

However, when he entered the vicinity of an ancestor, something about the chemistry of their interaction, whether physical or not, released their shared memories. Usually he could control it, functioning on one level while the memories poured through him. With Inanna he'd found it impossible to resist following the slender thread of memory so he could unravel more of the complicated weave.

Inanna had been insatiable during that long-ago night.

Silver moonlight, nearly bright as day, illuminated their gleaming bodies.

The warrior at last succumbed to the aphrodisiac and her strong allure, taking her maidenhead, surrendering his will to hers. Together, they howled as they climaxed, undeterred by any fear of detection. Her father, having fallen beneath the spell of her mother twenty years earlier, had recognized the need stirring in his daughter to take a mate.

Just as her mother had done before her, Inanna chose not to complete the blood-bond, knowing she would need the protection of a human mate in this sun-drenched climate, resisting by sheer force of will the instinct to feed from the man who would sire her child and thereby turn him into an immortal companion.

So substituting one hunger for another, she sated her appetite throughout the night, using a magical oil on his cock to make his desire impossible to ease. But the oil was not replenished this last time.

The room had become stifling hot, so they threw open the doors leading to the balcony outside his chamber. Inanna stood naked, her fingers curving around a smooth, marble railing, her back bent low as the man standing behind her rutted into her tightening sex.

Below her, moon-silvered fronds of date palms bordering the pool moved limply in the night air.

"Husband," she moaned, claiming him for her own. Her gaze lifted from the view of her father's palace garden to the endless expanse of

desert beyond the tall gates. This was her kingdom, her duty to her destiny about to be fulfilled.

"Inanna," he groaned, and then stiffened as his seed spurted deep inside her.

Inanna gasped at a cramp working its way through her womb. I have conceived, she thought triumphantly.

Her husband leaned over her, his strokes slowing. He kissed her shoulder, then withdrew from her body before turning her in his arms.

But not before Inanna saw the pale figure beside the pool, her face turned upward to watch the couple embracing. Her sister's face twisted with hatred.

Inanna smiled slyly, reaching between Dumuzi's legs to grasp his slick cock, causing him to moan loudly.

Alex had been released from the memory only after Inanna had been led away by Pasqual. He'd ignored Nicolas's questioning stare. He'd shaken off the lurid memory, feeling unclean, wondering what had become of Dumuzi and feeling sympathy for the warrior who'd been caught between two sisters' ambitions.

Alex slumped in a leather chair across from Simon, who sat at his wide, scrolled-legged desk doing his mystic-thing—staring at Alex over his steepled fingers as though he could sink into his mind. Not one of his talents, or so he'd often claimed.

Simon didn't really need to look into his mind, because he knew Alex would eventually cave and tell him everything he needed to know anyway. Alex just didn't like having to share tonight's unsavory details.

Where to start? With the visions he'd had of Inanna's past? The lover she'd drugged and stolen from beneath her sister's nose? And since when did she have a sister? Alex was bothered by the fact that he hadn't remembered that detail.

Should he tell Simon everything that had happened between

him and "Sarah"? He'd taken her because he'd had time on his hands and she'd amused him. Utterly selfish of him. That he'd found himself drawn to her and resentful of her previous lover—so much so that he'd abused her—sat like a heavy stone squarely in the center of his chest.

That he'd forgotten the one "Golden Rule" he'd adhered to all his life—"Thou shalt not fuck without a condom"—was most embarrassing of all. He never forgot; he'd forsworn the use of one only once, intentionally, with Chessa.

Now he'd impregnated a human woman, making her prey for the Underworld. So perhaps he should start there. Then maybe he'd never have to get to the part about kidnapping Gabriella and seducing her cooperation out of her, or talk about the wrestling match with Nic, or leaving Chessa in his escape pod . . .

"Busy night?" Simon asked, a small smile tipping one corner of his mouth.

Alex gave him a baleful glance. "Why don't you tell me?"

"You got her address?"

Alex didn't bother asking whose address. Simon already knew. "From the driver who took her home."

"Then why are you here?"

"Thought you should at least be apprised that—"

"Erika's dead and Chessa's in your special place?"

Alex narrowed his gaze. "Never mind. Guess it was a waste of time coming here." He raked a hand through his hair, annoyed with Simon and himself. "Tell me, Simon . . . was I supposed to impregnate her?"

Simon hesitated, then gave him a careful nod.

"Will she come to harm because of me?"

Simon's face remained inscrutable.

Alex's heart sank. "Is it already too late to save her?"

"You're following your path, Alex. Just let things happen. Act on your instincts."

Cold dread filled Alex. Simon had no reassurances to give him. "I don't accept that. I have to change it. It's possible. I have freedom of choice."

Simon's steady gaze softened. "But which choices will give you the outcome you desire?"

"It isn't always just about me, Simon. She's innocent."

"As a newborn." His agreement came too quickly.

Alex stared, sure there was some hidden meaning he should be able to ferret out. "Is there anything I *need* to know?" he asked, between clenched teeth.

"Go find your little bird."

Alex remembered the tattoo that stretched across Sarah's lower back. "You keep a journal, right? Is that how you remember the details? Hundreds of years have passed from the time you watched this unfold the last time. Tell me, you don't just remember it all."

Simon gave him an enigmatic smile. "I'll bring Chessa a warm meal."

Alex rose from his seat, frustration and growing dread weighing on him. "Simon, what if I don't want to do this? Don't want to be what you've all shaped me to be?"

"I'm not a puppeteer. You have free choice. Follow your heart. I'll go to Natalie and let her know about her mother."

At the door, Alex glanced back, catching a look on Simon's face that deepened his own churning emotions. Simon seemed tense, his bearded Templar's face set in stone. "We've had this conversation before, haven't we?"

This time Simon's smile was full, a generous flash of white . . . and genuine.

CHAPTER

14

A low, ominous growl rumbled from the shadows beneath the two-lane bridge spanning a narrow bayou. Almost at the end of the bridge and ready to turn and follow the dark, empty street toward a destination she couldn't quite recall, Miki felt her heart thud dully in her chest.

She walked faster, trying to keep her steps muffled, but the growling grew, slowly building to an ominous resonance that whittled at her courage. Turning onto the sidewalk beside the street, she spied a distant streetlamp, fixed her gaze and hopes on it, then freed her hands from the pockets of her jacket, her blackjack held tightly in one fist.

Closer now, the light was a golden beacon, but a scraping sound—no, several, like sharp claws digging at the pavement—came from behind her. The low-pitched growl *was now an ear-piercing whine. And the sounds were getting closer.*

She broke into a run, all thought of slipping silently past the menace fleeing as she raced forward. She couldn't look back, couldn't waste the precious second it might cost, didn't want to trip, didn't want to really know what sped after her.

When it barreled into her back, she fell forward, the weight of her pursuer crushing her into the dirt. Then they were slipping together down the muddy side of the embankment toward the murky swamp water. Her attacker slid past her, his body splashing loudly. Then, pivoting sharply despite the muddy depths, he turned to lunge toward her.

She had time only to roll onto her back and meet him, her arm raised.

Jaws opened, burrowing between her shoulder and her head. She battered his skull with the hardened leather weapon, but she couldn't dislodge him. Fangs sank into her neck; a steel maw opened and bit deeper again—jaws so long and wide that she knew she had seconds to live as blood spurted from her neck and soaked his fur.

Weakening, the sounds and knife-edged pain faded around her. Then something unexpected happened. Heat burst, singeing her from the inside out, flaring at the last moment, and she saw the beast's glowing eyes widen—

Miki bolted upward from her bed, drenched in sweat, the last remnants of her dream lingering in her mind so damn vividly that she still had the scent of singed fur in her nostrils.

The dream was getting stronger. It was filled with lurid details, which no longer crept back to hide in her subconscious when she wakened.

The details she recalled now made no sense at all. Sure she'd woken on the side of that embankment, but she hadn't been savaged by an animal. She'd had no wounds whatsoever, just an empty place inside where her past had existed. The circumstance that had brought her to that ditch, naked and shivering from the cold, was still undiscovered.

She was beginning to think her dream might be symbolic. Something her mind devised to replace the true horror she'd experienced.

With her heart still racing, she crawled out of bed, headed to her bathroom, and pulled another bottle of water from the box underneath the sink. She pulled her nightgown over her head, poured part of the water onto a washcloth, and blotted her face and chest to remove the sweat and soothe away the heat. The room was stifling hot.

She eyed the closed window. The screen had been removed when the plywood had been nailed over it to protect the glass, but she hadn't bothered replacing the screen when the plywood had been taken down. If she slid open the large plate window, she risked being eaten by insects. A few mosquitoes seemed a less uncomfortable choice at the moment.

Miki rummaged beneath her sink for a Citronella candle. She lit it and set it on her nightstand. Then she stepped toward the window, lifted the latch, and slid it to the side to open it halfway. Humid air gusted inside. Not much cooler than the air in her room, but fresh and moving. She stood naked in the darkness, closing her eyes as the breeze wafted over her.

The movement of the air sliding over her breasts felt like wicked little fingers, gusting against her nipples, slipping between her legs. Miki shivered, opened her eyes, and let the night's debauchery sift through her thoughts again.

Her intimate flesh was still sensitive, still abraded. She didn't dare slide a finger between her legs or cup a breast without hissing air between her clenched teeth. Instead, she lay down on her cool sheets, opened her legs, and stretched her arms out to her sides, letting the breeze soughing over her skin cool and soothe her to sleep again.

Should she dream of monsters with gnashing teeth or blood-sucking horn-dogs who fed their hungers on her flesh and blood? She touched her lips, slightly swollen from her lovers' passionate kisses, and drew the memory of Alex in the garden around her like a comforting blanket before she drifted back to sleep.

Alex landed on the windowsill, slipped his legs over the edge, and sat on the wide ledge while he folded his wings back into the slitted pouches between his shoulders.

Beneath him, stretched across her bed, lay the woman who called herself "Sarah." With moonlight silvering her bed, he watched her long legs shift restlessly in her dreams, gliding closed and apart. His cock stirred, filling to press ruthlessly against the stiff fabric of the fresh jeans he'd donned before seeking her out.

Her slender legs tensed, relaxed, then folded outward, teasing him with the thought that if he stood at the foot of her bed, he'd clearly see the soft folds he'd plundered. Instead, all he could see now was her soft, furred mound. His gaze swept upward, over the swell of her belly, the hollow beneath her ribs, the rise of her breasts, and the soft, round discs cresting at their centers.

With her arm outstretched, her pillowy breasts lay like small milky hillocks, and his palms itched remembering the softness of her skin and the way her breasts had quivered when he'd bounced against her bottom.

He eased to the floor, stepped out of his shoes, and walked

around to the foot of the bed to gaze raptly at her open cunt. *His to take, to own, to love.*

Looking at her now, he felt so different from how he'd felt when he'd shunted her into the car, thinking he'd never see her again. He'd been ready to forget her, only a little regretful he wouldn't have been the man to wake up to her every day. He'd enjoyed the vibrancy of her skin, hair, and body—and the curiosity that had shone in her soft eyes.

Now, knowing he'd filled her womb with his seed, a swell of possessive heat expanded his chest and filled his loins. What was done was done, no turning back. Fate had given her to him. A crazy, free-falling sensation buzzed through him at the thought that now he could let himself drown in her gaze and ease his body and his mind inside her embrace. There was true freedom in having all his options narrowed to one. *One woman.*

But how would he keep her safe? Lock her away in his little cavern for the rest of her days, spending stolen moments with her?

Again, it was all about him. All about being the Born male. Born to rule. Born to be miserable and make anyone who truly loved him the same.

How was any of this fair to her? She hadn't known that the cost of receiving his seed would be her freedom and, ultimately, her life. If she had the choice, would she even want him? He'd treated her badly. Abused her fragile, human body. How he wished he could start afresh with her.

The last time they'd met, she'd thought he was a human man—an average Joe. How he wished he had kept up that pretense. If he'd had the power, he would have turned back time to undo that last, revealing bite and woo her as any human man might, with flowers and attention—after he'd assuaged the unnatural desires raging in her body. She would have been grateful, embarrassed for a time, until he'd convinced her he'd been meant to find her, to meet her in that garden and rescue her—be the knight to slay her dragon of lust. How delightful a slow courtship would have been, giving them time to know each other, to discover their souls before he would ever have been forced to introduce her to the other half of himself.

The thing he'd always craved—human connection—had been there for him to nurture, his to have, if he hadn't been selfish, hadn't been afraid to try. His subconscious had acted on his desire, turned him from his duty for those brief, blazing moments when he'd entered her and marked her forever his.

His glance cut around the room, wanting to discover more about the woman who would be his consort. The room was functional, Spartan, without photographs of friends or lovers—immaculate except for the trail of clothing on the floor that she'd worn that night. A New Orleans calendar with a picture of Jackson Square was pinned to the wall above a white, built-in desk. He padded toward the desk, ignoring the laptop with its closed monitor and dangling cord. Instead, he reached for the neat stack of yellow legal pads.

Notes annotated with the dates since the onset of the storm contained short, graphic descriptions of everything she'd observed and experienced. The preparations by the building's tenants as they'd awaited the storm, the celebration when it had brushed past, and their growing horror as the water had risen, cutting them off from the rest of the world.

He flipped through the notes, looking for the previous day,

but her careful descriptions ended with the morning and a sketchy plan to check out the Quarter during curfew.

She hadn't made an entry since he'd spotted her in the alleyway. He wondered what she'd write about that.

But why the copious notes? His detective's instincts kicked in. He shuffled through envelopes in her in-box, where he found one with a local magazine's return address in the corner and cash inside. Was she a reporter, then? It would explain her curiosity and cagey reply when he'd questioned her about her interest in vampires.

Alex tossed the envelope back onto the top of her in-box. Her profession might be inappropriate for the life she would enter, but it was over as of now.

She shifted on the bed again, sighing, drawing his attention back to her. Her toes curled, stretching to point, then relax. He followed flexing muscles up her trim calves, past firm thighs. His gaze snagged on her open sex and the moisture that glimmered there like a thin layer of crushed pearls, iridescent and scented with her musk.

His body throbbed, his blood heated, rushing south, filling his cock, stealing caution from his mind. Returning to the end of her bed, he reached down and slowly wrapped his fingers around her ankles, succumbing to the ravenous demon inside him, again.

Miki's eyes slammed open to find the man in her dreams at the foot of her bed with his large hands slowly sliding open her legs. "A-Alex?" she stammered, recognizing him despite the shadows that painted his features in sinister darkness. Her startled glance swept his naked chest and the soft, faded blue jeans that hugged his trim hips like a lover. A carved, polished stone lay at the base of his throat, glinting dully in the moon-light.

"Your name," he rasped. "I want your real name."

"What?" she bit out, trying to close her legs and quiet her panic. Trying to think. "You didn't just decide to ransack my purse and check my driver's license while you were breaking into my apartment?"

"I'm not a thief."

"But you are a liar."

His head canted, his eyes narrowing.

"That bite you gave me . . . ," she said, realizing that maybe she shouldn't be blurting out every thought. Especially when he reacted so strongly. "You said . . . you weren't one of them," she finished haltingly.

His body went still, but his hands tightened painfully around her ankles.

"Ouch! Psycho much?" she gasped, trying again to pull her feet away, trying to hold onto her shock and fear at finding him here. Her traitorous body, however, was already melting inside, inspired by the heat of his low-lidded gaze and taut features.

He released her ankles, but before she could heave a sigh of relief, he was pressing her to the mattress, moving so fast that she hadn't seen the motions, could only gasp for breath at how quickly he covered her. Her nipples beaded instantly against his lightly furred chest.

"You shouldn't have remembered that," he growled. "If you were human, you would not. Even vampires can't resist that suggestion. Who are you, *Sarah*? What are you?"

She twisted her lips into a bitter smile. "I don't know what you tried to do to me besides fuck me raw, but the memories I have, I intend to keep."

His forehead wrinkled as though trying to grasp her meaning.

She tried to start again, to find a way to ease the suspicion crowding into his tight expression. If she could just get him to behave reasonably, maybe he'd let her go. "My name's Mikaela Jones, Alex. I assure you, I'm perfectly human—*unlike you*. Now, will you get the fuck off me?"

His chest expanded, deepening the pressure against her sensitive breasts. "I'm not leaving. Not until we've talked . . . *Mikaela*." He said her name as though savoring it, his voice roughening, rasping over the syllables.

Miki drew a shallow breath, forcing her breathing to remain even, hoping her body wouldn't heat in kind with the passion she saw entering his taut cheeks and jaws. The flair of his nostrils as he drew in her scent made her fiercely glad she'd washed away his and every other aroma she'd accumulated that night. "Miki," she bit out. "I prefer Miki."

"I know a little about your preferences, *Miki*. Shall I remind you?"

"Did you break into my apartment to insult me?"

Alex's expression softened. "Of course not."

"Then why? Did you come to finish me off?"

His eyebrows rose. "That sounded melodramatic. Why would you think that?"

"What am I supposed to think? You're here without my invitation—" She narrowed her gaze at him. "Hey, aren't you supposed to have to ask to come in?"

His lips slid into a sly grin. "Only when I'm worried about being polite."

"Not a rule, huh? Garlic doesn't do a thing for you?"

"Love it."

"Stake through the heart?"

He winced, then lifted his chest off hers, sliding to the side to rest his weight on an elbow while the rest of his body remained draped over her. "Sounds downright painful. Blood-thirsty little thing, are you?"

"Just figuring out the rules," she huffed, hating the fact that she was starting to enjoy the conversation. How did he do that? Make her forget to be afraid?

He lifted a hand and cupped her breast as though it was the most natural thing in the world for him to do . . . with her. "Miki, we have to talk."

She blinked, telling herself she wasn't going to let him see the tears beginning to burn the backs of her eyes. "We did that, remember? I dumped my woes on you. You pretended sympathy and offered to *help* me with my little problem—"

"And I frightened you," he said softly.

She swallowed, and despite her valiant attempt, moisture blurred her vision. "I wasn't scared. You hurt me."

His hand slid up her chest and slipped behind her neck, cradling her head. "I'm sorry—"

"You made me feel like an idiot," she said, her voice breaking.

His fingers rubbed her scalp in delicious, drugging circles. "Again, I'm sorry."

"Stop petting me, for God's sake!" she said, feeling her mouth draw downward. "I'm not a dog. Not your girlfriend. I was just a convenient meal and fuck."

"Baby, there's not a convenient thing about you."

Miki's fingers tensed against his warm skin, and she realized she'd been caressing his chest all the while. "Glad to hear it," she said, aiming for bitchy and hoping he hadn't noticed her unconscious fondling. "I'd hate for you to think I'm easy. I hope I gave you indigestion."

His slight, tight smile didn't jive with his thoughtful frown. Alex leaned close and sniffed along her collarbone, her neck, and then her hair.

"Uh . . . what are you doing?"

"I didn't taste anything different about you last night."

"Just one of a million girls you could have. How'd I get so lucky you decided to come to me for seconds?"

Alex shook his head, his eyebrows nearly meeting. "Do you always talk this much when you're scared?"

She swallowed and lifted her shoulders, giving him a strained smile. "It's like diarrhea of the mouth, isn't it?"

"Not a pleasant image."

"Um . . . not trying to be nice, here. I'm the one who's naked with a vampire stretched over her like a blanket."

Alex sighed, then shifted his lower body—no doubt to make room for the erection slowly filling against her belly. "I'm not a *Revenant*. I didn't lie to you."

Miki fought the urge to squeeze her thighs together. Blood was heading south to plump her burning folds. "There's a difference between kinds of blood drinkers?" she asked breathlessly, her thoughts beginning to unravel.

Alex's head lowered and he inhaled, trailing above her skin from her breast to her neck. "One's born; one's bitten, drained, and made." She felt his deep exhale all the way to her pussy.

She gasped, and her eyelids dipped. "Which kind are you?" she asked, hearing the tone of her voice rising as her whole body tightened beneath him.

"*Revenants* are the Undead," he said, his mouth hovering over hers.

"So you are the born one? You really weren't lying to me before?"

"I was being—"

"Evasive? Ambiguous?"

"Cautious."

Miki licked her lips. "Why? Aren't you all after the same thing?"

"We aren't about getting blood, any more than you're about hot dogs or tacos."

"I was talking about . . . the sex."

"Well, I guess we share some similarities." His hand closed around her breast again. "You're not as frightened as you were before."

"How do you know?" she whispered.

"I can hear your heart beating." His lips moved above hers, and Miki couldn't help following, hoping he'd close the distance between them. "Your heart's slowing down, sounding less panicked."

"What does it sound like now?" she said, feeling her nipple spike against his palm.

"A heavy thrum. You're aroused." He squeezed her breast.

Miki closed her eyes. "I shouldn't be. The aphrodisiac wore off."

"Could it be me?" he asked softly.

She opened her eyes, letting him see the desperation beginning to build inside her. "It's probably just the fact your cock is snuggled between my legs—muscle memory or something."

One corner of his mouth quirked upward. "Muscle memory?" he repeated, a silent chuckle vibrating against her.

Miki clamped her lips shut. Talking smack was what had gotten her into all this trouble in the first place.

Alex eyed her mouth, and then his penetrating gaze met hers again. Slowly, he lifted his hips and settled more squarely between her legs. The long, thick column filling the front of his jeans scraped her swollen labia. Miki stifled a moan.

Something of her distress must have shown on her face. "I'm hurting you?"

Her cheeks filled with fiery heat. Miki debated blurting out the cause, but she didn't think she could bear it if he laughed at her again. Instead, she tightened her lips and glared.

His hips flexed, giving her a shallow little dig, and this time she couldn't bite back the gasp.

He lifted off her in an instant.

Before her relieved sigh ended, he knelt between her legs, bending over to peer at her sex.

Miki slammed her hands over her pussy and tried to close her legs. "Enough, already!"

"Let me see," he said, prying away her hands and diving closer.

When she realized he wasn't giving up, she flung her hands away and closed her eyes, determined to live through the next humiliating minutes despite her desire to die right then and there.

His fingers trailed along her outer labia, and air hissed between his teeth. "Your skin's inflamed."

So was her clitoris, but he'd discover that soon enough.

Despite the chafing injury that caused her discomfort, the other parts of her genitalia had remained in a state of unabated arousal, likely reacting to the heat surrounding them.

She hadn't dared risk touching herself with her fingers—the rasp was too abrasive. Should she tell him? Beg him for release? He had to know better than she did how to alleviate the ache.

Something warm and wet, and unbelievably soft, stroked along her outer lips, leaving cooling moisture behind. His tongue. *God, his tongue.*

"Have you any aloe?" he asked softly.

"In my medicine cabinet," she said, her voice faint and breathy.

Alex rolled off the bed and walked barefoot to her bathroom, returning in a moment with a small container in his palm.

"Raise your knees and let them fall open."

She didn't think to disobey; instead, she opened eagerly. His fingers soothed over her skin, smearing cool gel up and down until he coated her outer lips. "Better?"

She nodded dumbly.

Something changed in his expression. It darkened. His jaw ground tight. With his fingers still resting on her inner thighs, he lifted a dry thumb and pushed up the hood protecting her engorged, perfectly erect clit. "Were you going to tell me you needed release?"

She shook her head in denial.

"Never hold back from me. I will never deny you."

Miki wondered at the passionate promise. Inside her starving, lonely soul she dared to let hope grow that maybe he intended to begin some sort of relationship with her. That he wouldn't abandon her after he'd achieved his own pleasure.

Was she so needy, so pathetic that she read something more than he intended in his solemn words? At the moment, she couldn't think beyond the agony clawing at her womb. "Alex . . . I ache."

"You shouldn't have washed so thoroughly. All those natural lubricants . . ."

She shook her head violently. "I didn't feel clean."

"I made you feel that way," he said quietly. Not a question. He knew he was responsible for the damage he'd done her psyche. A small, regretful smile lifted his lips. "Let me help you."

Without waiting for her consent—probably because he knew she couldn't tell him no—he reached for a pillow and dragged it down the bed.

She lifted her hips automatically, letting him slide it beneath her. Opened to him, her sex elevated like an offering, she closed her eyes and sighed as he once again bent between her legs.

When his tongue softly laved her clit, she trembled, her breath catching on a jagged sob. Slippery fingers opened her lips. A single digit traced her cleft and slowly dipped into her entrance.

Miki cupped her breasts and arched her back. Moisture seeped around the finger stroking gently inside. His tongue continued to swirl over the exposed knot of nerves, rasping softly while he tunneled into her.

Miki's pussy clasped him, making succulent little sounds that seemed to excite him, because he began to murmur against her, and his tongue flicked faster.

His gentleness was almost more than she could bear. Despite the raw heat burning around her entrance, she began to chant, to beg him to enter her. To fuck her.

"God, please, Alex," she moaned, lifting her feet from the bed and widening her legs.

Alex shook his head, and his lips closed around her clitoris. He suckled the knot, forcing it to rise higher, creating a painful fullness that kept her on the edge of exploding while his finger twisted and skimmed inside her clenching walls.

When his lips slid toward the base of her clit and tightened around it, tugging it firmly, Miki's legs straightened, her hips curled, and suddenly she cried out, jerking her hips against his mouth as he teethed the base of her clit and swirled his tongue over the top.

How long he tortured her through her orgasm, she couldn't know. She flew outside herself, colors exploding behind her tightly clenched eyelids, until she fell back, her legs easing toward the mattress, her body trembling. Only then did he gently enfold her in his arms.

CHAPTER

15

Miki lay on her side atop crisp white sheets, hands tucked beneath her cheek like a child. The late afternoon sunlight streamed through the open window, glinting in the gold and red strands of her thick hair.

Alex couldn't wait for her to open her eyes so that he could find the answer to the question that had been bothering him ever since he woke. What color were her eyes, anyway?

A silly thing to consume his thoughts, but so much more enjoyable than recalling the dream that had disturbed his sleep. Just when he'd touched innocence, hoping to escape his sordid world in the arms of an uncomplicated woman, Inanna's dark, cruel past had reached out to bite him in the ass again. He needed to see Simon. To show him what he'd discovered.

He trailed his fingers along her cheek. "Time to wake up, Miki."

Her forehead wrinkled and she muttered, but she rolled to her back and slowly pried open her eyes, squinting at him through her dark, auburn lashes. Her gaze widened as she stared at him standing next to the window with the sunlight warming his back. "Are you supposed to do that?"

Green. Darker than the color of grass—more the deep, lush shade of a primordial forest. "Do what?" he asked, trying to remember the question.

"Be in the sunshine. Shouldn't you be smoldering, at least?" She sniffed as though seeking a hint of smoke.

His lips stretched, and he released a short, gusting laugh. "I told you I'm different. Did you sleep well?"

A blush flooded her cheeks with an adorable pink.

"I think the aloe did the trick," he said smugly, giving her body a possessive sweep.

Miki's hands shot down, clutched the edge of the sheet, and pulled it up to cover her breasts. "You didn't . . . um . . . I fell asleep. Sorry about that."

"I didn't what?" he teased, pretending not to understand.

"Come," she said, her tone flat.

"Well, I'm a man. Half, anyway. Yes, I was aroused," he said, nodding, "but I enjoyed giving you pleasure."

Her glance slid away. "Did you do something . . . ? Just curious."

Alex sat on the bed beside her and lifted her hand to hold inside his. "Trying to ask me if I masturbated myself?" At her distressed moue, he relented. "Yes, I'm not made of stone. You came so completely undone, I was inspired. Couldn't sleep until I took care of it."

Her vivid green glance flirted beneath her eyelashes. "I would have helped."

"Nice to know," he replied dryly.

She sat up, raking her hair back, and secured the sheet beneath her arms. "Do we have any more of that aloe?"

"Need me to apply some more?" he said, letting his voice slide deep to see her reaction.

She didn't disappoint. Her breath hitched, and rose bloomed brighter in her cheeks. "I can manage—"

He squeezed her hand. "I'd enjoy it. Just say yes, if you want me to."

Her blush intensified, spilling down her throat to tint the tops of her breasts, but she lifted her face. "Yes. I'd like that."

"That's better." Alex stood, turning away to adjust himself inside his jeans. He could do this. Perhaps afterward he could even manage to walk without a noticeable limp.

"I hope you don't think I'll always be this agreeable," Miki said behind him, her voice recovering some of her trademark starch. "I don't think I'm the submissive kind of woman or anything."

Scraping the jar off the top of the dresser, he turned. "I didn't assume you were." He waggled his eyebrows. "I thought you just deliciously sated."

"What man talks like that?"

"I'm not metrosexual, if that's what you're thinking. I've just been around a while."

Her eyebrows lowered, but he could tell she fought a smile; her lips twitched. "Maybe I should do this myself," she said, holding out her hand.

Alex slowly shook his head and tugged the sheet from her tight grasp, his amusement fading immediately. In sunlight, her pale, creamy skin shone like mother-of-pearl, the golden highlights in her deep auburn hair burnished like a fiery halo. Even her lips, slicked by her tongue, gleamed.

Looking at her, with her legs curled beneath her, her hands rising to cover her breasts, all the shadows in his life seemed to burn away in the brilliance of her beauty.

He sat beside her again and lifted his hand to cup her cheek, smoothing his thumb over her full lower lip.

Her pink lips parted, her tongue darting out to touch him. Her eyelids dipped as she tilted her head, her expression, one filled with painful longing, begging for his kiss.

Alex set the jar on the mattress and bent to take her mouth. Miki's lips opened, welcoming him inside, her tongue stroking into his mouth to mate in a wild tangle with his.

He thrust his fingers through her hair to cup the back of her head and slanted his mouth across hers to deepen the kiss.

She leaned into him, sighing, and then jerked back, her lips closing. "You brushed your teeth."

"I used your toothbrush."

"That's not the problem. I didn't."

"Use my toothbrush?"

"No, you idiot," she said with a roll of her eyes. "I haven't brushed my teeth."

Alex smirked. "I don't mind."

"I do. I must taste—"

"Delicious."

"Liar."

"Okay, a slight exaggeration, but I don't mind. Perhaps

you'd prefer I kiss something besides your lips?" he asked, lifting one brow.

Again she glanced at him from beneath her lashes, her chest lifting to her shallow inhalations. "Maybe—"

Alex leaned closer, nuzzling her neck. "The aloe first?"

A soft hand smoothed around the back of his neck, teasing through the hair at his nape. "The aloe . . . after?"

Alex couldn't resist sliding his tongue along her sleek shoulder, halting at the corner of her neck so he didn't alarm her. "I'm not coming inside you. You're sore."

"Then let me pleasure you."

He lifted his head while arousal flared, filling his loins with heavy, throbbing anticipation. "You'd do that? After everything . . ."

"You made a very pretty apology. I'm still quivering inside."

God, how she pleased him. Alex stared into her eyes, finally understanding why the phrase was called "falling in love." The combination—a perfect moment, the perfect lover, and complete surrender of self—made him wish he could make time stand still. "Mikaela . . ."

"I want to do this. Just show me what you like."

"You already know. You took me in your mouth in the garden."

"You forced me to swallow you whole, and I wasn't really taking notes. I'd like to do better."

"You had never done it before?"

Her expression turned suddenly stark, haunted. "Besides that *very brief* moment with Nic, I don't know."

Sensing an opportunity to learn more, and a chance to deepen her trust in him, he tamped down his arousal and scooted closer to her on the bed, slowly bringing his arms around her waist while keeping his gaze locked with hers. "Tell me what you mean."

A slight, unfunny smile thinned her lips. "A couple of years ago, I woke up." She shrugged. "I was lying in tall grass on an embankment. Naked. Shivering, although it was about as warm as it is now outside. When I crawled up to the road, a car stopped, the couple took me to the hospital. They ran tests, a rape kit—nothing seemed to be wrong with me. But I couldn't remember my name or how I got there."

"Your name's not Mikaela, then?"

"I chose it from a book of names. I liked the sound of it."

"Pretty choice," he said, tucking her hair behind her ears. "No one came to claim you? No missing person reports were ever filed?"

"The police checked it all out. Took my statement, looked around the bayou where I was found, but came up with nothing." Miki rested her head on his shoulder.

Alex hugged her closer and smoothed his hands up and down her back. "I'm going to come off sounding like the biggest jerk ever, but I kind of like the idea that most anything I show you, anything I do, will seem like a first."

"I like believing you were my first," she said, her voice muffled against his skin. "You would have been my only, except for Nic—"

Wanting no reminders, he interrupted. "Did he rub you with aloe?"

A soft, feminine snort was followed by a quiet, "No."

"There's another first," he said, smiling into her hair. He

rubbed her back again and took a deep breath. "Did he tell you he might be in love with you?"

"Of course not." Her head fell back, her eyes widening. "We hardly know each other . . ."

Not wanting to scare her off, he gave her a little half smile. "Well, then, there's another first I'll reserve. *For later.*"

A shallow crease formed between her dark brows. "You're not worried my past will come back to haunt me?"

Alex cupped her chin in his palm. "You have no past that doesn't begin with me."

She wrinkled her nose. "Now you do sound a bit like a jerk. But oddly, that turned me on."

"Which is a very nice segue back to our original discussion."

Her lips slid easily into a teasing smile. "We were talking about something?"

"You . . . pleasuring . . . me."

"But I'm the one turned on now."

"Who says we can't pleasure each other at the same time?"

"Without you coming inside me?" At the wicked rise of his eyebrows, her gaze rounded. "Oh! You mean you and me . . . our mouths . . ."

Alex lowered his eyebrows and gave her smoldering look. "I'll go down on you while I fuck your mouth."

A soft sigh slipped between her lips. "Not the way I would have phrased it, but could we do that? Please?"

"Maybe I'll let you be on top. I might forget myself and choke you to death. I was a gentleman last night."

"You have your limits?"

"Stretched to the breaking point, sweetheart."

"I can do that to you?" she asked, wonder in her voice.

"Effortlessly, so it seems," he murmured, caught again by her amazing green eyes.

"What do I do?"

"I'll show you." Alex stood, stripped off his jeans and boxers in one enthusiastic push, and crawled onto the bed. She scooted to the side, her hands still covering herself.

He eyed her covered breasts and lifted an eyebrow. "You know I've seen every inch of you."

"Not in the daylight. I feel really . . . exposed."

"Sexy, isn't it?"

She licked her lower lip and stared at his cock, which jutted toward her. "Very. And impressive. I only had a glimpse before. And the shadows . . ."

"The shadows hid many delights. I didn't know your true colors. Green eyes," he said, staring into hers. "Lovely . . . like moss."

Her nose wrinkled. "Sounds slippery and spongy."

"They're beautiful. So are your nipples," he said, prying her hands from her breasts. "Peach, with rose tips."

"Sounds like a tea."

"I'll take a sip or two," he said, fingering a nipple, then bending to draw it delicately into his mouth.

She moaned and he drew away instantly, cupping her breast gently. "Are you sore here as well?"

"No, just aching. I liked it."

"Lie back, then."

"I thought I was going to be on top."

"We'll get there. I promise."

Miki lay down, letting her hands flutter to the mattress. When his lips closed around the opposite peak, she gasped and squeezed her thighs together, which reminded her of the ache between her legs. Moisture seeped slowly from inside her. "I like that. *So much*."

His tongue circled her areola, lapping over the tip, dragging it upward before he latched his lips around it and suckled gently.

Miki's belly trembled and her legs shifted restlessly. Alex's hands smoothed over her skin, warming her, shaping her curves, petting her as though he gentled an animal, which she realized she needed, because her whole body shivered with nerves and delight.

He traced the indention of her waist, molded over the flare of her hip, followed the sleek lines of her outer thighs, but never ventured between them. Too soon, it wasn't enough. The tug of his lips sent little shock waves throughout her body, and intense heat curled around her womb.

She shifted her legs again, opening them, lifting her hips to invite him to explore, but he ignored her plea, instead switching breasts and gently torturing her with more hot licks and tugs that had her nipples ripening into painful points, which he toggled and teethed on until her mewling cries lifted endlessly into the air around them.

"Alex, please. You're killing me, I need more. I need you inside me, now!"

His tongue fluttered at her tip, and he lifted his head. His cheeks were stained with ruddy color; his nostrils flared. "You'll have to straddle me. Put your knees on either side of my shoulders and lower yourself over my face."

She bit her lip, heat filling her own cheeks. "Inelegantly put. And now I'm thoroughly embarrassed."

Alex's hand glided down her belly, and he slid one finger

between her folds, swirling in her moisture, then plunging into her.

She couldn't hide her wince.

"You didn't give Nic a blow job?" he asked, his face tense and darkening.

Wishing he hadn't asked that question, she couldn't lie. "Like I said, Nic put his penis in my mouth—but not for long."

"I'll kill him. No, I'll let Chessa do it for me."

"I wish I hadn't been with him."

"Not your fault." He flashed a cocky smile. "And how could you know you'd see me again? You ready?" he asked, tunneling his finger deeper inside her.

Miki clasped his hand with her thighs, trying to keep him right there, needing him deeper. Needing his thickness to fill her. "Will it be enough? For you?"

"The only thing better would be for me to watch your mouth swallow my dick again. Another time for that. Seems you're getting wet, Ms. Jones."

Her hips lifted to deepen his touch. "Hurry?"

Alex pulled out his fingers and lay down, then waited patiently while she gingerly turned and lifted a leg over his upper body. "You have no idea how uncomfortable I am doing this," she grumbled.

"Why are you concerned? You're lovely—all rosy and glistening." He inhaled deeply. "And fragrant."

"I really wish you'd shut up," she said as he guided her with gentle nudges of his hands. His thumbs hooked under her hips, his fingers splayed to cup her bottom. When at last he seemed satisfied, she bent over him, trying to find the right place for her hands to support her weight.

"Lie over me. I can take your weight. You'll want to be free to handle me."

Miki made a face, feeling awkward and frustrated, then something hot and moist stroked over her swollen clit. She gasped and bent over him, eager now to taste him, as he was tasting her. But there was so much of him.

"Lick your palms and slide them around me," he said, his voice taut. "Don't be afraid you'll exert too much pressure. So long as you don't try to wring me like a dishrag, I swear I'll like it."

Miki did as he suggested, wetting her palms, then reaching for the long, thick shaft thrusting from a nest of dark curls. How grotesque and oddly lovely it all was. Below his shaft lay the sac with two hard stones, so vulnerable, so suddenly appealing. She cupped the sac and leaned low to inhale his musk and feel the softness of his skin and hair against her cheek. She gave him an experimental lick and was rewarded with a husky groan.

Encouraged, she opened her lips and sucked one ball into her mouth.

Alex's thighs widened and his hips lifted, his cock sliding under her chin as she mouthed him, laving his ball inside her mouth as tension shivered through his thighs. She let him go, then cupped his sac and opened her mouth wider to take both inside, gobbling them delicately with her teeth shielded behind her lips.

Again, Alex moaned, and a muffled, desperate laugh gusted against her moist flesh. Then he speared into her, lapping at the cream flowing in a trickle to greet his ravaging tongue.

Miki tilted her hips, scooting into his mouth, wanting him

deeper. Her pussy spasmed, caressing his tongue, and he murmured against her, the soft sound vibrating.

Knowing now how delicious sound felt, she let her own voice go, moaning freely as she tugged and licked at his balls, growing so excited herself that she had to taste the rest of him. She moved up to smooth her cheek along his shaft.

When she was looking down his length, she knew she could only take so much of him inside, but she didn't want to disappoint. She knew instinctively that she had to warm every inch of his cock, like a moist, hot cunt swallowing him whole. So she wet her palms, set one hand atop the other, and sank her mouth over the tip, squeezing her hands up and down his satiny, veined shaft.

Alex's legs shifted. He planted his feet firmly in the mattress and began to pump into her mouth, countering her downward glides to force himself deeper into her mouth. He glided along her tongue, butting the back of her throat as she twisted her hands and pumped them up and down.

So enthralled was she with her efforts that she almost missed the moment when his fingers entered her vagina, thickness filling her at last, hard knuckles twisting in her hot tissues, coaxing more liquid excitement from her depths as he pushed in and out, all the while giving her clit a wild lashing of his tongue.

Miki sobbed around him. His cock thrust into her and saliva built inside her mouth, until the urge to swallow couldn't be ignored. She did so and discovered that the movement caressed his blunt crown. So she did it again and knew she pleased him when his thrusts quickened.

His strokes deepened, nearly gagging her, but she opened her throat, finding she could accommodate more of his length, and she relaxed around him, suctioning her lips around his shaft as he did the work, fucking in and out of her mouth while she braced herself to hold still above him.

When the rhythm of his thrusts grew a little erratic, almost frantic, she knew he was close, so she reached beneath his cock and kneaded his balls, reveling in the wildness that tightened his whole body as he bucked beneath her.

Low, guttural grunts gusted against her sex as his mouth fell away from her pussy, his release making him selfish in those last moments.

Miki didn't care; she held onto him, swallowing again to encourage him. Finally she felt the hot jets of his orgasm streaming into her throat.

She gulped it down, her breaths labored, choked, but she wouldn't let him pull away as he tried to do. Instead, she squeezed his balls and drove her mouth downward, taking him, forcing him to completion.

When his thrusts finally slowed, she bobbed slowly over him, soothing him with her gliding tongue and lips, before coming slowly off his cock and dragging in deep, reviving breaths.

Alex shuddered beneath her, his hands stroking her bottom aimlessly. "*Goddamn.*"

Miki smiled, knowing how he felt. Completely wrung out. Boneless. She lifted her leg, ignoring his resistance, and climbed off him, rolling to the side to look up his body as she braced her head on one hand and caressed his cock with the other. "How'd I do?"

Alex speared her with an incredulous glare. "If it had been any better, I would have been incinerated."

Miki gave him a cheeky grin. "You, however, fell down on the job."

His eyes narrowed and he rolled up to sit, pushing her hand from his cock. "An oversight I'll take care of now."

Miki squealed when he suddenly came to his knees and grabbed her thighs, jerking them apart. When he pushed two pillows beneath her hips, the blood rushed toward her brain, leaving her head swimming for a moment.

Sunlight gleamed brightly through the window and directly at her open pussy.

Alex's thumbs spread her inner lips and he stared. "You have no idea how much I wish I could bury myself right here."

"I'm wishing it too. Can't we?"

Alex shook his head regretfully, then reached for the pot of aloe. He twisted off the lid, dipped two fingers inside, and painted her lips again. "When you're recovered, I promise to fuck you raw again. Often."

"Sounds like you plan to be around," she said lightly, but hoping with all her heart it was true.

"Baby, I'm never letting you go."

CHAPTER
16

"Ω ico, stay a while with me," Innana said, patting the plum-colored cushion of the love seat beside her.

Nicolas stiffened. Since the night his small army of *Revenants* had swarmed *Ardeal*, Inanna had remained distant, her communications with him brittle, her long gazes assessing and filled with distrust. He preferred it that way, not liking the fact that he and Chessa shared the same roof with the woman who'd been party to his turning, his blood-mate. He feared she would try to wield her power over him to force a tear in his deepening relationship with Chessa.

Did she know Chessa had escaped? His presence had been requested in Inanna's bedroom suite. In the room he shared with Chessa, Nicolas left the bathroom door locked in case anyone checked.

"Pasqual," Inanna said, without looking behind her. "Leave us."

Pasqual's already dour expression darkened as he shot a bitter glance Nicolas's way, but he left the room, closing the door quietly behind him.

"Sit beside me. I don't like it when you loom."

Nicolas would have liked to use some excuse to escape. The look on Inanna's face was one he knew too well. She wanted sex. His brand of sex.

Since Chessa had reentered his life, Inanna had seemed obsessed with having what he gave Chessa. Did she think that he would love her as much if she let him dominate her like Chessa preferred? Didn't she know that the dynamics of his relationship with Chessa had been built on trust and an attraction that had grown despite a lack of supernatural blood-bonds?

"Inanna, I really should get back to the guests. We aren't finished questioning them."

Inanna's dark gaze speared him. "You've found nothing."

Nicolas nodded. "That's true. Nothing that tells us who was the last person with Erika. The blood trail was destroyed, and her body wasn't discovered until several minutes past the moment of her death. The killer had time to bathe away the blood."

"He chose his victim well. So many scents contaminated her—all working to diffuse his. He's very clever."

"I've told my team to work in pairs and never let the other out of sight. It must be one of us. The *sabat* is clear of suspicions, so too the guests brought in for the party."

"One of us," she said, toying with her black choker. "Any of us. For all you know, it might be me."

"I think The Devourer is a man."

"Why are you sure?"

"Because Erika straddled him, fell off him backwards. I think if she'd been with a woman—"

"She would have knelt in front of her or vice versa. You're right." Her hand dropped from her necklace and her liquid brown eyes pleaded with him. "Nico, I'm afraid."

Some of Nicolas's wary caution bled away. He blew out a deep breath. "So am I."

"This brings back all those memories. Of the last time he escaped. Of sweet Anaïs—and your brother."

Preferring not to wallow in his own pain and remorse, he changed the subject. "Have you spoken with any of the council members since it happened?"

"They've taken to their rooms, preferring to keep to those they know. They think I'm completely incompetent."

"What about the wolf?"

"She was shown her room earlier, and a guard was placed at her door. For her protection, of course."

Nicolas snorted. "She didn't seem the sort to need it."

"She's imposing, is she not?" Her gaze slid sideways, a calculating gleam in her eyes. "Did you find her beautiful?"

"She wasn't to my taste," he said carefully.

Inanna stretched her arms across the back of the love seat. The gesture plumped the tops of her breasts rising above the edge of her sari. "Am I . . . still to your taste?"

Nicolas felt a slight heaviness invade his cock and ruthlessly ignored it. "Inanna," he said, tired of playing games, "what do you want?"

"You . . . like you've always been with me. I've missed you," she said, her voice girlish and lilting. "I was angry with you, but I'm over it. I understand why you and your little army rose up against me." Her lips twisted into a wry smile. "I think I was even aroused by it."

He shot her an incredulous stare. "You were aroused by my insurrection?"

"It took courage, and you know how I admire a fearless man." She trailed a finger over the tops of her breasts, then scraped one nail downward, tugging the edge below her nipples. "I would have you love me now. I would know your heart is still mine."

But I love Chessa! he wanted to shout. Inanna knew it, but she still insisted on carving out a piece of his heart for her own—drawing him back with subtle threats and tugging at his emotions, reminding him of what they'd been to each other for centuries.

Knowing well that Inanna might take revenge on Chessa if he refused her, Nicolas was well and truly caught.

"Why are you still dressed?" he asked, lowering his voice to a growling rasp—due not to arousal but rather to his own frustration with the situation. Let her interpret his actions however she chose.

Inanna's eyes widened; her nostrils flared. She rose quickly, unwinding her sari from around her body and letting it drop at her feet. She assumed a subservient posture with her head lowered and her hands cupping her sex.

Nicolas sighed. Her thighs were already slick, and yet he'd have to work up a hard-on to give her what she wanted. Strange, but this was the first time in their long lives together that he didn't find her naked body attractive.

Her skin was too burnished—he much preferred Chessa's pale, creamy color. Her dark, oval nipples with their long stems weren't the shy pink tips he loved to coax into spikes. Nothing about her body stirred him.

But he could never let Inanna guess. Her wrath would be deadly.

Nicolas stood and unbuttoned his shirt, shrugging out of it. He stripped away his shoes and trousers, then stood with his flaccid cock dangling, giving her a look that dared her to do something about it. "I think I'm bored, Inanna. Unless you can stir me, I'm afraid I won't be able to give you what you wish."

Inanna stared at his cock, her expression darkening, then suddenly growing detached—

"You cannot cast for me!" he bit out. "I forbid it."

Her eyes blinked, and her gaze, when it met his, was anguished. "I never thought I'd need it," she whispered. "Not with you."

"Perhaps I've learned some control. You know how I love to be in control. I need persuasion." He fisted his hands on his hips. "Wet persuasion. Your tongue and lips, servicing me. *Now*."

Inanna's shoulders straightened and her face tightened. Nicolas knew her first reaction was to balk, to fly at him for his insolence. She was the Born of this relationship, but her body began to tremble, and her nipples sprang taut and dimpled. Arousal flooded her body, heating the air around them, carrying the scent of her need wafting in the air.

She strode toward him, then slowly sank in front of him to rest on her knees with her head bent. "Tell me what pleases you," she said softly in her musical voice.

Nicolas closed his eyes, remembering how they'd been together. Centuries of loving, centuries of her manipulating him to her will. "Use only your mouth. Start with my balls. Make them ache."

Inanna's shoulders lifted, her mouth firmed, but she obeyed, lifting her face to nuzzle aside his penis and engulf one testicle with her wet mouth.

He braced his legs, widening them to provide her access. "Must I describe in detail what you have to do to arouse me?"

She murmured around him, laved his ball with her tongue, and tugged gently with her lips, suckling him.

Nicolas closed his eyes, drawing on his memories—of Inanna reaching for Chessa's belly at the moment she discovered her pregnancy. Remembering the cold fear that held him frozen, he kept his cock from reacting to the sweet heat of her mouth. He opened his eyes and pinned her with a hard glare.

For several long moments she continued to suckle. Then she opened her mouth wide to suck the other testicle inside. Her gaze lifted to his and widened.

Did she read his rage? Did she know how he wished that any other woman knelt before him? That her mouth on his body no longer gave him pleasure?

Her teeth raked a testicle, drawing blood, but he wouldn't allow himself to flinch. "How clumsy, Inanna," he grated.

She opened her mouth, releasing him, and glanced away. "Forgive me."

For what? Scraping his ball? Or was she apologizing for causing the rift that grew ever wider between them with each passing day?

"Perhaps you haven't the expertise to pleasure a man. You have only to command him, to cast your allure, and he'll do your bidding. You've become lazy." He stepped back from her and her reaching hands.

Inanna's eyes glittered and narrowed, then swept sideways as though to hide her true thoughts. "I'll do whatever you wish. Show me how to please you."

Nicolas leaned down and thrust his hand into her hair, pulling back her head so that she was forced to meet his glance. "I think I can only take from you. After all, you trained me."

Her tongue wet her lips. Her eyelids dipped. "Take from me, then. Whatever you wish."

He pushed her back. "Go to the bed and wrap your hands around the rail at the foot of the bed. Bend over so that I can see how much you want me."

She rose slowly, awkwardly, for once. Her feet shuffled toward the large ebony bed, with its slender, scrolled bedposts and rich silk covering, as though her mind raced before her, wondering what he would do.

"Don't look back. I won't be pleased."

He went to her closet, pulling gowns from hangers until he found one particularly beautiful silk gown with layers of scarves that floated from a banded waist. He ripped several of the scarves away and approached her from behind, reaching past her shoulders to tie her hands to the rail, then arranging her body to receive him.

Pressing between her shoulders, he forced her head beneath her stretched arms, then shoved apart her feet so that his view was unimpeded.

Her bare pussy glistened with moisture; her small dark hole glinted just above it. Looking at her bent, subjugated, willingly offering him anything he chose, Nicolas felt a stirring in his cock. He allowed it to rise at last, anticipating the clutch of her silken muscles all along his shaft as he hammered into her body.

Would he let her come? Could he control his own rising passion to prevent her from taking her pleasure? Nicolas wasn't sure how deep the anger was that rode him now. He'd savaged her body once before. He'd hated himself for it afterward.

Still, the urge to punish her was hard to ignore. He glanced at the trousers he'd abandoned, his gaze narrowing on his leather belt. He strode toward it, pulled it slowly from the loops, placed the buckle in his palm, and wound the leather around his fist.

Inanna glanced over her shoulder, her eyes widening on what he held in his hand.

"Will you cry out?" he said tonelessly. "Will you call for Pasqual to rescue you?"

"Nico. *No!*" she pulled against the restraints, wriggling wildly as he approached.

Her distress was a lie. She was strong enough to break free, to rip the silk to shreds if she truly feared him. Instead, her body trembled with anticipation.

Nicolas's lips pulled back from his teeth and he raised his arm, swinging downward to deliver the first stinging blow to her buttocks.

Inanna froze in shock.

Nicolas waited to see how she would react after she processed the fact that he'd actually struck her. Their centuries-long affair had taught him a lot about her desires. Only recently had he discovered her need to be dominated, her fascination with pain.

"Shall I give you everything you deserve, *Mistress*?" he said, snarling as he gave her the formal address she'd demanded when they'd been in company.

"Will you be ruthless?" she whispered.

"If that is what it takes to teach you, I will not be ruled."

Inanna's teeth bit into her lush, lower lip. "I have never taken instruction very well. As I am the one who should mold you."

Nicolas whipped out his arm, stinging her with another slap of leather.

Her mouth gaped open, but her eyes slid shut. She paused as though savoring the lash.

"Why do you test my resolve? You have only to surrender to me, *Mistress*."

Her gaze met his, her lips lifting in a strained smile. "If I am weak, you will not be impressed with my courage."

"And you think that if you allow me to stripe your sweet ass that I will be impressed?"

"Won't you?"

Nicolas wanted to wrap his hands around her neck and shake her. She'd forced him to do this, but now he wished she'd release him. Rage made his body tremble. "Perhaps I will be destroyed."

"Because you have always been gentle?" she taunted.

"I will hate myself because being with you, whatever I do, will sully the memory of our love." He didn't specify whose love, but she knew.

"But you have no choices here, do you, Nico? If you do not love me, you risk my displeasure. And it is only my pleasure that keeps her alive."

Nicolas shuddered, fighting the urge to tell the witch that Chessa was no longer hers to play against him, but he needed to delay that revelation for as long as possible. Until he'd found the monster and could clear the estate of the *sabat*.

If he was dutiful, duplicitous enough to fool her into believing he still loved her, there might be a chance that he and Chessa could remain together. Long enough that Alex could wrest leadership of the coven from Inanna.

Nicolas knew now that Alex coming to power was their only chance at living in peace.

He pulled the strap tighter around his fist. He'd give her what she wanted. What she craved from him. Later, he would beg forgiveness from God for relishing the task so much.

A soft cloth swept between Miki's legs, bringing her instantly awake.

"Like that, do you?" Alex murmured next to her ear.

The terry cloth gently abraded her flesh, a reminder of their sexy play. Embarrassed, Miki muttered and rolled to her stomach, burying her head in her pillow and pretending to sleep.

A sharp pinch nipped her hip and she yelped, lifting her head to glare at a grinning Alex, who spun the cloth between his hands.

"That hurt," she complained, reaching back to rub the spot he'd flicked.

Alex's smile slipped. "Time to get up. We're leaving."

She raised her arms to stretch, then let them drop immediately when his sharp, blue gaze dropped to her naked breasts. "Where are you taking me?" she asked, suddenly breathless. "I'm starved. Will you feed me?"

"We'll find something later. Get dressed."

"Where are we going?"

"Somewhere safe."

Something in the way his features hardened—his jaw firming and his gaze growing more remote—made her nervous. "That implies we're not safe here. What's going on, Alex?"

Drawing a deep breath, Alex sat on the mattress beside her and cupped her cheek. "There are some things about me that I should have mentioned before."

Trying to dispel some of the gloom entering the room, she gave him a small smile. "Are they more interesting than the fact that you're insatiable?"

His quick smile didn't reach his eyes. "They have to do with my being a Born vampire. I'm the only one, by the way."

"You're saying you're special?"

A smirk lifted one corner of his lips. "Did you ever doubt it?"

"Not for a moment. But what does that have to do with us not being safe?"

His gaze locked with hers, probing and intense. "I didn't use a condom when we made love. Did you notice that fact?"

Miki lifted her chin. "I thought you were done with the pretense of being an average kind of guy."

"I didn't use the condom as a ploy. Miki, I've always used them to protect my partners."

Feeling the pleasurable bubble she'd inhabited since she'd woken fade away, Miki cupped her hand against the outside of his and brought it down to her lap. She threaded her fingers slowly through his, stalling while she gathered the fraying edges of her courage around her. "Protect us from what? I thought you were all sterile and disease-free."

"I'm not sterile."

Her eyes widened. "Well then, shouldn't we have to wait until a little time has passed to see whether I'm in trouble? Besides, it's not that time of the month for me."

Alex squeezed his fingers against hers. "Read my lips, sweetheart. I'm special. You don't have to wait for ovulation.

I induce it. It's one of my *gifts*." The way he stressed the word indicated that he considered it anything but a gift.

"You're saying I'm pregnant? You're sure about that?"

At his nod, her free hand smoothed over her tummy. "What will it be?"

"You mean beyond a little girl? A Born vampire. Whatever else she is won't be clear until she matures."

Feeling as though the room was tilting beneath her, she shook her head. "And I'm not safe because I'm pregnant? I'm not following your logic."

"There are people scouring the city for me while you're lying in this bed. They'll destroy me and any who have harbored me. They'll seek out any child I've fathered and destroy it, too. Now do you understand? You're not safe here anymore, Miki."

Miki pulled her fingers from his and wrapped both arms around herself. "But no one knows. If you keep away from me, no one will."

"There are metaphysical ways for our child to be discovered. I'm sorry I didn't use better judgment when I loved you. I would have preferred to never involve you in my problems."

"Did you come here because of the child?" she asked, firming her lips against the trembling creeping through her body.

Alex shut his eyes for a moment, then glanced away. "I would never have exposed you to further danger. But that doesn't mean I wouldn't have wanted to come to you—if I'd been free to pursue you."

Tears slipped down her cheeks, and she ruthlessly scraped them away. "What am I supposed to believe? And who? The man who teased me and manipulated me into begging for release? Or the man who took me ruthlessly on the floor of that gazebo? I don't know who you are."

"And we haven't the luxury of time for you to find out. If you believe only this, I'll be satisfied for now—you aren't safe. Our child isn't safe." He held out his hand.

Miki looked at his broad palm, his long fingers. So much strength resided in his hands. He could pull her from the bed, force her into her clothes, and make her come whether she wanted to or not.

He preferred her acquiescence. Miki's mind raced, turning over the possibilities. Since she'd entered his world, she'd operated on instinct, followed her curiosity. At this point, her lost past didn't seem nearly as intriguing as the future stretching before her—all resting in the palm of his hand.

She slipped her hand inside his, closing her eyes briefly when he squeezed hers in approval.

He didn't love her. Maybe he couldn't. But she belonged to him now. Connection was something she'd dreamed of finding. Instead, it had found her.

She climbed off the mattress, catching her breath when she found herself standing pressed against his body.

Glancing up, she caught a glimpse of some strong emotion darkening his gaze. He raised his hands to her face and tilted her chin upward with his fingers. His kiss was soft, a little tentative, and, after all the passionate ones they'd shared, somehow more meaningful. "I don't know what the future holds for us," he said softly, "but I want your happiness."

"You trapped me—whether you planned it or not," she said as she met his gaze with a glare. "But Alex . . . I don't really care. Promise me you mean to do right by me, and I'll be patient and wait to see how this plays out."

Alex kissed her hard, then pushed her gently away. "Clothes. Now!"

His impatience filled her with a restless, gnawing fear. His glances toward the sky outside her window had her wondering if the coming darkness was the reason for his concern.

"You didn't seem to be in a hurry today. Are you worried because it's getting dark?"

"The others need darkness to roam freely. It's when they hunt."

"That's all I needed to know," she muttered. "Could have given me a clue." She pulled on a pale blue T-shirt and blue jeans, then caught the running shoes he tossed. She got the message—be prepared for anything.

When they were both dressed, he walked around the apartment, closing windows, pulling curtains closed. Miki grabbed her jacket with its deep pockets and shrugged into it, scraping the keys from the hook beside the door.

As she locked the door behind them, she gave Alex a quick glance. "I have to tell my super I won't be back for a while."

Old Man Mouton opened his apartment door after unlocking the series of dead bolts he must have just installed. He peeked around the door and blinked at her, then his gaze widened on Alex. "Didn't I warn you 'bout closin' those windows?"

"I'm all right," Miki said, wondering how he'd guessed. "Just wanted you to know I'll be gone for a while."

"You find those monsters you been lookin' for?" he said, eyeing Alex with a hard glare.

Alex returned the look with a steady one of his own. "I'll do my best to keep her safe."

As they climbed down the stairs, Alex flashed a smile over his shoulder. "Looks like you're not so all alone after all."

Miki's steps felt lighter as she realized it was true.

* * *

The drive back to his apartment took longer than Alex would have liked. The few civilian vehicles rolling through the city were a target for every checkpoint. They pulled to a stop beside his building just after sunset.

"This where you live?" she asked, glancing up at the white-washed brick building with its wrought-iron balconies. "Nice."

"Glad you like it. You'll be staying here a while."

"Shouldn't I have packed some clothes?"

"I have some things in the apartment you can use," he murmured, not mentioning the fact that they were his mother's clothes, abandoned and forgotten when she'd been on the run from rogue vampires seeking to destroy her before she became pregnant—with him.

He passed his own doorway and headed straight for Simon's. The door opened just as they reached it. Simon wore his Templar's face, his beard neatly trimmed around his chin and mouth, his long hair brushing his shoulders. He wore olive jeans and a tee with a marijuana leaf on the front. Miki would probably think he looked like a member of a cult. Which he did. Just not any modern religious flavor of sects.

"Simon," Alex nodded and slipped quickly inside, pulling Miki behind him.

"What took you so long?" Simon asked, a sly smile stretching his lips beneath his dark moustache.

Alex ignored his jibe, knowing Simon already understood exactly what had kept him occupied all day. "I have something to show you."

"Come into my office. Bring Mikaela, too." Simon turned and led the way down the hallway to his office.

Miki gasped behind him. "How does he know my name?" she whispered.

"It's a long story. One I'm sure he'll tell you. Later."

Simon seated himself in a low-backed upholstered chair. "We haven't much time. Show me," he commanded, his fingers gripping the padded arms.

"I don't know why we have to do this," Alex muttered. "You've already lived this."

"You know well why we go through the motions. Something might have changed."

Alex lifted his chin toward another chair, beside Simon's desk. "Miki, have a seat. Don't be frightened by what you see."

He stepped behind Simon as the mage tilted his head to the side. Alex swept aside his long brown hair and bent close, closing his eyes to focus his thoughts on the dream he'd had, centering his mind on Inanna and the white palace in the midst of the sand dunes.

Then he inhaled, seeking the heated, heavy throb of Simon's heartbeat in the vein just beneath his skin at the side of his neck. He leaned closer, letting his fangs slide down from the roof of his mouth. Then he opened his jaws wide and sank into his mentor's flesh, ignoring Miki's loud gasp.

CHAPTER
17

Inanna paced the length of her bedchamber, wringing her hands while her father's old wizard stood stone-faced, watching. "He'll return any time now. You know what you must do?"

Ninshubur pulled the object from a roughly woven bag, brushing away straw. He set the base of the relic on a low table and carefully extracted the black crystal, polishing it with his sleeve before setting it on the base.

Inanna circled the table, staring at the dark orb clutched in the talons of a dragon's claw. "You're sure this will work?"

"We have only the promise Irkalla made to you."

"My sister hates me," Inanna muttered, her stomach knotting with tension. "Anything can happen."

"I told you that you were being reckless, foolish to bid a

favor from the Underworld. Why could you not be satisfied with the child you have?"

Inanna had asked herself the same thing a dozen times. The greed for power, to increase her stature among the Born, had driven her, forcing her to take extreme measures.

"I must have a female child," she said. Then, and only then, could she destroy the abomination she'd bred. Her daywalking son made her shudder. Born with memories that looked back on her every misdeed, he'd poisoned her husband against her, cutting at the foundation of their fragile relationship with cautionary tales of her manipulations.

Dumuzi no longer looked at her with lust and love. He kept to his own chambers, openly cavorting with whores rather than bedding her.

Not that she'd deprived herself of blood or sex. Still, his insult could not be ignored. He'd even refused her offer to turn him. They'd never shared the strongest of blood-bonds, because she'd left him human during her season, but he would have been tied to her just the same.

Yet he'd refused, preferring to age and spend his days with their son.

Their whispered conversations, halting when she'd approached, and the long hours—even days—they'd spent away from the palace, had only served to deepen her anger.

They'd forced her to make this devil's deal. With her sister.

Irkalla had disappeared all those years ago after spying on them from the garden, only to reappear when the wizard had sent prayers to the demon's world on Inanna's behalf, asking that she might conceive another child to replace the creature she'd born with Dumuzi, opening a doorway between the realms for Inanna to enter and offer her plea.

To say that Inanna had been dismayed to see her sister standing beyond the portal after all those years was an understatement. And to see her bedecked in priceless gemstones and rich silks had sent her into a silent fury. "*Where have you come from?*" she'd asked, as the whirling portal had pulsed behind her.

"*Where your plotting sent me,*" Irkalla had said silkily, her sloe eyes glinting with dark humor. "*I prayed for a means of revenge. I prayed for the return of my one true love. You have been long in giving me the means.*"

"*I did not summon you.*"

"*You thought The Master would attend you?*" Irkalla's head had canted, amusement curving her lush lips. "*Did you think he would be the one to fill your womb?*"

Inanna had felt her spine stiffen. She had indeed hoped the most powerful of the demons would have been the one to grant her wish.

Irkalla had tsked. "*Sister, you still overreach your destiny. You will be given a second season, another chance to breed—with a human bond-mate.*"

Inanna's teeth had ground tight. Not what she'd wanted, but she would accept the offer. Anything to rid herself of her spawn. "*What will be the price?*"

Irkalla had smiled. "*I think you know. One cannot enter the Underworld and hope to escape, unless she lures another soul to take her place.*"

Inanna had sucked in a deep breath. "*After all this time, you still desire him? He has grown old.*"

"*He will be given another form. Made demon.*"

Knowing she could not withdraw her plea and hope to escape this dimension, Inanna had stared at her sister, her twin, feeling as though the heat and suffocating air of this terrible place would consume her if she didn't escape quickly. "*What must I do?*"

Irkalla had given her the relic and the instructions for its use. Now, it sat upon a table in her bedchamber. Once she opened the door, one soul would have to pass through the portal. It would not be hers.

She pulled a silken rope to ring the bell and bring a chambermaid to attend her. When the girl bowed her way inside, Inanna asked for her husband to attend her.

Dumuzi arrived moments later, looking annoyed, dust still clinging to his boots and ankles. He halted when he saw the aging wizard inside her room. "What do you want?" he asked, his tone curt.

When they'd first wed, he hadn't spoken to her in such harsh tones. He'd been attentive, insatiable. She would never admit to missing the forceful warrior. "Can a wife not request the company of her husband?" she asked, her voice sliding like silk.

Still handsome, despite the years that had carved harsh lines around his mouth and the corners of his eyes, she felt a moment's sensual thrill at the lift of one of his dark brows as his gaze swept her body.

Knowing she retained a remarkable beauty, she touched her bottom lip with her tongue, wetting it. Perhaps she would take him one last time. . . .

Impatience stamped his cold features. "I'm tired and dusty, Inanna. Can this wait?"

She glanced back at the wizard. "We are done."

The wizard raised the crystal, warming it in his hands, and began the incantation Irkalla had included with the relic.

Dumuzi's glance slammed into hers. His mouth opened to speak, but suddenly a glimmering circle, like a vertical pool of pale blue water, opened beside him. His head turned to peer inside, and long, slithering arms reached through to wrap around his legs and arms, pulling him toward the opening.

His scream was sucked into the glowing circle as his body disappeared. The light blinked out and the room looked as it had before, undisturbed by the bright storm that had engulfed it moments before.

Inanna let out a breath, staring at the place where Dumuzi had disappeared.

The door to her bedchamber opened and her son stepped inside. "Where is father?" he said, his gaze wary and hard as he eyed his mother.

"Gone, son," she said. "You just missed him." She smiled briefly, knowing one more task lay ahead of her before she could seek her next mate.

Alex withdrew his teeth, breathing hard and trembling as he clasped the backs of Simon's shoulders. "The bitch! She consigned her husband to Hell and murdered her own son. Why could I not see it before?"

Simon reached back to pat his hand. "This memory was particularly well guarded. Perhaps by Inanna herself. What woman would want to remember her own hideous crimes?"

Feeling sick to his stomach, Alex strode to the window overlooking the boulevard, staring sightlessly out into the darkness. "I hate that they live inside me now."

"Alex," Simon said softly, "the memories give you infinite power. You have delivered us the means to defeat her."

Alex's gaze swung back to Simon, whose lips curved into a half smile. "You mean the black crystal? Can it be used again? Do you think she still has it?"

"With her thirst for power, do you really believe Inanna would ever let such a powerful instrument out of her possession?"

"Of course not. How will we find it?"

"Now that I know what I seek, the rest should be simple. But I'll need certain herbs for such a spell."

Alex straightened, knowing his moment had finally arrived. Seven centuries of waiting and preparing, and now he had to react on the fly. "We don't have any time to lose. Inanna has more help than she wants in broadening her search for me. I can almost feel them closing in around me."

Simon's expression sharpened, seeming to gauge his determination. "You have your special key. You can escape at a moment's notice."

Alex drew his lips into a snarl. "I don't want to run and hide. I want to face her, to confront the whole damn council. They all hold responsibility for helping her maintain her power through murder. Other males have been born, yet none survived."

"Only you."

Alex caught sight of Miki's expression. Her green eyes were narrowed, but she leaned forward in her chair, curious and probably confused. But where was the fear? "Miki, you'll remain here in Simon's home. You should be safe."

Simon nodded, pushing himself up from the chair. "I won't be gone long, but Alex, you must get to Nicolas right away. Let him know it's time for him to make a choice. He has access to her."

Alex felt his jaw grind tight. "Do you think he's ready? Could he really do Inanna harm?"

"He loves Chessa. There is no other choice."

Alex stepped around the chair and reached down, pulling Miki up into his arms. "I know you're feeling a little lost," he said, smoothing his hands over her back. "Bear with us. Don't go out. I don't need to be worrying about you."

Miki bracketed his face with both hands. "Alex, I only caught part of what the heck's going on here, but I'm not dumb. You both look worried as hell. I'll be here when you get back."

His kiss was hard and over way too soon. Without a backward glance, he headed to his car. A stop by his parents' house for a couple more reinforcements, then he'd go straight to *Ardeal.*

The time had finally come to beard the lioness in her den.

* * *

Nicolas dragged the end of the leather belt down Inanna's slender back. "Tell me, *Mistress*," he said softly, "can you hold back your cries?"

"If that's what you wish," she replied in mock submission, her buttocks flexing, anticipating the sting of the leather that had already produced a thin trickle of cream to coat her inner thighs.

The ancient bitch hadn't a clue how much he hated her. She thought this was a sexy game he played. He lashed out, leaving a long red mark that spanned both cheeks.

Air hissed between her teeth, but her jaw tightened, and her brows lowered in pretended rage. She flung back her head, letting her hair settle along her shoulders like a pretty mane, and stared straight ahead.

While she bit her lips to still her cries, Nicolas didn't curb his anger or the strength of his blows. He let the belt fall fast and hard—snapping the leather to raise welts that crisscrossed her tender bottom until her breaths gusted fast in jagged sobs. The raised, reddened stripes gave him a deep, growling satisfaction, but they only assuaged a small part of the bitter enmity he found welling inside him.

Inanna had lured his brother and himself into her realm, seducing Armand with the promise of a higher purpose to serve, seducing Nicolas himself with a glimpse of life served with endless lust and happiness. Both promises had proved empty.

Armand had been murdered, his body invaded by the beast, who'd used the face they'd shared as a means to seduce Nicolas's wife, who'd had no clue she'd lain down with a demon.

Inanna had then failed to steer his sweet wife, Anaïs, from destroying herself after The Devourer had raped her, never offering her another option. Instead, Inanna had waited in the shadows after Nicolas had pulled Anaïs from the sunshine to offer to fill all the lonely places in his soul.

Yet Nicolas admitted he shared responsibility. He hadn't wanted to look too closely at Inanna's actions and motives because he'd been alone, without family for solace. He'd stayed with the powerful matriarch, becoming her paramour, her right hand as she'd dragged the clan and the monster's sarcophagus to the New World to find a place they could rule without competition and without long memories of what she'd done.

Now, because he'd finally fallen in love again, finally found the woman who would be his last love, he could no longer turn a blind eye to her machinations. He would not continue to service her and serve her ambition.

Nicolas gave Inanna's bottom a casual, passionless caress, noting the warmth beneath his palm. "Open your legs wider. I would see whether you've learned your lesson."

She stomped her feet apart but raised her bottom, inviting his inspection. Her labia were swollen and moist. Her clit peeked from beneath its hood, slick and red.

Nicolas dangled the belt between her legs, then flicked it upward, catching her pussy with a sharp, glancing slice.

Inanna screamed, and her knees buckled. She caught herself and straightened her knees, her legs and buttocks quivering as she waited for another slap.

Instead, Nicolas rolled the belt into a tight circle and pushed it inside her vagina.

Inanna moaned, but her cunt clasped the balled, warmed leather, holding it inside her.

Nicolas pushed two fingers behind the roll and pulled the buckle to unwind the belt, until it finally slipped free. With the leather slippery from her juices, he painted her thighs with quick, wet flicks before giving her one last sharp crack against her cunt.

He dropped the belt on the bed in front of her, then guided his cock to trail the crevice between her buttocks. He paused at her tight back entrance. "Shall I fuck you here, *Mistress*?" He slapped her with his penis.

Her buttocks squeezed, trapping the head of his cock, then releasing it as she widened her stance again. "*Please*, Nico. Fuck my ass," she hissed.

Gathering his cock inside his fist, he held it against her tiny puckered hole and flexed his hips, pushing against her opening until it eased around the blunt tip of his cock.

Heat surrounded him, and he pumped inside, pushing past the ring that banded his cock, squeezing around him like the caress of a tiny mouth. Finally mounted, he began to stroke inside, tunneling deeper, closing his eyes to savor the clasping, pulsing sensations that engulfed him.

He speared deep, ignoring the shudders and whimpers that racked her slender body, concentrating instead on the pleasurable sensations that stoked a smoldering fire in his loins. Inanna didn't provide him pleasure; any woman's ass would have done.

His hands clutched her warm bottom, his fingers splaying and digging into her soft flesh to pull her buttocks apart so he could sink deeper. His hips pistoned hard and sharp, thrusting his cock into hot tissue while his balls banged her slippery cleft.

Inanna's head sank further between her shoulders and she rose on her toes, tilting her buttocks higher, inviting him to slam inside her body. She rocked on the balls of her feet, forward and back, countering his quickening motions, gasping and grunting with each of his forceful strokes.

It wasn't enough. Not enough punishment. She enjoyed it too much.

Nicolas pulled out and stepped back, smiling mirthlessly when Inanna's legs crumpled and she knelt, breathing hard beside the end of the bed.

He tore the scarves from her wrists and bent to lift her from the floor, tossing her into the middle of the bed. He leapt onto the mattress and stared down at her, letting his rage paint his features with heat, letting her see the glinting anger in his eyes.

Her gaze widened, and she scrambled backwards, trying to escape, but he planted a foot in the center of her belly to pin her. "Open your legs wide, *Mistress*."

Inanna's entire body quivered and her lips trembled, but she slowly unfolded her legs and opened them wide atop the plum and gold coverlet.

Nicolas reached for the long, scrolled finial at the end of one bedpost and pulled it free. He knelt quickly, lifting her thighs and pressing them forward until her knees met her chest. Then he placed the end of the finial between her folds and shoved it inside her vagina.

Inanna's lips drew away from her teeth, her face tightening against the pain of the harsh invasion, then easing as he pulled it out and shoved it deep again. Her cunt sucked it inside, clasping moistly to hold it.

Nicolas cupped her buttocks, lifting them. He placed his thumbs on either side of her back entrance, stretching it open, then leaned toward her, fitting his cock against her and pushing inside. With the wooden end of the finial snug against the top of his groin, he began to stroke into her again, ramming the finial into her cunt, and his cock deep inside her rectum.

Inanna keened, her hands clutching the backs of her thighs, her knuckles whitening as he hammered her. He drew his knees closer to her body, rolling her hips upward so that both entrances pointed toward the ceiling and he dropped his hips hard, slapping his groin against the slick saddle of her sex with each harsh thrust.

"Nicooooo!" she screamed as her orgasm exploded, tightening her asshole around his dick, and cutting off his own release with her strong inner spasms. Nicolas shuddered, continuing to slam into her, while her cries grew hoarse, until at last the clasp of her inner muscles eased and cum jetted from his cock deep into her ass.

Nicolas fell over her, pressing her knees tighter against her chest while she gasped and shuddered beneath him, her screams dying away into noisy sobs.

Suddenly, he went still, his gaze slamming into hers as silence fell around them. "Inanna," he said softly, "what have you done?"

Her gaze shuttered, her features tightened as wariness crept across them. "What do you mean? I wasn't the one doing anything."

Nicolas planted both fists into the mattress beside her shoulders and leaned closer, trapping her with his cock still embedded in her ass and the wooden dildo shoved deep against her womb. "As close as Pasqual has hovered around you these past few days, I expected him to burst through those doors at your screams. Why didn't he?" he asked softly, a clawing fear tightening every fiber of muscle in his body.

Her mouth opened, perhaps to tell him a lie, but his gaze stabbed, daring her to try.

Her shrug was a casual affectation. "He does what you will not bring yourself to do, lover."

"What have you done?" he repeated between clenched teeth.

She licked her lips, then curved them in a little smile. "Pasqual is making a sweep. Gathering up the traitors who harbor the daywalker."

Nicolas pulled slowly out of her body, his muscles quivering hard because he fought the temptation to shake her, to fly at her and rip open her throat. "What traitors?" he asked carefully.

"For a start . . . Simon."

His breath caught. "You've made a mistake."

"We don't think so." Inanna's chin came up as she lowered her legs slowly and reached between them to pull out the finial. "And why would you care? You have said yourself he's no longer your friend."

"I would not have him harmed."

"And he won't be, if he cooperates. You know yourself that he protects the daywalker. All signs point to a powerful mage—he is the strongest on this continent."

"And that didn't give you a moment's pause? Do you know what he can do to you? What his Order will do to you? They have always been neutral."

Her lips twisted in an ugly snarl. "He crossed the line when he helped Natalie escape. You think I didn't figure that out? And that Chessa helped her and the human? And now he aids this abomination—this daywalker."

Her expression turned remorseful, pleading—so quickly

that it raised the hairs on the back of his neck. "The secrets you've kept from me, Nico," she whispered. "They make me weep. I had hoped you would see how dangerous your path is and that you would seek my help to make amends."

Nicolas shook his head, disbelieving. "You conspired with Pasqual. Did you use my own Security Force?"

"Those who are resentful of the rogues you brought. They are with him now."

Nicolas rolled from the bed, striding straight for the door. He had to warn Simon . . . and Alex.

"You won't be allowed to leave. It is already too late."

With his hand on the doorknob, Nicolas leaned his head against the door, calling himself a fool. He'd let her do this, manipulate his emotions to distract him. "You purposely seduced me. Made me linger here so that he could sneak away and take care of your dirty little business."

"I did what I must," she said hoarsely. "Tell me you didn't enjoy it. When this is all over, you will be glad, lighter of heart. I know how keeping secrets from me weighs on you."

He glanced over his shoulder to meet her gaze. "If you believe I've betrayed you, why not just kill me?"

"Because I love you, Nico." Her smile was beatific, made eerier because he knew she meant it. "Because you're mine. *Forever*. For now, go back to your Chessa. You will be called when the *sabat* reconvenes. Darling, think hard on which side you will choose. You risked much for the power you craved. Do not waste it. You must side with those who know better, who've lived longer than you."

Because he needed to think, as well as the freedom to move around the compound, he nodded and left the room . . . and her alive.

CHAPTER

18

Miki didn't mind being left behind in Simon's home. Her curiosity prickled into hyper-drive as she circumvented his apartment. There were too many intriguing secrets for her to discover among the books and objects crammed into his shelves and on every table in the sprawling, high-ceilinged rooms. Books and papers lay opened everywhere, long passages underscored in red. History books sat next to astrological charts. Metaphysical treatises and mythological works with dog-eared pages and notes scribbled in the margins held more clues to Simon's preoccupation with the occult. Some books were dated editions; some were so old that the yellowed pages spoke of their age.

The scent of dusty books, sandalwood incense,

and a dozen burning beeswax candles, as well as a pleasant cologne and male musk, permeated the place. Simon had lived here a while.

His scent, his personality, was stamped on every frightening and playful object. In a cupboard behind his desk, she found bones—small animal bones, human finger bones, some intact, some crushed and splintered. Mortar dishes held ground powders and dust; she guessed that some of the "spells" he concocted used more than the herbs he hunted now.

She didn't feel the slightest bit guilty rummaging through his things. She'd been invited to make herself at home, but, as far as she could recall, she'd never been in such a curious one. She found a drawer filled with small cloth bags and opened a few to find crystals and polished gemstones. Everything pointed to an inescapable and tantalizing conclusion—Simon must be some sort of witch.

Besides his strange collection and the aromas that tickled her nose, there was also a subtle femininity underlying everything. A mirror perched above a sofa—ornate, gilded, a little ostentatious—hung below Simon's height. Feminine toiletries were bunched on a mirrored tray on the dresser in his bedroom, immaculately dusted, as though waiting for the woman to return to pick them up and apply them. A lady's robe in thick embroidered silk hung on the back of the master bathroom door.

Miki pressed her nose to the silk and picked up a fading floral scent. Simon's lady-friend was a visitor in his life, not a true companion.

His choice of pets gave her pause. She gave the bird clinging to a natural tree branch perch in the living room a wide berth, because she felt uncomfortable beneath its constant stare.

Something about the small raptor's posture made it seem . . . more than a bird. Intelligence gleamed in its golden eyes.

"We'll be fine," Miki said, "so long as you keep to your perch. Any beaks come pecking my way and we'll have a problem."

Small and hawklike with a curved beak, the bird flapped its black-spotted brown wings, then settled down again to preen its feathers.

"So long as we understand each other," Miki murmured and continued her exploration.

She wondered if she'd find Alex's home as interesting, as filled with clues about his life and interests. Had he lived as long as it appeared Simon had to have collected so many ancient books and relics? She hadn't thought to ask him.

Recalling what little she did know made her grow appalled with herself. She was a reporter, a writer with a natural inclination to observe and question everything around her. It was how she'd accomplished so much since her awakening. Curiosity about her world, as well as the mystery that had made her, was what had fed her and driven her to explore.

Yet she'd failed to learn so many basic facts about the man she'd made love with numerous times since they'd met last night. Since he was born to a vampire, did that mean he had family? Did they live nearby?

Was he married? *Did* vampires marry? If he'd lived a long life, how many wives or lovers might he have had?

How did he support himself? Did he have a job, or did he just frequent vampire parties and seek blood donors to fill his appetite to the exclusion of anything else? He'd slyly mentioned once before that those who lived long had the time to accumulate wealth—was he rich? Would he use that wealth to fund an endless orgy of blood and lust?

Somehow, she didn't think he was a hedonist. Something about him spoke of a man with a deep well of compassion and drive. When this was all over, when he'd conquered whatever demons he sought now, she'd have to ask him. Maybe she should make a list. The questions just kept coming.

She wondered if he'd been as curious about her and what he might have thought about the lack of clutter inside her own small apartment. What had he made of her lack of "things" that defined a person? Since she was still rediscovering her own tastes, she'd refrained from decorating or collecting. Beyond the supplies and equipment she needed to pursue the one talent she'd uncovered rather quickly, her clothes and furniture were strictly utilitarian and comfortable.

Maybe in the end there wasn't really anything all that interesting to learn about herself. After all, she wasn't a Born vampire or a re-hatched *Revenant*. Maybe she should just be satisfied she had a foot in the door into the adventure of a lifetime.

After snooping through everything short of Simon's underwear drawer, Miki strolled back into the living room, paused to pick up a candle, and settled down in an armchair with one of the tantalizing mystical books she'd pilfered from his library.

Just when she was about to admit the archaic language stumped her completely, scuffling footsteps sounded from beyond the short hallway leading to the door of the apartment.

Thinking it might be Simon, she set aside the book and started to rise.

An explosion of noise—the crack of a splintering door, shouts as armed men spilled into the room—froze her where she stood. Before she even formed the thought that maybe she should run, a streak of gray flashed toward her, halting suddenly to reveal a man dressed in black SWAT-like clothing.

She recognized him from the party. He'd mingled in the crowd, his dark, alert gaze sweeping over the many guests, but never resting long. Tonight, his dark brown hair was scraped back in a ponytail. His harsh, but handsome, features were set, emotionless; his eyes stared at her as though she'd been a curious insect—and just about as insignificant.

A shiver bit her spine.

He stepped so close that his boots touched the tips of her tennis shoes. "Where is the mage?" he asked in a thick Cajun accent.

"Mage?" *That's what Simon is?* "Not here," she said, trying to catch a full breath, but he stood too close, looked too lethal for her to do anything but hold herself rigid and pray he didn't take an instant dislike to her.

He shot a glance over his shoulder at the men fanning out around the apartment. Already a couple were returning from the bedroom and office, shaking their heads.

"Grab the goddamn bird." His gaze narrowed on her. "Perhaps we should leave him our callin' card."

The way he said it—low and rasping, a glint of true evil darkening his eyes while his lips thinned into a smile—had the hairs on her arms and neck lifting.

A feminine hand slipped over the top of the vampire's shoulder. The hand pulled him back, but he resisted. He shot an acid-filled glance behind him.

Miki broke with the man's eyes only to lock gazes with the

woman who'd worn the crystal-studded blue dress the night before.

The woman lifted an eyebrow and stared him down.

The man backed up a step and the woman walked around him, leaned close to Miki, and drew in her scent. Her head drew back quickly, and she knelt, her nose skimming down Miki's breasts to the juncture of her thighs.

Shocked into stillness, Miki could only wonder at her crude behavior.

Tension straightened the woman's shoulders as she slowly rose. "There was a man at the estate last night. A vampire who remained aloof from the others. She wears his scent," she said, her voice roughening.

"Do you think he might be the daywalker?"

She shrugged as though the answer didn't matter. "Perhaps. But if he is, she might be the bait we need to trap him. Do not harm her." Her gaze returned to Miki, narrowing.

Miki felt as though she'd been marked somehow, that the woman's pointed stare held more than curiosity—her enmity was a physical thing that washed over Miki in a hot-cold rush of dread.

The dark-haired man flashed a feral smile. "We'll bring her along. If she's not important, at least we can have a snack."

Miki swallowed hard. The polite but debauched crowd she'd circulated in last night hadn't prepared her for the icy reality of being at the mercy of vampires. She'd seen them move— she didn't have any hope of escaping them. She knew their strength could easily overpower her if she resisted. She had no choice. Although she knew the wise path would be to keep quiet and not raise anyone's hackles, her jaw came unhinged in her nervousness. "I don't suppose you're going to tell me where you're taking me and why? I really do have a life to get back to—you know, friends and family who will be wondering what's keeping me so long. They might even call the police."

But the one who'd spit out the orders was already storming out, the tall woman in his wake.

"You gonna give me a clue?" she whispered to herself. "Guess not."

As another man dressed in black wrapped his large hand around her upper arm and dragged her forward, her only silent thought was, *Thank God Alex isn't here.*

Gabriella quivered with rage. The scent of sex clung to the human woman.

Alex, the bastard, had played her. He'd made her believe he wasn't like all the other vampire whores who fed and fucked whenever their appetites twisted their insides. But he'd left her, promised he'd seek her out—had let her believe he'd needed the release an old lover would give him.

She should have remembered his tryst with the demon-whore—the one he'd seduced after he'd left her bed in order to get his hands on his precious stone. Alex pretended he held himself above his instincts, that the teachings of his monkish mentor had made him more discerning, less ruled by his baser nature. What a goddamn hypocrite.

Outside the apartment building, she held back while the Security Force escorted the woman and the mage's familiar into paneled trucks. Pitch darkness shrouded their movements and hid their kidnapping from the other tenants in the building.

Pasqual strode to the lead vehicle and shot her a questioning glance over his shoulder as he held open the door. "Are you coming?"

Gabriella didn't like Pasqual. Didn't like the way he looked at her, as though he wished he could carve out her heart. Something dark and repulsive lurked inside him. She was glad she didn't have to share another long, tense drive with him. It was time to shake her fur loose.

"I've found a scent trail," she said, keeping her anger with Alex banked. As volatile as she felt at the moment, she might let something slip to alert this cagey vampire that she knew more than she admitted. "I'll follow it for a while. I can make my own way back."

"If you find him, what will you do?"

"Deliver the message," she said, with a small, tight smile.

When the vehicles pulled away, she stepped into the walled courtyard beside the apartment building and stripped off the borrowed uniform. Alex's scent was strong. She'd already noted where his car was parked, and she thought she had a good chance of following it to wherever he'd escaped. She'd find him before Inanna's henchmen did.

What happened after that was entirely up to how well Alex explained himself. The human couldn't be important—she had to be a diversion, a sex toy. Surely he wouldn't be so foolish as to elevate her to their world.

Alex waited impatiently inside the Broussard home as his parents armed themselves. He wondered at the discipline they'd exercised these last strained months as they'd waited for the events that would cast their former selves into the eye of a storm they'd escaped when they'd crossed through a portal and landed in Scotland during the Middle Ages to bide their time and raise him.

How had his tender mother resisted the urge to warn her

foster parents and her college friend of the attacks that would take their lives? Instead, they'd waited on the outskirts of New Orleans, biding their time until no chance remained of them catching a glimpse of themselves as they stumbled through their harrowing journey to find each other.

Simon had stayed in close contact with all of them crisscrossing his own path, using his memory, or perhaps the journals Alex suspected he kept, to ensure he didn't meet himself coming or going. Simon wasn't certain what might happen if their paths did collide, but he feared the consequences might be too great to risk satisfying his own curiosity.

Rene entered the kitchen, where Alex had helped himself to coffee. His father's stern jaw looked like granite as he closed the buckle on his utility belt and sank a handgun into the holster.

"You know," Alex said dryly, "bullets will only piss them off."

"It's backup," Rene bit out, lifting a short, tactical crossbow from the kitchen table. What he didn't need to say was that their weapons would be the only backup they could expect.

Alex knew from his father's terse words and his jerking movements that he was worried.

"I want to hit Simon's one last time. To make sure he found what he needs for the spell," Alex muttered, not liking how long he'd already been away. Miki should be safe, but she was probably frightened and questioning why she'd listened to anything he'd had to say.

He hadn't mentioned her to Rene and Natalie, telling himself there was time for introductions later.

Natalie strolled inside, dressed in dark, close-fitting camouflage, as Alex and Rene were. "It's odd. Seems like we've waited for this moment forever, and now it's still too soon."

Rene hooked an arm around her waist and pulled her close. "I wish you'd stay here," his deep voice rumbled.

Natalie slid her hand along his cheek. "Our son needs us both there. We're going to be sorely outnumbered as it is."

Rene kissed her, his face slanting to capture her mouth.

Natalie gave a sexy little moan that never failed to make Alex uncomfortable—no matter how many centuries he'd witnessed the passion that still sprang hot between them.

"We'll have Nic and anyone who stands with him," Alex said, wrinkling his nose and wishing they'd leave their little displays of affection strictly private.

Rene lifted his head and one dark eyebrow. "You've already gotten his promise?"

"Of course not. The man's every bit as stubborn as Chessa."

The two shared crooked smiles, both being intimately familiar with just how stubborn and volatile Chessa Tomas could be. "Sounds like you and Nic have bonded."

Alex shrugged. "Share a couple punches and a couple women—we're brothers now."

Natalie raised an eyebrow. "A couple of women?"

Alex winced at the slip. She already knew about Chessa. The last thing he needed was a twenty-questions interview all the way to *Ardeal*. "Ah . . . we should head out."

Entering the garage just off the kitchen, Alex pressed the button and waited impatiently for his parents to follow. When the door rose, Natalie and Rene filed out, heading straight for the car.

"*Merde!*" Rene suddenly spat, pulling his weapon from his holster and crouching low, his gaze and weapon pointing toward the mouth of the garage.

Alex glanced over his shoulder to find a wolf standing at the entrance. "Rene, no!" he said, reaching out to pull down his father's arm. "She's a friend."

"A friend?" Natalie asked, her voice tight.

Alex approached Gabriella slowly, ignoring her menacing growl. "Gabi, sweetheart, why are you here?"

His mother gasped behind him. Alex hoped she didn't take aim on the wolf as well. She knew the whole story of Gabriella's attempted assassination.

Alex continued toward Gabriella, crooning softly. "I need you to transform, now."

Gabriella's growl cut off and she shook her coat, her form stretching, morphing into her gorgeous human skin. She rose slowly, eyeing the pair behind his shoulder with undisguised distrust.

Alex reached out and caught her hair, winding it around his fist and pulling her close. "Why are you here?"

Gabriella shook free of his hold and took a step back. "I have just one question. Who is the woman you stashed at the mage's house?"

His whole body froze. "You've seen Miki? What the hell were you doing at Simon's apartment?"

Gabriella's eyes glittered in the moonlight. "Who is she to you?"

He thought about lying, but only for a moment. Gabriella deserved better. "She's the mother of my child."

Gabi's mouth opened, then snapped shut. Her back stiffened. "How inconvenient for you," she bit out. "She's been misplaced."

"What are you talking about? Dammit, Gabi. No games. What's happened?"

Gabriella stepped back, shaking her head and her shoulders.

Alex lunged for her, taking her to the concrete. "Transform, and I swear I'll let them kill you." He straddled her naked body, holding her arms above her head.

"You said you would seek me out. You led me to believe we would be something to each other."

"We are, Gabi. *We're allies. Friends.*"

"With *fucking* benefits?"

Then he saw the hint of moisture welling in her gold-brown eyes. "I didn't plan this, I swear," he said gently. "I'm sorry, but you really need to get over it and quick. Tell me what the hell has happened."

"Why should I help you?" she asked, her voice ragged.

"Because you still have your clan's interests to uphold. We have a business arrangement."

"That's all I am to you?"

"It's all I can offer you now."

Her lips trembled a moment before she drew them tight against her teeth. "I fucking hate you, Alexander Broussard."

"Hate me all you like. But fear me, too. You know what I am, but you have no clue what I can do to you and yours."

Gabriella swallowed, gasping beneath him as she struggled fruitlessly to ease from his grip. Finally, she fell still. Her head turned to the side, her eyes breaking with his gaze. "Inanna sent a patrol to capture you. I accompanied it, hoping to warn you. To somehow intervene."

"Was anyone harmed?"

"The mage wasn't there. But they've taken the woman and his familiar to *Ardeal*. I convinced Pasqual not to kill your *girl-friend* on the spot. Told them she might have value to you."

"Do they know who I am?"

"Only that you attended the party under their noses last night."

Alex swept down and kissed her cheek. "Thank you."

Her head turned, her gaze locking with his. "You're welcome. Now will you get the hell off me?"

"Will you promise not to run away?"

"Are you inviting me to come with you?"

"You said you wanted to see Inanna taken down."

Her slow smile this time was genuine. "That would be a hell of a consolation prize."

Alex grinned and climbed off Gabriella, then offered her a hand up. "You won't need clothing. Just get in the car and we'll keep the AC down."

Rene walked up behind him as Gabriella took a seat in the back next to his mother. "You trust her?"

"Of course not. But she will help us to a point."

Rene shook his head. "And I thought Nicolas was a whoring bastard. When did you have time to screw a human woman?"

Alex snorted, unwilling to spill the whole story with Gabriella so close. "You drive. I need to keep my eyes on Mother. Her trigger finger gets a little itchy around *weres*."

The ride back to Simon's was made in total silence. Simon was waiting on the side of the street as they pulled up. His glance snagged on Gabriella, then returned to Alex. "I found what I need."

"Want to come with us?"

Simon smiled. "I'll be there an hour ahead of you."

"Should I fly?"

Simon shook his head. "Mikaela and my kestrel are fine for now. I'll need the time to locate the relic and prepare the spell. Be vigilant. Do you have a plan for when you get there?"

"A brilliant plan. I'm walking through the front gates." Alex looked for a sign of disapproval, but Simon only smiled. "Guess you already knew that."

Simon lifted a hand, and then winked out.

"I fuckin' hate it when he does that," Rene growled.

Alex shook his head. "He always likes having the last word."

Back inside the car, he sat sideways in the seat to keep an eye on the females in the backseat. Natalie's gaze never wavered from Gabriella.

"These are your parents?" Gabriella asked, her gaze slipping from Natalie and Rene and back to Alex. "I can see the resemblance."

"Surprised I have any?" he asked wryly.

"I guess I'm just surprised you are all here in New Orleans. Inanna would be furious to know you've been right under her nose all along. The *sabat* was right to question her authority."

"None of those women would have known any better."

"Is this all you have to do battle? An old mage and your mom and dad?"

Alex smiled. "I have the truth."

"And you think that makes me feel better about the fact I'm riding into Hell with you?" Gabriella asked, although she didn't look particularly worried.

Alex loved her confidence. "You can always claim I kidnapped you."

She arched an eyebrow. "If things go sour for you, don't think I won't. I'll just take a walk to the other side."

"Gabi . . ."

"Don't give me that look. I don't want your pity."

"Seems you've been a very busy man, son," Rene drawled. "Gonna tell us all about it?"

Alex turned in his seat, satisfied for now that the women wouldn't be going for each other's throats.

CHAPTER

19

Natalie, Rene, and Gabriella parked the car alongside the highway, deciding it would be safer to hump it the rest of the way to the compound, as Alex stepped in front of the closed gates and waited. While the radios buzzed the news, the trio jumped the fence at the rear of the compound. Or so that was how the scenario was supposed to work. Otherwise, they were screwed.

"Damn, I feel like a rock star," Alex said, pasting on a carefree smile as Pasqual and his crew surrounded him like army ants covering an elephant's carcass.

When Pasqual grabbed his arm to pull it back and cuff him, Alex resisted, balling his hand into a fist and holding up his arm, keeping it rigid.

Pasqual attempted once again to pull it down, but he couldn't budge it. His gaze narrowed with deadly intent.

Alex leaned close and whispered, "Kill me now and you'll have to face the wrath of the entire *sabat*. I'm here of my own free will, asshole. Now, do your job and escort me to them."

Pasqual bit out a low, filthy epithet, but he dropped Alex's arm and signaled to the men to surround him. As though they led a prisoner to his execution, they kept their gazes straight ahead, allowing themselves only quickly darting glances to satisfy their curiosity.

Alex made his own surreptitious assessment of the men leading him toward the house.

All Nicolas's men, but no doubt ones who'd been culled for their devotion to Inanna. Their loyalties would be tested in the next hour.

Alex drew a deep breath of the humid air and glanced around. How different *Ardeal* appeared as compared to the previous night.

Sure, the genteel, stately grounds surrounding the white Victorian mansion were still meticulously manicured, but lights didn't beckon visitors to the house; the doors weren't opened in welcome; and music and laughter didn't spill from the windows.

Drapes were pulled tight, and the lights inside were as muted as the noise.

Except for the crunch of booted feet on the pebbled driveway, there were no sounds. An expectant hush lay over the party escorting him and the people watching him from the windows of the house.

They expected blood to flow. *His.*

Despite the menace permeating the air, a dead calm settled

over him. For the first time in his life, Alex felt the swell of pride in his birth and a certainty that this was the moment of his destiny.

As they neared the house, the memories from the generations that preceded him crystallized, taking away his breath as he peered into the past—beyond Inanna and her attempt to seize a kingdom in ancient Sumer, all the way back to the birth of their species.

The stone that sat heavy at the base of his throat pulsed against his skin. Gifted by angels to protect him as a child, the carving on it held the secret of their conception: the mating of the *lilum*—a race of demons born to Lilith and her legion of demon lovers—and angels expelled from heaven for daring to defy God and his wish to elevate man above them.

"Explains the wings," he whispered, his steps slowing.

Which made them even less demon than he'd always supposed . . . perhaps they possessed the same potential for good or evil as Man.

A hand shoved between his shoulder blades to hurry him along.

Alex stuck his hands inside his pockets, and he briefly touched the crystal key to his private cavern. He curled his fingers away from it. He wouldn't escape. Now he didn't even want to escape whatever The Fates and God had planned.

Inanna would be served her punishment. Hopefully, he'd be there as witness and master strategist to recraft the Nation's ragged bonds into a force capable of facing the coming battle.

After he'd retrieved his woman.

The front doors opened wide, and he crossed the black and white marble tiles, heading for the chamber where the *sabat* waited.

Two files of armed guards lined up on either side of the chamber doors. Without hesitating, he stepped inside the shadowy room, his gaze sweeping the chamber, lighting briefly on Nicolas, whose face seemed set in stone, then landing on Inanna, who stared at him as though he were a creature who'd stepped out of her worst nightmare. They were seated at a black, round table with the other *sabat* members, men in SWAT gear standing beside every window and doorway. As though they could prevent intrusion or protect the members from his wrath.

Alex almost smiled—until he spied Miki standing beside a rustling canvas bag with her hands bound behind her.

Pasqual strode straight for her and took up position beside her, his hands sliding behind his back as he assumed a military stance.

Alex held Miki's glance for only a moment. He was unable to telegraph a message, but he hoped she knew how much he regretted bringing her into this.

Time for the game to begin.

Taking a fortifying breath, he glanced back at Inanna, whose beautiful face seemed to glow in the candlelight. *"Grandmère,"* he said with a slight inclination of his head.

"Don't you call me that," she hissed, her lips lifting into a snarl as her fingers tightened around the arms of her ebony chair.

"How kind of you to extend me this invitation."

Her contemptuous snort pleased him. However she might posture and pretend that she held all the power, he had her measure now. He let his gaze land on every member of the council, pausing to challenge each of them with a quick, dismissive glance.

"Stop with the theatrics," one of the council members spat.

Her dark eyes gleamed with satisfaction. "The only reason you aren't already dead is because we're curious."

"About me? I'm flattered," he drawled.

"Cecily," Inanna interrupted, "I'll handle this." Her gaze slid to Alex's, narrowing, then raking over his body. "I remember you. From last night."

"We met briefly."

"You attended our party. How did you gain entry?"

"I was invited by Erika."

The glittering anger in her eyes didn't dim at the mention of her murdered granddaughter. "Erika was never very selective," she murmured.

"Or discerning . . ."

"You think you're clever. And yet you walked right up to the gates. What did you think would happen?"

"That you'd throw a party for your prodigal grandson?"

A deep breath lifted her chest. "Before we decide whether to plan a feast," she snarled, "I would know your true nature." She settled back into her seat, her fingers twisting on the arms. "Please take off your shirt."

He snorted. "Now who's practicing theatrics? You know what I am." But he unbuttoned his shirt, stripping it down his arms. When he dropped it to the floor, he locked his gaze with Inanna and released his wings, letting them flare wide behind him, brushing away the guards who stood too close.

Gasps escaped from several of the *sabat* members.

When the din died down, Inanna asked, "Who is your mother? How have we missed her?"

"You were careless and lost her, Inanna. Just days ago."

Her chin lifted, and her lips thinned. "Natalie," she said evenly. Her gaze sliced to Nicolas, and she gave him a measuring, guarded look. To the others, she said, "Do you see why we seek Simon now? He's at the bottom of this abomination."

"I am Born. Not an abomination," Alex said, lifting his chin and pinning her with an emotionless stare. "Same as you."

"We must kill him," Cecily said, playing with her necklace.

Inanna looked her way but didn't respond. Her gaze again slipped to Nicolas.

"You hesitate, Inanna," Alex said softly.

"You sired Chessa's child," she said, responding to him, but still staring at Nicolas.

Cecily's mouth gaped. "Chessa is pregnant again? Why weren't we informed?"

Inanna gave the woman a dismissing wave of her hand. "It was very recent."

"We must destroy him," the woman seated beside Cecily said. "He upsets the balance of things, the order we've maintained."

Inanna's lips twisted. "Madrigal, you're shortsighted. He might prove useful."

Cecily's gaze narrowed on him. "As a stud?"

"The rogues hunted our offspring these past four decades and killed many of our breeders. Without him, we can't conceive enough to replenish our ranks. We can destroy him when we no longer have a use for him."

"Seems a little incestuous to me," Alex drawled.

"You fucked your father's best friend," Inanna bit out. "Don't tell me you have any scruples concerning whose womb you fill."

Alex kept his attention on Inanna and hoped like hell Miki didn't give away the secret she carried in her own belly. "Why should I cooperate?"

"I believe we hold something precious to you," she said,

nodding toward Miki. "If you would see her live a little while longer, you will cooperate."

Alex resisted the urge to follow her gaze to Miki, hoping the women would believe she didn't matter. All this talk of breeding made his skin crawl. He had no intentions of giving these bitches what they wanted, but he needed to stall for time. "You would share me with your council members?"

Inanna sat perfectly still for so long that the other members glanced toward her.

"Do you intend to keep him for yourself?" Cecily asked, her voice incredulous.

"Cecily," Alex said softly, "she fears what I might tell you if I were alone with you."

"Shut up," Inanna said, two bright spots of color darkening her cheeks.

Glancing at the rest of the council, he said, "Do you even know why you fear your male children?"

"You're stronger," the one called Madrigal said hesitantly. "Prone to dominate and to wage war." She looked to Cecily for approval before continuing, "We prefer rule by consensus. We're more civilized."

"It's a lie," he said flatly.

"Silence!" Inanna shouted. "Pasqual, take him out of here."

Into the quiet that followed her order came a deep masculine voice. "Perhaps," said Nicolas, "the council would find what he says to be needful before we decide his fate."

"Be careful, Nico," Inanna said, her voice rising toward the end with warning.

"You made him a member of this council, *Grandmère*," Cecily said sweetly. "Did you intend him to only second your every command?"

Inanna glanced wildly at Nicolas, whose gaze remained pinned on Alex. Her eyes began to fill.

Alex almost felt sorry for her, knowing she finally realized that Nicolas was no longer bonded to her. No longer hers to command.

Alex met Nicolas's gaze, careful to keep any emotion from revealing a relationship between them. "Male Born have unique gifts." He turned to Madrigal and bowed slightly. "It is true that we are marginally stronger than you, but we aren't unconquerable. We can also impregnate our partners, regardless of their species or fertility."

Encompassing the rest of the council with his gaze, he lifted his chin. "But the gift that makes us truly dangerous is our clear vision of the past . . . an innate ability that makes us more qualified to rule."

"Do you hear what he's saying? He thinks he should rule us all," Cecily exclaimed. "I told you he would upset everything we've worked to maintain."

"You've murdered to maintain your rank," Alex said, beginning to choke on the rage rising inside him. "Every one of you has participated in killing male progeny to ensure your own positions. *How greedy, how shortsighted.* You don't have the Nation's best interests at heart, only your own."

"What is the nature of this gift that you think makes you more suitable to rule?" Cecily asked, her nose sniffing.

"I inherited the memories of every one of my forebears. I can see into their pasts as if they were my own. My memory is longer than even Inanna's, richer, because it does not begin and end with you; it stretches beyond our species' birth."

"What advantage does that give you?" Cecily grated. "What

gift is that? The ability to bore us like an old man relating tales of his youth?"

"I know many useful things," he said slowly, turning to pin the ancient matriarch with a glare. "Don't I, Inanna?"

Her chin sank toward her chest, and her glare stabbed him. "Be quiet or I will kill you myself."

Alex ignored her threat, instead aiming a glance that included the entire group—even the *Revenants* standing around the room. "Aren't you the least bit curious about why the *Grizashiat*, The One Who Devours, is so intent on stalking Inanna? Here's a demon, freed from Hell. He could go anywhere, operate in the open as anyone, but he tracks her here, torments her by leaving bodies at her door to make sure she knows he's coming for her. Why?"

"He's a beast," Inanna gritted out, her eyes flashing a warning. "He wants revenge for me imprisoning him so long."

"You know that's a lie," Alex said, impaling her with a glance. "He comes for you because you're responsible for him being made demon in the first place—he wants revenge against you and yours because you gave him to Hell and murdered his son in order to remove any challenge to your authority."

Inanna's hand went to her throat. Her eyes widened and grew moist. She opened her mouth, perhaps to deny the charge, but she slowly closed it.

Cecily's head swung to Inanna and she leaned away. "You are responsible for his existence?"

Sensing that Inanna's defenses were crumbling around her, Alex drew a deep breath and let his wings flare again, knowing that the dark, widening span made him seem sinister, larger than he already was. "Tell them all who he was when he was human, Inanna," he said, keeping his voice toneless and even.

"He was my husband," she whispered.

"Your bond-mate?" Cecily's skin paled. "How could you have done that?"

"Inanna never turned him during her season," Alex answered for Inanna, who trembled. "She kept him human so that he could do her bidding during the day and run her kingdom for her. She thought her own beauty and persuasion would be enough to keep him in line."

Inanna lifted her chin, defiance curving her lips. "This is all very interesting, I'm sure. But I still don't see how it is useful. It's ancient history. I made a mistake—one I've regretted."

Alex shook his head, exaggerating his surprise at the way she tried to downplay her crime. "You made a monster who hunts our kind—who murdered one of our *family* only last night."

"Your family?" she scoffed.

"She would have been if I hadn't been denied my birthright."

Silence fell like a suffocating blanket around the occupants of the room. Inanna's gaze skittered from one *sabat* sister to another, only to find them turn away, their disapproval a palpable, breathing entity.

While a deep, burning satisfaction flooded Alex's veins with an adrenaline spike, he knew he still teetered on a sharp edge that could turn vicious and bloody in a second.

Wishing Simon would hurry it up, he had to drag out the drama just a little longer.

"Enough of rehashing the past," he said smoothly. "We have time for that later. Right now we have more urgent matters to deal with." He paused, waiting to see if anyone would resist his attempt to continue his interrogation.

When the room stayed quiet and all eyes turned his way, he felt another rush of power. Their faces were still wooden, their expressions pale and shocked as they digested everything they'd learned, but they seemed willing to listen, to let him lead the discussion while they continued to sort through it.

Only Nicolas seemed relaxed. He slouched back in his chair, his gaze narrowed, but one corner of his mouth lifted in a wry smile.

Alex cleared his throat. "I possess the means of identifying your monster and destroying him once and for all."

Cecily sat forward, her glance darting around the table before she opened her mouth. "Tell us how you would go about doing this." For the first time, her tone, when she addressed him, was civil.

"I have a talisman," Alex said. "One that has protected me from the demon all my life. When that talisman is worn by him, he can be killed and prevented from invading another body to effect an escape."

"Are you speaking of the stone you wear?" she said, her gaze dropping to the amulet lying at the base of his throat. "Why can't we just take it from you and use it ourselves?"

Alex rested his hands on his hips and smiled. "You and who else?"

"Use it!" Madrigal burst out. "Find him now!"

Nicolas sat forward. "We should think about this a moment, narrow our focus to likely suspects. Now that we know the extent of his connection with Inanna, think what you would do if you were him and able to skip bodies. Where would you position yourself?"

"You would want to be as close as you could be to the object of your obsession . . . ," Alex began, and then halted when he saw Nicolas's head draw back.

"A lover . . . ," Nicolas said softly.

"It could be you!" Madrigal gasped. "Put the necklace on him!"

Alex shook his head. "It can't be Ni—him. We fought last night. He was unaffected by proximity to the stone while we wrestled."

Inanna roused herself. "You fought?" she asked Nicolas. "You know him?"

"It was a misunderstanding," Alex said quickly, not wanting to tip his hand regarding their relationship so soon.

"You fought," Inanna said, looking at Nico as though she'd never seen him before. "He's the father to your woman's child. What else aren't you telling me, Nico?"

"Let's stick to the subject of your demon first," Alex interrupted. "Who else besides Nicolas are you intimate with here, Inanna? Who do you trust? Because he would want to be that close."

Her gaze slid slowly from Nicolas and swept the crowded room until it landed on Pasqual. "Dumuzi?" she whispered.

Pasqual stood perfectly still, not breathing as his eyes flickered from Inanna to Alex and back to his mistress again. When it appeared no one would intervene on his behalf, he straightened, his arms coming forward and his palms turning upward in supplication. "Have I tried to harm you in any way, Mistress? Haven't I seen to your every need? How can you think it'd be me?"

"You've been different these past days," Inanna said, her voice sounding hollow. "When we are alone you've been . . . more aggressive . . ."

Pasqual's chest rose and fell more quickly, and his face tightened. "Because I saw that you enjoyed it. I watched you with Nic—"

Inanna rose from her chair, her eyes boring into his. "Is it really you?"

Pasqual's head swung toward the door, which was blocked by too many guards, toward the windows, which were also covered. Then he crouched, his hands balling into fists. "I won't be taken," he said, his voice devoid of any Cajun drawl.

"You can't escape this room," Nicolas said, his voice even and deadly, already on his feet and moving toward him. "You're going to pay for what you did to my brother and my wife."

Alex closed in, pushing back the Security Force members who were already crowding toward that end of the room. He had to get close enough to shove Miki out of harm's way. No one else would care as much if she got in the way.

Before anyone could get near him, Pasqual's arm snaked around Miki's waist and pulled her close.

"Take him now!" Cecily shouted.

"Not if you wish for her to live," Pasqual said, his gaze locking with Alex's.

"She's human, she can be sacrificed," Cecily spat.

Alex consigned Cecily to the same slag heap on which he intended to toss Inanna. He held up his hands and said quietly, "Take it easy. If you hurt her, I'll pull you apart, limb by limb."

Miki's eyes were wide, her face as pale as parchment, but she kept silent, for once, her gaze on Alex's—open and trusting.

"She's important to him!" Pasqual shouted back. "She carries his child!"

Alex bit back a curse.

"Which makes her mean even less to us!" Cecily said, her tone becoming strident.

Pasqual brought Miki in front of him, turning her to face him. He cupped his hand like a shovel and pointed it toward her belly. "I will kill her if you do not let me leave this room. I could scoop out your child at the same time I rip her heart from her chest."

"There is another solution," a calm voice said, rising above the noise of skittering chairs, scraping feet, and despairing murmurs.

Alex closed his eyes briefly, thankful to be hearing Simon's quiet tones. When he opened his eyes, he found them—Simon, his mother and father, and Gabriella in her wolf's skin— standing behind Inanna.

"How did they get in here?" Madrigal asked in a trembling voice.

"He's a mage," Nicolas said. "How do you think? He doesn't need a door."

"This is outrageous," Cecily wailed. "And just another reason why you've become ineffective, Inanna. Your schemes invite our enemies to pour through our doors."

"I just said he doesn't need doors," Nicolas said, giving Cecily a look filled with disgust.

"Shut up!" Pasqual screamed. "What other solution, mage?"

"You can go back to where you came from."

Pasqual's chest heaved. "I think not."

Simon met the demon's wild gaze with a quiet smile. "You can bring your wife with you."

"No!" Inanna said, shaking her head. "You can't do this."

"Rene, grab her," Alex said, swinging back to gauge Pasqual's expression.

The demon straightened, his eyes narrowing on Inanna while a gleeful smile began to stretch his lips. "You can do this?"

While Rene clasped the upper arms of a wriggling Inanna, Simon stepped around her and slipped the loop of the satchel he carried over his head.

Inanna moaned when she saw the bundle.

"Yes, Inanna," he said calmly. "You were foolish to keep it. You should have smashed the orb into a million pieces."

Simon opened the satchel and carefully extracted the dragon claw base, setting it on the table. Then he pulled out the black crystal, which seemed to glow with an inner light. He set it on the base and stood back. "Dumuzi, you must come toward me."

Pasqual, keeping Miki snug beside him, shoved past the guards surrounding him and came to a stop in front of Simon.

"You can let her go now," Alex said softly. "The woman . . . let her go."

"Once he opens the portal," Pasqual said, not looking his way, his gaze instead locking with Inanna's. "Bring her to me."

Rene dragged Inanna forward, only letting go of her arms when she stood beside Pasqual. Looking wildly around the room for an ally, Inanna flung back her head, but she met only cold condemnation everywhere she looked. "I did this for us. To make us strong. A male would have led us like a king. He would have forced us to serve him."

"You had your chance to lead, Inanna," Alex said, feeling suddenly tired. "Besides the methods you employed, you failed because you couldn't see what has been and what will come. You have left us all unprepared."

"You talk in riddles. Like a bloody mage."

"Enough talk for now," Simon inserted. "I'm ready. How convenient you saved the incantation, too."

As Simon began to chant, he lifted the orb from its bed and held it in his open palm. The crystal blinked and began to glow, shedding arcs of light that brightened the room like a thousand shards of moonlight. Turning, he faced the back of the room, empty except for the shimmering circle that seemed to suck the fragmented beams toward it, curving them into a vertical pool.

"Pasqual, take Inanna and go!" Simon shouted.

Pasqual shoved Miki an arm's length away and stepped toward the circle. Then his head swung back to Alex, and he flashed a white, feral smile.

As horror bent him double, Alex felt as though his feet had been glued to the floor. Too late, he watched as Pasqual thrust his hand beneath Miki's ribs and reached deep into her chest, the force of his blow lifting her from her feet.

Miki's eyes squeezed shut, then her body slumped until Pasqual shrugged her off his arm, lifting her beating heart in his fist. Then he grabbed Inanna's hand and leapt into the portal.

Bright light flashed, blinding Alex for a moment. He recovered a split second later and leapt atop the table, landing on the other side, beside Miki's bloodied body. He began to gather her up, but arms surrounded him, pulling him back. He struggled wildly to free himself, but the arms tightened.

"Wait, Alex," Simon said urgently in his ear. "Look at Mikaela."

Miki's skin lost its ashen pallor and began to glow—lit by a golden inner fire that ignited her body in an instant. The fireburst flashed, ashes exploding into the air and catching in an updraft to swirl like a tiny devil wind above the place where her body had fallen.

With his mouth gaping, Alex watched as the whirling ashes slowed, then fell, settling on the ground. He lurched forward, reaching out, but drew back his hand when the ashes billowed outward into a shape—hers—at first a thin dark layer of sooty black that smoothed, then stretched. Another light burst from inside the fragile black skeleton, and when it blinked out, Miki lay there, her body whole again.

Alex thrust away Simon's hands and bent over Miki's naked body, his hand sliding over her chest. A heartbeat stuttered and then began a steady throb. Her eyes blinked and opened, then widened as she caught sight of the many people leaning over her.

A cry wrenched from her and she jackknifed up, scooting to put her back to the wall.

Nicolas thrust a shirt into Alex's hands. Still kneeling, Alex reached out, offering the shirt. "Take it."

Miki's frightened gaze darted from his hands to his eyes, then she thrust out her hand and grabbed the shirt, covering her chest with the garment while she eyed the crowd like a wary animal.

"Explain this, Simon," Alex whispered urgently.

Simon's hand fell on his shoulders. "She's a Phoenix—cursed to be reborn."

"Cursed by whom?" When Simon didn't answer, Alex shot him a sour glance. "Is that really all you know? No more crap about what I need to know. I *have* to know."

"It had to have been a powerful demon," Simon said quietly. "And probably a long time ago, since Phoenixes aren't exactly plentiful."

By Simon's tone and steady gaze, Alex accepted that was all he did indeed know. He blew out a deep breath and turned back to Miki, who was listening carefully to their conversation. "She doesn't remember anything, does she?"

"Not you. Not even who she is. She'll know how to speak, how to get about. But she doesn't remember her life or the places and people she's met along the way."

"She's not human, then?"

"Completely so, but cursed."

"She doesn't remember *us*."

"Now, I took you for a smart boy."

Alex glanced up to find Simon's gaze leveled on him, waiting. . . .

For him to realize another purpose for his gift.

Inside, Alex began to shake. For the first time in what seemed an eternity, he felt tears fill his eyes. "I can show her us."

CHAPTER
20

All eyes turned toward Miki, whose breaths were short and labored, her fear leaving an acrid scent. Alex slowly extended his hand to her, palm up. "Let me help you with the shirt," he said softly.

Miki's moss-green eyes stared in rapt fascination at his hand, as though it was a snake poised to strike. His stomach plummeted. She didn't remember him, didn't remember a damn thing about their short acquaintance.

Perhaps it was a blessing, because she didn't know she'd carried his child, a daughter now lost to the inferno that had engulfed Miki's body.

Her gaze slowly lifted beyond him, widening.

"Your wings," Simon whispered.

Alex slowly folded them inward and withdrew them completely. Then he waited while her choppy breaths evened. "Father, Nicolas . . ." he directed over his shoulder.

"We'll see to everything," Rene said, his voice gruff. "Take care of your little firebird."

Alex crawled closer on his knees and reached for the shirt she clutched against her breasts.

Miki sank against the wall, trying to evade his reach, her frantic gaze seeking an escape.

"I promise I won't harm you, sweetheart." He dragged the shirt from her stiffened fingers and lifted it above her, holding her gaze.

Slowly, she leaned forward and let him drop it behind her, slipping her arms into the sleeves, her wary stare fixed and unblinking.

He concentrated on closing the buttons, cursing silently because his fingers trembled and it took longer than he wished.

When he'd finished, he slowly stood and held out his hand again. "I'll take you someplace private where we can talk. I promise to answer all your questions. I know you're curious—it's one of your most endearing qualities."

She stared at his hand again, then lifted her gaze to lock with his. "Who are you?" she asked slowly, as though not trusting the sound of her own voice.

"My name's Alex. I'm yours, and you belong to me."

Her gaze darted around the room that was slowly emptying as Rene and Nicolas quietly took charge and ushered people away. Perhaps she only judged him the least frightening option, but eventually, she drew a deep breath and slid her palm inside his hand. He drew her up, then bent and lifted her from the floor, ignoring her soft gasp as he clutched her close to his chest.

Alex strode swiftly for the door, leaving behind the scent of scorched flesh and miasma of despair that lingered inside the room.

He chose Chessa's bedroom on the second floor. The one his parents had occupied before her, and where he'd been conceived. He hoped that the pale flowers of the lavender wallpaper and the soft, feminine furnishings would soothe Miki's alarm.

Sitting her on the edge of the bed, he knelt beside her and drew her hand between his. "Do you remember anything at all?"

She shook her head. "Where am I?"

"At *Ardeal*, just outside New Orleans. Do you know where that is?"

"Louisiana," she said tentatively.

Alex smiled. "You remember something, see?"

"Who am I?" she asked, lifting her chin. "Besides yours."

"Mikaela Jones. Although you told me it was a name you chose for yourself."

"Why can't I remember it?"

"Baby, it will take me longer to tell you than if you let me show you."

A wrinkle bisected her brow as she frowned. "Should I understand what you mean?"

"If you let me come closer, I can give you parts of our past. But I have to hold you close."

She sucked her bottom lip between her teeth while her green gaze studied him.

Alex held himself perfectly still, hoping she'd decide to trust him. The last thing he wanted to do was force her to submit to this bite. He didn't want her first memories sullied by a violent act.

"Are you an angel?"

Alex felt a smile tug his lips. "A distant relative."

"What do you want me to do?"

"Tilt your head to the side and let me come closer."

"Are you going to kiss me?"

"Yes."

Her nose wrinkled. "Is that all you want of me?"

"This isn't about what I want, sweetheart. It's about what you will receive."

Her breath huffed out, her frustration evident in her frown. However, she tilted her head to the side.

The challenge in her gaze amused him. Her personality was intact. Defiance and curiosity overcame her fear.

Alex rose slowly, brushed away the strands of red hair clinging to her skin, and leaned close.

Her inhalation was sharp. Her body stiffened.

"Don't be afraid. This might sting."

"A kiss will sting?"

Rather than take more precious moments during which her anxiety would mount, he glided his lips along the smooth skin. His tongue found her throbbing pulse, then he opened his mouth and let his teeth slide inexorably down.

Her breath hissed between her clenched teeth and her hands shoved at his chest, but Alex didn't let go. He concentrated, ignoring her spicy, womanly scent and the salt and metal flavor of the blood that filled his mouth, tamping down his pleasure to ensure this first bite wouldn't elicit a sensual thrill to distort the memories he gave her—or use them to bind her to him.

Their first chance meeting in the dark, dank alleyway . . . "Not gonna ask me what a nice girl—"

His seduction of her in the shop beside the blood bar . . . "You had to know I'd want answers. Can we talk? Face-to-face, this time. I don't even know what you look like." "Conversation isn't free . . ."

His manipulations that had led to their lovemaking in the gazebo on this very estate . . . "I already gave. Twice," she'd bitten out. "So no tricks—keep those damn pheromones and fangs to yourself." "I'm not a Revenant," he'd replied. "I don't care what the hell you call yourself, no more 'gifts' are happenin' here," she'd responded.

The long, hot night they'd spent together in her apartment, where he'd set free his heart to love her. . .

And at last her death and rebirth.

When he drew back, he closed his eyes briefly, knowing she'd seen herself through his memories, known his every thought. Would she hate him for his arrogance?

Miki's eyes glittered with unshed tears, and her body quivered. "All those memories are yours?"

"Yes. I can only let you see what I've experienced."

"That was me burning?" she asked, her eyes awash in misery. "I'm cursed?"

Alex tenderly enfolded her small hands. "I see it as a gift."

"A gift?" She tried to pull away her hands, her lips twisting in a bitter grimace. "Do you see me as a woman you can remold each time I flare up?"

Alex bent his head and took a deep breath, hoping he could find the right words to reassure her. "I'm a man who's lived my life alone, knowing any woman I choose as my mate will be endangered. You can never be destroyed."

"Again, I'm not seeing the advantage from my perspective. It's all about you, isn't it?"

Alex shook his head. "We are made for each other. You're a woman without memories. I have an infinite store of memories that I will share with you."

"Your memories, not mine."

"If we stay close, always, they will be ours."

"Why would you show me how we met? Why would you let me know you only used me? How does it serve your interests?"

"Don't you see? It doesn't serve *me* at all. But I want you to know me. The good and the bad."

"Because you think you can love me? Because I'm the one woman who can't be taken from you?"

He bowed his head. Newborn she might be, but Miki's mind was sharp. She'd cut straight to the one point he couldn't deny. He gently squeezed her hands and lifted his gaze. "Don't you think there's a hint of fate in our meeting? That we were meant to find each other and love each other?"

"What future do we really have if we must repeat this conversation a thousand times?"

The hint of weary exasperation in her tone wasn't a rejection—it was just her way of sorting through what she'd learned and trying to discover his true feelings. If she cared about his motives . . .

He gave her a smile. "That's where your talent will come to play, love. You're a writer, a storyteller. Capture our lives together so that you will understand our journey. Capture your own memories, your own thoughts. Then we can skip this whole conversation the next time."

Her gaze fell to his smiling lips. "I guess it's not all bad," she said, her mouth curving into a sweet smile. "I'll be a virgin each time we renew our relationship. Sex will never be boring."

Alex couldn't contain his wolfish grin. He started to rise, coming closer to her sweet mouth.

"Don't you 'cast' for me," she warned.

"You caught onto that?"

"You thought it; I remember it," she said, narrowing her eyes. But she didn't resist as he pushed her back on the bed.

"Guess secrets will be impossible for me to keep forever," he murmured, his fingers sure this time as he flicked open the row of tiny buttons.

Her hand shoved at his chest. "I'm a reporter! I work for a newspaper."

"Worked," he growled. "You hardly think you'll be able to tell a soul what you learn."

Miki lifted one dark brow as he opened the shirt and bared her creamy skin. "Maybe I'll try my hand at writing a novel."

Gabriella landed on her knees in the middle of the Persian carpet. Once again facing the crudely carved stone walls of Alex Broussard's magical bolt-hole. "Alex, you lousy bastard, you can't do this to me—"

Her shout was cut short when the object of her bitter tirade grabbed the hand of the pregnant woman who'd been resting on a deep sofa inside the cavern when they'd flashed inside. He cast Gabriella an apologetic smile, palmed the crystal key to the room, and they both blinked out in a narrow flash of white light.

"Sonofabitch," she muttered, reaching up to grab the silver-linked choker from her neck that he'd used to subdue her and ripping it off. How could he do this, leave her in his bolt-hole, after everything she'd done to help him in his quest to usurp command of the vampires?

While he'd disappeared for hours, clutching the phoenix-creature he appeared to love against his chest, she'd helped round up the sabat, *nipping at the council-members' heels to herd them toward their rooms where Nicolas posted guards to keep them in lock-down.*

Malcolm, Nicolas's next-in-command, had led away Inanna's private security force to the barracks for "debriefing" and posted their own men around the compound to keep things quiet while Alex's closest advisors sorted through the chaos that was the aftermath of Inanna's expulsion into Hell.

When Alex had at last returned, looking like he'd just had the sweetest sex of his life, Gabriella shook her fur, pulling on her human skin, ready to remind Alex about their agreement when his gaze fled up the staircase, again.

The look on his face, one filled with a mixture of impatience and tenderness, had made her heart sink. When she'd cleared her throat to remind him she was still standing there, another look crossed his face—one that had her backing up a step and stammering.

The collar had been a real kick in the ass. He'd pulled it from his pocket and apologized, all the while grappling her to the ground to loop the damn thing around her neck. "I swear. It's just for now," he'd ground out as she wriggled beneath him. "Just until I get everything sorted out."

If he thought she'd be in any mood to talk to him, to negotiate a transaction to ensure the peace between their nations remained in place—well, he'd have to do a whole lot of begging, preferably on his knees and naked, before she agreed.

The thought of Alex, nude and serving her up a dish of submission, soothed her dented pride for all of a second. Her shoulders slumped, and she released a dejected sigh.

Gabriella never lied. Not even to herself. Alex was lost to her, for good. Once long ago, she'd hired an assassin to kill him, and she'd grieved for centuries, believing she'd killed him in a fit of jealous rage and lost the only lover who'd ever completely fulfilled her dark, sensual fantasies. The past few days, fighting and loving with him had been a bitter reminder of what she'd missed most—but he'd only been playing her, using her to get what he needed from her. When his other lover had "died," it took only one glance at the desperation tightening his face and the tears filling his eyes to know she'd never hold his heart.

She shook out her hair and glanced toward the bureau standing against the far wall of the cave. With time to kill, she could at least empty his liquor cabinet.

With a glide, she pushed off the floor and strode to the cabinet, lifting one bottle and another until she found a cognac to her taste. Pouring a beaker full of the warm amber liquor, she glanced at herself in the mirror and lifted her glass to toast her reflection.

Noting the red ring around her neck, she wrinkled her nose. Wasn't the first time she'd accepted a noose. Maybe the Dom in Atlanta would be amenable to a little retraining. Her nipples prickled and extended, spiking at the thought of the nasty things she'd beg him to do. As soon as she settled her business with Alex, she'd give him a call.

Her features tightened and the corners of her lips curved downward. She shut her eyes and downed the contents of her glass. When she opened them again, she stared at the mirror and set down her drink.

How many times had Alex stared into the glass, looking into that dreadful room—the hall where the demons and the dead feasted on each other in Hell. Remembering Alex's warning about the mirror, she reached up and gingerly touched only the frame.

The hall shimmered into sight. The same scene replayed—people in glittering, bejeweled costumes sitting at long benches in a Medieval-style hall. She shifted to the side to catch a glimpse of The Master's entrance—the handsome creature whose black aura resembled a dragon's. With Alex behind her, she'd watched The Master stride into the room, felt a tingle of awareness for his masculine beauty, and shuddered

*for the power he wielded over the orgiastic bloodletting that had fol-
lowed. She wouldn't deny the man fascinated her.*

*The hellhounds once again stood like sentries at either side of the
plank door. She waited for a long while, watched the couple nearest the
mirror savage each other on the floor, but still he didn't appear.*

*Just when she'd decided to drop her hand, a figure stepped in front
of the glass.*

*Her eyes widened as she found herself staring directly into The Mas-
ter's golden eyes. The narrow, slitted pupils slowly expanded, engulfing
the irises entirely in black.*

*Gabriella told herself he couldn't see her. Perhaps he looked at his
own reflection in a matching mirror. Gathering calm around her, she
stared back, noting the thick black hair that fell to the tops of his broad
shoulders, the neatly trimmed beard and moustache that framed his
chin and mouth, drawing her gaze to his lips—full for a man, sensual,
and beginning to smile.*

A chill gnawed at her spine, causing her to quake.

*As though she stared into a cobra's mesmerizing stare, she couldn't
break with his gaze as he slowly raised his hand and pressed it to the
glass, his long fingers splayed.*

*Gabriella felt as though she stood outside herself, watching as she
reached up, spreading her own fingers to match his, and pressed her
hand against the glass.*

*The glass began to warm, and then dissolved between them . . . and
their fingers met . . .*

Until recently, award-winning romance author **DELILAH DEVLIN** lived in south Texas at the intersection of two dry creeks, surrounded by sexy cowboys in Wranglers. These days, she's missing those wide-open skies and starry nights but loving her dark forest in central Arkansas, with its eccentric characters and isolation—the better to feed her hungry muse! For Delilah, the greatest sin is driving between the lines because it's comfortable and safe. Her personal journey has taken her through one war and many countries, cultures, jobs, and relationships to bring her to the place where she is now—writing sexy adventures that hold more than a kernel of autobiography and often share a common thread of self-discovery and transformation. To learn more about Delilah, visit www.delilahdevlin.com.